**W9-AHA-983**

# QUICKER THAN THE EYE

*Also by Ray Bradbury*
*in Large Print:*

Death Is a Lonely Business

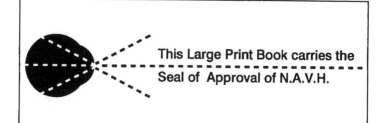

# QUICKER THAN THE EYE

## Ray Bradbury

**Thorndike Press • Thorndike, Maine**

Published in 1997 by arrangement with Avon Books, a division of The Hearst Corporation.

This is a collection of fiction. Any similarity to actual persons or events is purely coincidental.

Thorndike Large Print ® Basic Series.

The tree indicium is a trademark of Thorndike Press.

The text of this Large Print edition is unabridged. Other aspects of the book may vary from the original edition.

Set in 16 pt. Bookman Old Style by Minnie B. Raven.

Printed in the United States on permanent paper.

**Library of Congress Cataloging in Publication Data:**

Bradbury, Ray, 1920–
   Quicker than the eye / Ray Bradbury.
     p.    cm.
   ISBN 0-7862-0945-3 (lg. print : hc)
   1. Large type books.    I. Title.
  [PS3503.R167Q53    1997]
   813'.54—dc21                      96-39257

To Donn Albright,
my Golden Retriever,
with love

# CONTENTS

# Unterderseaboat Doktor

The incredible event occurred during my third visit to Gustav Von Seyfertitz, my foreign psychoanalyst.

I should have guessed at the strange explosion before it came.

After all, my alienist, *truly* alien, had the coincidental name, Von Seyfertitz, of the tall, lean, aquiline, menacing, and therefore beautiful actor who played the high priest in the 1935 film *She.*

In *She*, the wondrous villain waved his skeleton fingers, hurled insults, summoned sulfured flames, destroyed slaves, and knocked the world into earthquakes.

After that, "At Liberty," he could be seen riding the Hollywood Boulevard trolley cars as calm as a mummy, as quiet as an unwired telephone pole.

Where was I? Ah, yes!

It was my *third* visit to my psychiatrist. He had called that day and cried, "Douglas, you stupid goddamn son of a bitch, it's time for beddy-bye!"

Beddy-bye was, of course, his couch of pain and humiliation where I lay writhing in agonies of assumed Jewish guilt and Northern Baptist stress as he from time to time muttered, "A fruitcake remark!" or "Dumb!" or "If you ever do *that* again, I'll kill you!"

As you can see, Gustav Von Seyfertitz was a most unusual *mine* specialist. Mine? Yes. Our problems are land mines in our heads. *Step* on them! Shock-troop therapy, he once called it, searching for words. "Blitzkrieg?" I offered.

"*Ja!*" He grinned his shark grin. "That's *it!*"

Again, this was my third visit to his strange, metallic-looking room with a most odd series of locks on a roundish door. Suddenly, as I was maundering and treading dark waters, I heard his spine stiffen behind me. He gasped a great death rattle, sucked air, and blew it out in a yell that curled and bleached my hair:

"Dive! Dive!"

I dove.

Thinking that the room might be struck by a titanic iceberg, I fell, to scuttle beneath the lion-claw-footed couch.

"Dive!" cried the old man.

"Dive?" I whispered, and looked up.

To see a submarine periscope, all polished brass, slide up to vanish in the ceiling.

Gustav Von Seyfertitz stood pretending not to notice me, the sweat-oiled leather couch, or the vanished brass machine. Very calmly, in the fashion of Conrad Veidt in *Casablanca*, or Erich Von Stroheim, the manservant in *Sunset Boulevard* . . . he . . .

. . . lit a cigarette and let two calligraphic dragon plumes of smoke write themselves (his initials?) on the air.

"You were saying?" he said.

"No." I stayed on the floor. "*You* were saying. Dive?"

"I did not say that," he purred.

"Beg pardon, you said, very clearly — Dive!"

"Not possible." He exhaled two more scrolled dragon plumes. "You hallucinate. Why do you stare at the ceiling?"

"Because," I said, "unless I am further hallucinating, buried in that valve lock up there is a nine-foot length of German Leica brass periscope!"

"This boy is incredible, listen to him," muttered Von Seyfertitz to his alter ego,

11

which was always a third person in the room when he analyzed. When he was not busy exhaling his disgust with me, he tossed asides at himself. "How many martinis did you have at lunch?"

"Don't hand me that, Von Seyfertitz. I know the difference between a sex symbol and a periscope. That ceiling, one minute ago, swallowed a long brass pipe, yes!?"

Von Seyfertitz glanced at his large, one-pound-size Christmas watch, saw that I still had thirty minutes to go, sighed, threw his cigarette down, squashed it with a polished boot, then clicked his heels.

Have you ever heard the *whack* when a real pro like Jack Nicklaus hits a ball? *Bamm.* A hand grenade!

That was the sound my Germanic friend's boots made as he knocked them together in a salute.

*Crrrack!*

"Gustav Mannerheim Auschlitz Von Seyfertitz, Baron Woldstein, at your service!" He lowered his voice. "Unterderseaboat —"

I thought he might say "Doktor." But:

"Unterderseaboat *Captain!*"

I scrambled off the floor.

12

Another crrrack and —

The periscope slid calmly down out of the ceiling, the most beautiful Freudian cigar I had ever seen.

"No!" I gasped.

"Have I ever *lied* to you?"

"Many times!"

"But" — he shrugged — "little white ones."

He stepped to the periscope, slapped two handles in place, slammed one eye shut, and crammed the other angrily against the viewpiece, turning the periscope in a slow roundabout of the room, the couch, and me.

"Fire one," he ordered.

I almost heard the torpedo leave its tube.

"Fire *two!*" he said.

And a second soundless and invisible bomb motored on its way to infinity.

Struck midships, I sank to the couch.

"You, you!" I said mindlessly. "It!" I pointed at the brass machine. "This!" I touched the couch. "*Why?*"

"Sit down," said Von Seyfertitz.

"I am."

"*Lie* down."

"I'd rather not," I said uneasily.

Von Seyfertitz turned the periscope so

its topmost eye, raked at an angle, glared at me. It had an uncanny resemblance, in its glassy coldness, to his own fierce hawk's gaze.

His voice, from behind the periscope, echoed.

"So you want to know, eh, how Gustav Von Seyfertitz, Baron Woldstein, suffered to leave the cold ocean depths, depart his dear North Sea ship, flee his destroyed and beaten fatherland, to become the Unterderseaboat *Doktor* —"

"Now that you mention —"

"I never mention! I declare. And my declarations are sea-battle commands."

"So I noticed . . ."

"Shut up. Sit back —"

"Not just now . . ." I said uneasily.

His heels knocked as he let his right hand spider to his top coat pocket and slip forth yet a fourth eye with which to fasten me: a bright, thin monocle which he screwed into his stare as if decupping a boiled egg. I winced. For now the monocle was part of his glare and regarded me with cold fire.

"Why the monocle?" I said.

"Idiot! It is to cover my *good* eye so that *neither* eye can *see* and my intuition is free to work!"

"Oh," I said.

And he began his monologue. And as he talked I realized his need had been pent up, capped, for years, so he talked on and on, forgetting me.

And it was during this monologue that a strange thing occurred. I rose slowly to my feet as the Herr Doktor Von Seyfertitz circled, his long, slim cigar printing smoke cumuli on the air, which he read like white Rorschach blots.

With each implantation of his foot, a word came out, and then another, in a sort of plodding grammar. Sometimes he stopped and stood poised with one leg raised and one word stopped in his mouth, to be turned on his tongue and examined. Then the shoe went down, the noun slid forth and the verb and object in good time.

Until at last, circling, I found myself in a chair, stunned, for I saw:

Herr Doktor Von Seyfertitz stretched on his couch, his long spider fingers laced on his chest.

"It has been no easy thing to come forth on land," he sibilated. "Some days I was the jellyfish, frozen. Others, the shore-strewn octopi, at *least* with tentacles, or the crayfish sucked back into my skull. But I have built my spine, year on year, and now I walk among the land men and survive."

He paused to take a trembling breath, then continued:

"I moved in stages from the depths to a houseboat, to a wharf bungalow, to a shore-tent and then back to a canal in a city and at last to New York, an island surrounded by water, eh? But where, where, in all this, I wondered, would a submarine commander find his place, his work, his mad love and activity?

"It was one afternoon in a building with the world's longest elevator that it struck me like a hand grenade in the ganglion. Going down, down, down, other people crushed around me, and the numbers descending and the floors whizzing by the glass windows, rushing by flicker-flash, flicker-flash, conscious, subconscious, id, ego-id, life, death, lust, kill, lust, dark, light, plummeting, falling, ninety, eighty, fifty, lower depths, high exhilaration, id, ego, id, until this shout blazed from my raw throat in a great all-accepting, panic-manic shriek:

" 'Dive! Dive!' "

"I remember," I said.

" 'Dive!' I screamed so loudly that my fellow passengers, in shock, peed merrily. Among stunned faces, I stepped out of the lift to find one-sixteenth of an inch of pee on the floor. 'Have a nice day!' I said, jubilant with self-discovery, then ran to self-employment, to hang a shingle and next my periscope, carried from the mutilated, divested, castrated unterderseaboat all these years. Too stupid to see in it my psychological future and my final downfall, my beautiful artifact, the brass genitalia of psychotic research, the Von Seyfertitz Mark Nine Periscope!"

"That's quite a story," I said.

"Damn right," snorted the alienist, eyes shut. "And more than half of it true. Did you listen? What have you learned?"

"That more submarine captains should become psychiatrists."

"So? I have often wondered: did Nemo really die when his submarine was destroyed? Or did he run off to become my great-grandfather and were his psychological bacteria passed along until I came into the world, thinking to com-

17

mand the ghostlike mechanisms that haunt the undertides, to wind up with the fifty-minute vaudeville routine in this sad, psychotic city?"

I got up and touched the fabulous brass symbol that hung like a scientific stalactite in mid-ceiling.

"May I look?"

"I wouldn't if I were you." He only half heard me, lying in the midst of his depression as in a dark cloud.

"It's only a periscope —"

"But a good cigar is a smoke."

I remembered Sigmund Freud's quote about cigars, laughed, and touched the periscope again.

"Don't!" he said.

"Well, you don't *actually* use this for anything, do you? It's just a remembrance of your past, from your last sub, yes?"

"You think that?" He sighed. "Look!"

I hesitated, then pasted one eye to the viewer, shut the other, and cried:

"Oh, Jesus!"

"I warned you!" said Von Seyfertitz.

For *they* were there.

Enough nightmares to paper a thousand cinema screens. Enough phantoms to haunt ten thousand castle walls. Enough panics to shake forty cities into ruin.

My God, I thought, he could sell the film rights to this worldwide!

The first psychological kaleidoscope in history.

And in the instant another thought came: how much of that stuff in there is me? Or Von Seyfertitz? Or both? Are these strange shapes my maundering daymares, sneezed out in the past weeks? When I talked, eyes shut, did my mouth spray invisible founts of small beasts which, caught in the periscope chambers, grew outsize? Like the microscopic photos of those germs that hide in eyebrows and pores, magnified a million times to become elephants on *Scientific American* covers? Are these images from other lost souls trapped on that couch and caught in the submarine device, or leftovers from *my* eyelashes and psyche?

"It's worth millions!" I cried. "Do you *know* what this is!?"

"Collected spiders, Gila monsters, trips to the Moon without gossamer wings, iguanas, toads out of bad sisters' mouths, diamonds out of good fairies' ears, crippled shadow dancers from

Bali, cut-string puppets from Geppetto's attic, little-boy statues that pee white wine, sexual trapeze performers' *allez-oop,* obscene finger-pantomimes, evil clown faces, gargoyles that talk when it rains and whisper when the wind rises, basement bins full of poisoned honey, dragonflies that sew up every fourteen-year-old's orifices to keep them neat until they rip the sutures, aged eighteen. Towers with mad witches, garrets with mummies for lumber —"

He ran out of steam.

"You get the general drift."

"Nuts," I said. "You're bored. I could get you a five-million-dollar deal with Amalgamated Fruitcakes Inc. And the Sigmund F. Dreamboats, split three ways!"

"You don't understand," said Von Seyfertitz. "I am keeping myself busy, busy, so I won't remember all the people I torpedoed, sank, drowned mid-Atlantic in 1944. I am not in the Amalgamated Fruitcake Cinema business. I only wish to keep myself occupied by paring fingernails, cleaning earwax, and erasing inkblots from odd beanbags like you. If I stop, I will fly apart. That periscope contains all and everything I have seen and known in the past forty years of observing pecans, cashews, and almonds. By staring at them I lose my own terrible life lost in the tides. If you won my periscope in some shoddy fly-by-night Hollywood strip poker, I would sink three times in my waterbed, never to be seen again. Have I *shown* you my waterbed? Three times as large as any pool. I do eighty laps asleep each night. Sometimes forty when I catnap noons. To answer your millionfold offer, no."

And suddenly he shivered all over. His hands clutched at his heart.

"My God!" he shouted.

Too late, he was realizing he had let me step into his mind and life. Now he was on his feet, between me and the periscope, staring at it and me, as if we were both terrors.

"You saw nothing in that! Nothing at all!"

"I did!"

"You lie! How could you *be* such a liar? Do you know what would happen if this got out, if you ran around making accusations — ?

"My God," he raved on, "If the world knew, if someone said" — His words

21

gummed shut in his mouth as if he were tasting the truth of what he said, as if he saw me for the first time and I was a gun fired full in his face. "I would be . . . laughed out of the city. Such a goddamn ridiculous . . . hey, wait a minute. You!"

It was as if he had slipped a devil mask over his face. His eyes grew wide. His mouth gaped.

I examined his face and saw murder. I sidled toward the door.

"You wouldn't *say* anything to anyone?" he said.

"No."

"How come you suddenly know *everything* about me?"

"You *told* me!"

"Yes," he admitted, dazed, looking around for a weapon. "Wait."

"If you don't mind," I said, "I'd rather not."

And I was out the door and down the hall, my knees jumping to knock my jaw.

"Come back!" cried Von Seyfertitz, behind me. "I must kill you!"

"I was afraid of that!"

I reached the elevator first and by a miracle it flung wide its doors when I banged the Down button. I jumped in.

"Say good-bye!" cried Von Seyfertitz, raising his fist as if it held a bomb.

"Good-bye!" I said. The doors slammed.

I did not see Von Seyfertitz again for a year.

Meanwhile, I dined out often, not without guilt, telling friends, and strangers on street corners, of my collision with a submarine commander become phrenologist (he who feels your skull to count the beans).

So with my giving one shake of the ripe fruit tree, nuts fell. Overnight they brimmed the Baron's lap to flood his bank account. His Grand Slam will be recalled at century's end: appearances on *Phil Donahue*, *Oprah Winfrey*, and *Geraldo* in one single cyclonic afternoon, with interchangeable hyperboles, positive-negative-positive every hour. There were Von Seyfertitz laser games and duplicates of his submarine periscope sold at the Museum of Modern Art and the Smithsonian. With the superinducement of a half-million dollars, he force-fed and easily sold a bad book. Duplicates of the animalcules, lurks, and curious critters trapped in his brass viewer arose in pop-up coloring books, paste-on tattoos, and inkpad rubber-stamp nighmares at Beasts-R-Us.

I had hoped that all this would cause him to forgive and forget. No.

One noon a year and a month later, my doorbell rang and there stood Gustav Von Seyfertitz, Baron Woldstein, tears streaming down his cheeks.

"How come I didn't kill you that day?" he mourned.

"You didn't catch me," I said.

"Oh, *ja.* That was it."

I looked into the old man's rain-washed, tear-ravened face and said, "Who died?"

"Me. Or is it *I*? Ah, to hell with it: *me.* You see before you," he grieved, "a creature who suffers from the Rumpelstiltskin Syndrome!"

"Rumpel—"

"—stiltskin! Two halves with a rip from chin to fly. Yank my forelock, go ahead! Watch me fall apart at the seam. Like zipping a psychotic zipper, I fall, two Herr Doktor Admirals for the sick price of one. And which is the Doktor who heals and which the sellout bestseller Admiral? It takes two mirrors to tell. Not to mention the smoke!"

He stopped and looked around, holding his head together with his hands.

"Can you see the crack? Am I splitting again to become this crazy sailor who desires richness and fame, being sieved through the hands of crazed ladies with ruptured libidos? Suffering catfish, I call them! But take their money, spit, and spend! You should *have* such a year. Don't laugh."

"I'm not laughing."

"Then cheer up while I finish. Can I lie down? Is that a couch? Too short. What do I do with my legs?"

"Sit sidesaddle."

Von Seyfertitz laid himself out with his legs draped over one side. "Hey, not bad. Sit behind. Don't look over my shoulder. Avert your gaze. Neither smirk nor pull long faces as I get out the crazy-glue and paste Rumpel back with Stiltskin, the name of my next book, God help me. Damn you to hell, you and your damned periscope!"

"Not mine. Yours. You wanted me to discover it that day. I suppose you had been whispering Dive, Dive, for years to patients, half asleep. But you couldn't resist the loudest scream ever: Dive!

25

That was your captain speaking, wanting fame and money enough to chock a horse show."

"God," murmured Von Seyfertitz, "How I hate it when you're honest. Feeling better already. How much do I owe you?"

He arose.

"Now we go kill the monsters instead of you."

"Monsters?"

"At my office. If we can get in past the lunatics."

"You have lunatics outside as well as in, now?"

"Have I ever lied to you?"

"Often. But," I added, "little white ones."

"Come," he said.

We got out of the elevator to be confronted by a long line of worshippers and supplicants. There must have been seventy people strung out between the elevator and the Baron's door, waiting with copies of books by Madame Blavatsky, Krishnamurti, and Shirley MacLaine under their arms. There was a roar like a suddenly opened furnace door when they saw the Baron. We beat it on the double and got inside his office before anyone could surge to follow.

"See what you have done to me!" Von Seyfertitz pointed.

The office walls were covered with expensive teak paneling. The desk was from Napoleon's age, an exquisite Empire piece worth at least fifty thousand dollars. The couch was the best soft leather I had ever seen, and the two pictures on the wall were originals — a Renoir and a Monet. My God, millions! I thought.

"Okay," I said. "The beasts, you said. You'll kill them, not me?"

The old man wiped his eyes with the back of one hand, then made a fist.

"Yes!" he cried, stepping up to the fine periscope, which reflected his face, madly distorted, in its elongated shape. "Like this. Thus and *so!*"

And before I could prevent, he gave the brass machine a terrific slap with his hand and then a blow and another blow and another, with both fists, cursing. Then he grabbed the periscope as if it were the neck of a spoiled child and throttled and shook it.

I cannot say what I heard in that instant. Perhaps real sounds, perhaps imagined temblors, like a glacier cracking in the spring, or icicles in mid-night. Perhaps it was a sound like a great kite breaking its skeleton in the wind and collapsing in folds of tissue. Maybe I thought I heard a vast breath insucked, a cloud dissolving up inside itself. Or did I sense clock machineries spun so wildly they smoked off their foundations and fell like brass snowflakes?

I put my eye to the periscope.

I looked in upon —

Nothing.

It was just a brass tube with some crystal lenses and a view of an empty couch.

No more.

I seized the viewpiece and tried to screw it into some new focus on a far place and some dream bacteria that might fibrillate across an unimaginable horizon.

But the couch remained only a couch, and the wall beyond looked back at me with its great blank face.

Von Seyfertitz leaned forward and a tear ran off the tip of his nose to fall on one rusted fist.

"Are they dead?" he whispered.

"Gone."

"Good, they deserved to die. Now I can return to some kind of normal, sane world."

And with each word his voice fell deeper within his throat, his chest, his soul, until it, like the vaporous haunts within the peri-kaleidoscope, melted into silence.

He clenched his fists together in a fierce clasp of prayer, like one who beseeches God to deliver him from plagues. And whether he was once again praying for my death, eyes shut, or whether he simply wished me gone with the visions within the brass device, I could not say.

I only knew that my gossip had done a terrible and irrevocable thing. Me and my wild enthusiasm for a psychological future and the fame of this incredible captain from beneath Nemo's tidal seas.

"Gone," murmured Gustav Von Seyfertitz, Baron Woldstein, whispered for the last time. "Gone."

That was almost the end.

I went around a month later. The landlord reluctantly let me look over the premises, mostly because I hinted that I might be renting.

We stood in the middle of the empty

room where I could see the dent marks where the couch had once stood.

I looked up at the ceiling. It was empty.

"What's wrong?" said the landlord. "Didn't they fix it so you can't see? Damn fool Baron made a damn big hole up into the office above. Rented that, too, but never used it for anything I knew of. There was just that big damn hole he left when he went away."

I sighed with relief.

"Nothing left upstairs?"

"Nothing."

I looked up at the perfectly blank ceiling.

"Nice job of repair," I said.

"Thank God," said the landlord.

What, I often wonder, ever happened to Gustav Von Seyfertitz? Did he move to Vienna, to take up residence, perhaps, in or near dear Sigmund's very own address? Does he live in Rio, aerating fellow Unterderseaboat Captains who can't sleep for seasickness, roiling on their waterbeds under the shadow of the Andes Cross? Or is he in South Pasadena, within striking distance of the fruit larder nut farms disguised as film studios?

I cannot guess.

30

All I know is that some nights in the year, oh, once or twice, in a deep sleep I hear this terrible shout, his cry,

"Dive! Dive! Dive!"

And wake to find myself, sweating, far under my bed.

# ZAHAROFF/RICHTER MARK V

In the twilight just before sunrise, it was the most ordinary-looking building he had seen since the chicken farm of his youth. It stood in the middle of an empty field full of cricket weeds and cacti, mostly dust and some neglected footpaths in the half darkness.

Charlie Crowe left the Rolls-Royce engine running at the curb behind him and babbled going along the shadowed path, leading the way for Hank Gibson, who glanced back at the gently purring car.

"Shouldn't you —"

"No, no," Charlie Crowe cut in. "No one would steal a Rolls-Royce, now, would they? How far would they get, to the next corner? Before someone else stole it from *them!* Come along!"

"What's the hurry, we've got all morning!"

"That's what you think, chum. We've got —" Charlie Crowe eyed his watch. "Twenty minutes, maybe fifteen for the

32

fast tour, the coming disaster, the revelations, the whole bit!"

"Don't talk so fast and slow down, you'll give me a heart attack."

"Save it for breakfast. Here. Put this in your pocket."

Hank Gibson looked at the coupon-green diploma.

"Insurance?"

"On your house, as of yesterday."

"But we don't need —"

"Yes, you do, but don't know it. Sign the duplicate. Here. Can you see? Here's my flashlight and my pen. Thatsa boy. Give one to me. One for you —"

"Christ —"

"No swearing. You're all protected now, no matter what. Jig time."

And before he knew it, Hank Gibson was elbow-fetched through a paint-flaked door inside to yet another locked door, which opened when Charlie Crowe pointed his electric laser at it. They stepped into —

"An elevator! What's an elevator doing in a shack in an empty lot at five in the morning —"

"Hush."

The floor sank under them and they traveled what might have been seventy

33

or eighty feet straight down to where another door whispered aside and they stepped out into a long hall of a dozen doors on each side with a few dozen pleasantly glowing lights above. Before he could exclaim again, Hank Gibson was hustled past these doors that bore the names of cities and countries.

"Damn," cried Hank Gibson, "I hate being rushed through one god-awful mystery after another. I'm working on a novel and a feature for my newspaper. I've no time —"

"For the biggest story in the world? Bosh! You and I will write it, share the profits! You can't resist. Calamities. Chaos. Holocausts!"

"You were always great for hyperbole —"

"Quiet. It's my turn to show and tell." Charlie Crowe displayed his wristwatch. "We're wasting time. Where do we start?" He waved at the two dozen shut doors surrounding them with labels marked CONSTANTINOPLE, MEXICO CITY, LIMA, SAN FRANCISCO on one side.

Eighteen ninety-seven, 1914, 1938, 1963 on the other. Also, a special door marked HAUSSMANN, 1870.

"Places and dates, dates and places.

34

How in hell should I know why or how to choose?"

"Don't these cities and dates ring any bells, stir any dust? Peek here. Glance there. Go on."

Hank Gibson peeked.

To one side, through a glass window on the topmost part of a door marked 1789, he saw:

"Looks like Paris."

"Press the button there under the glass."

Hank Gibson pressed the button.

"Now look!"

Hank Gibson looked.

"My God, Paris. In flames. And there's the guillotine!"

"Correct. Now. Next door. Next window."

Hank Gibson moved and peeked.

"Paris again, by God. Do I press the button?"

"Why not?"

He pressed.

"Jesus, it's still burning. But this time it's 1870. The Commune?"

"Paris fighting Hessians *outside* the city, Parisians killing Parisians *inside* the city. Nothing like the French, eh? Move!"

They reached a third window. Gibson peered.

"Paris. But *not* burning. There go the taxicabs. I know. Nineteen sixteen. Paris saved by one thousand Paris taxis carrying troops to fend off the Germans outside the city!"

"A-One! Next?"

At a fourth window.

"Paris intact. But over here. Dresden? Berlin? London? All destroyed."

"Right. How do you like the three-dimension virtual reality? Superb! Enough of cities and war. Across the hall. Go down the line. All those doors with different kinds of devastation."

"Mexico City? I was there once, in '46."

"Press."

Hank Gibson pressed the button.

The city fell, shook, fell.

"The earthquake of '84?"

"Eight-five, to be exact."

"Christ, those poor people. Bad enough they're poor. But thousands killed, maimed, made poorer. And the government —"

"Not giving a damn. Move."

They stopped at a door marked ARMENIA, 1988.

Gibson squinted in, pressed the button.

"Major country, Armenia. Major country — gone."

"Biggest quake in that territory in half a century."

They paused at two more windows: TOKYO, 1932, and SAN FRANCISCO, 1905. Both whole, entire, intact at first glance. Touch the button: all fall down!

Gibson turned away, shaken and pale.

"Well?" said his friend Charlie. "What's the sum?"

Gibson stared along the hall to left and right.

"War and Peace? Or Peace destroying itself without War?"

"Touché!"

"Why are you showing me all this?"

"For your future and mine, untold riches, incredible revelations, amazing truths. *Andale. Vamoose!*"

Charlie Crowe flashed his laser pen at the largest door at the far end of the hall. The double locks hissed; the door sank away to one side, revealing a large boardroom with a huge table forty feet in length, surrounded by twenty leather chairs on each side and something like a throne, somewhat elevated, at the far end.

"Go sit up at the end," said Charlie.

Hank Gibson moved slowly.

"Oh, for Christ sake, shake a leg. We've only seven more minutes before the end of the world."

"End — ?"

"Just joking. Ready?"

Hank Gibson sat. "Fire away."

The table, the chairs, and the room shook.

Gibson leaped up.

"What was that?"

"Nothing." Charlie Crowe checked his watch. "At least not yet. Sit back. What have you seen?"

Gibson settled in his chair uneasily, grasping the arms. "Damned if I know. History?"

"Yes, but what *kind?*"

"War and Peace. Peace and War. Bad Peace, of course. Earthquakes and fire."

"Admirable. Now, who's responsible for all that destruction, two kinds?"

"What, *war?* Politicians, I guess. Ethnic mobs. Greed. Jealousy. Munitions manufacturers. The Krupp works in Germany. Zaharoff, wasn't that his name? The big munitions king, the grand mullah of all the warmongers, films of him on the newsreels in cinemas when I was a kid. Zaharoff?"

"Yes! What about the other side of the hall? The earthquakes."

"God did it."

"Only God? No helpers?"

"How can anyone help an earthquake?"

"Partially. Indirectly. Collaboratively."

"An earthquake is an earthquake. A city just happens to be in its way. Underfoot."

"Wrong, Hank."

"Wrong!?"

"What if I told you that those cities were not accidentally built there? What if I told you we had planned to build them there, on purpose, to be destroyed?"

"Nuts!"

"No, Hank, creative annihilation. We were up to these tricks as far back as the Tang dynasty earthquakewise on the one hand. Citywise? Paris, 1789 *warwise*."

"We? We? Who's *we?*"

"Me, Hank, and my cohorts, not in crimson and gold, but good dark cloth and decent ties and fine architectural school graduates. We did it, Hank. We built the cities so as to tear them down. To knock them apart with earthquakes or kill them with bombs and war, war and bombs."

"We? *We!?*"

"In this room or rooms like it, all across the world, men sat in those chairs on the left and right, with the grand mucky-muck of all architects there where you sit —"

"Architects!"

"You don't think all of those earthquakes, all of those wars, happened by mere accident, pure chance? We did it, Hank, the blueprint urban-plan architects of the world. Not the munitions makers or politicians, oh, we used them as puppets, marionettes, useful idiots, but we, the superb hired city architects, set out to build and then destroy our pets, our buildings, our cities!"

"For God's sake, how insane! Why?"

"Why? So that every forty, fifty, sixty, ninety years we could start over with fresh projects, new concepts, renewed jobs, cash on the line for everyone — blueprinters, planners, craftsmen, builders, stonemasons, diggers, carpenters, glaziers, gardeners. Knock it all down, start new!"

"You mean you — ?"

"Studied where the earthquakes hid, where they might erupt, every seam, crack, and fault in every territory, stage, land in the world! That's where we built the cities! Or *most* of them."

"B.S.! You couldn't do that, you and your planners! People would find out!"

"They never knew or found out. We met in secret, covered our tracks. A small klan, a wee band of conspirators in every country in every age. Like the Masons, eh? Or some Inquisitional Catholic sect? Or an underground Muslim grot. It doesn't take many or much. And the average politician, dumb or stupid, took our word for it. *This* is the site, here's the very place, plant your capital here, your town there. Perfectly safe. Until the next quake, eh, Hank?"

"Poppycock!"

"Watch your language!"

"I refuse to believe —"

The room shook. The chairs trembled. Half out of his chair, Hank Gibson sank back. The color in his face sank, too.

"Two minutes to go," said Charlie Crowe. "Shall I talk fast? Well, you don't think the destiny of the world would be

41

left to your ordinary farm-beast politico, do you? Have you ever sat at a Rotary/ Lions lunch with those sweet imbecile Chamber of Commerce stallions? Sleep and dreams! Would you let the world jog along with Zaharoff and his gun-maker-powder experts? Hell, no. They only know how to fire steel and package nitro. So *our* people, the same people who built the cities on the earthquake fault lines to ensure new work to build more cities, we planned the wars, secretly.

"We provoked, guided, steered, influenced the politicians to boil over, one way or t'other, and Paris and the Terror followed, dogged by Napoleon, trailed by the Paris Commune in which Haussmann, taking advantage of the chaos, tore down and rebuilt the City to the madness of some, delight of others. Consider Dresden, London, Tokyo, Hiroshima. We architects paid cold cash to get Hitler out of jail in 1922! Then we architects mosquito-pestered the Japanese to invade Manchuria, import junk iron, antagonize Roosevelt, bomb Pearl Harbor. Sure, the Emperor approved, sure the Generals knew delight, sure the kamikazes took off for oblivion, joyously happy. But behind the scenes, we architects, clapping hands, rubbing palms for the *moola,* shoved them up! Not the politicians, not the military, not the arms merchants, but the sons of Haussmann and the future sons of Frank Lloyd Wright sent them on their way. Glory hallelujah!"

Hank Gibson exhaled a great gust and sat, weighted with an ounce of information and a ton of confusion, at the head of this table. He stared down its length.

"There were meetings here —"

"In 1932, 1936, 1939 to fester Tokyo, poison Washington for war. And at the same time make sure that San Francisco was built in the best way for a new downfall, and that California cities all up and down the cracks and seams nursed at the mother fault, San Andreas, so when the Big One came, it would rain money for forty days."

"Son of a bitch," said Hank Gibson.

"Yes, aren't I? Aren't *we?*"

"Son of a bitch," Hank Gibson repeated in a whisper. "Man's wars and God's earthquakes."

"What a collaboration, eh? All done by the secret government, the government of surprise architects across the world and into the next century."

The floor shook. The table and the chair and the ceiling did likewise.

"Time?" said Hank Gibson.

Charlie Crowe laughed, glancing at his watch.

"Time. Out!"

They ran for the door, ran down the hall past the doors marked TOKYO and LONDON and DRESDEN, past the doors marked 1789 and 1870 and 1940 and past the doors marked ARMENIA and MEXICO CITY and SAN FRANCISCO and shot up in the elevator, and along the way, Hank Gibson said:

"Again, why've you *told* me this?"

"I'm retiring. The others are gone. We won't use this place again. It'll be gone. Maybe *now.* You write the book about all this fabulous stuff, I edit it, we'll grab the money and run."

"But who'll *believe* it!?"

"No one. But it's so sensational, everyone will buy. Millions of copies. And no one will investigate, for they're all guilty, city fathers, Chambers of Commerce, real estate salesmen, Army generals who thought they made up and fought their own wars, or made up and built their own cities! Pompous freaks!

Here we are. Out."

They made it out of the elevator and the shack as the next quake came. Both fell and got up, with nervous laughter.

"Good old California, yes? Is my Rolls still there? Yep. No carjackers. In!"

With his hand on the Rolls doorframe, Gibson stared over at his friend. "Does the San Andreas Fault come through *this* block?"

"You better believe. Wanna go see your home?"

Gibson shut his eyes. "Christ, I'm afraid."

"Take courage from the insurance policy in your coat pocket. Shall we go?"

"In a moment." Gibson swallowed hard. "What will we name our book?"

"What time is it and date?"

Gibson looked at the sun about to rise. "Early. Six-thirty. And the date on my watch reads February fifth."

"Nineteen ninety-four?"

"Six-thirty A.M. February fifth, 1994."

"Then that's the title of our book. Or why not *Zaharoff,* add Richter for the earthquake Richter scale at Cal-Tech. *Zaharoff/Richter Mark V*? Okay?"

"Okay."

The doors slammed. The motor roared.

"Do we go home?"

"Go fast. Jesus. Fast."

They went.

Fast.

# REMEMBER SASCHA?

Remember? Why, how could they forget? Although they knew him for only a little while, years later his name would arise and they would smile or even laugh and reach out to hold hands, remembering.

Sascha. What a tender, witty comrade, what a sly, hidden individual, what a child of talent; teller of tales, bon vivant, late-night companion, ever-present illumination on foggy noons.

Sascha!

He, whom they had never seen, to whom they spoke often at three A.M. in their small bedroom, away from friends who might roll their eyeballs under their lids, doubting their sanity, hearing *his* name.

Well, then, who and what was Sascha, and where did they meet or perhaps only dream him, and who were *they*?

Quickly: they were Maggie and Douglas Spaulding and they lived by the loud sea and the warm sand and the rickety bridges over the almost dead canals of Venice, California. Though lacking money in the bank or Goodwill furniture in their tiny two-room apartment, they were incredibly happy. He was a writer, and she worked to support him while he finished the great American novel.

Their routine was: she would arrive home each night from downtown Los Angeles and he would have hamburgers waiting or they would walk down the beach to eat hot dogs, spend ten or twenty cents in the Penny Arcade, go home, make love, go to sleep, and repeat the whole wondrous routine the next night: hot dogs, Penny Arcade, love, sleep, work, etc. It was all glorious in that year of being very young and in love; therefore it would go on forever . . .

Until *he* appeared.

The nameless one. For then he had no name. He had threatened to arrive a few months after their marriage to destroy their economy and scare off the novel, but then he had melted away, leaving only his echo of a threat.

But now the true collision loomed.

One night over a ham omelet with a bottle of cheap red and the conversation loping quietly, leaning on the card table and promising each other grander and more ebullient futures, Maggie suddenly said, "I feel faint."

"What?" said Douglas Spaulding.

"I've felt funny all day. And I was sick, a little bit, this morning."

"Oh, my God." He rose and came around the card table and took her head in his hands and pressed her brow against his side, and looked down at the beautiful part in her hair, suddenly smiling.

"Well, now," he said, "don't tell me that Sascha is back?"

"Sascha! Who's *that?*"

"When he arrives, he'll *tell* us."

"Where did that name *come* from?"

"Don't know. It's been in my mind all year."

"Sascha?" She pressed his hands to her cheeks, laughing. "Sascha!"

"Call the doctor tomorrow," he said.

"The doctor says Sascha has moved in for light housekeeping," she said over the phone the next day.

"Great!" He stopped. "I *guess.*" He considered their bank deposits. "No. *First* thoughts count. Great! When do we meet the Martian invader?"

49

"October. He's infinitesimal now, tiny, I can barely hear his voice. But now that he has a name, I hear it. He promises to grow, if we take care."

"The Fabulous Invalid! Shall I stock up on carrots, spinach, broccoli for *what* date?"

"Halloween."

"Impossible!"

"True!"

"People will claim we planned him and my vampire book to arrive that week, things that go bump and cry in the night."

"Oh, Sascha will surely do *that! Happy?*"

"Frightened, yes, but happy, Lord, yes. Come home, Mrs. Rabbit, and bring *him* along!"

It must be explained that Maggie and Douglas Spaulding were best described as crazed romantics. Long before the interior christening of Sascha, they, loving Laurel and Hardy, had called each other Stan and Ollie. The machines, the dustbusters and can openers around the apartment, had names, as did various parts of their anatomy, revealed to no one.

So Sascha, as an entity, a presence growing toward friendship, was not unusual. And when he actually began to speak up, they were not surprised. The gentle demands of their marriage, with love as currency instead of cash, made it inevitable.

Someday, they said, if they owned a car, it too would be named.

They spoke on that and a dozen score of things late at night. When hyperventilating about life, they propped themselves up on their pillows as if the future might happen right *now*. They waited, anticipating, in seance, for the silent small offspring to speak his first words before dawn.

"I love our lives," said Maggie, lying there, "all the games. I hope it never stops. You're not like other men, who drink beer and talk poker. Dear God, I wonder, how many other marriages play like us?"

"No one, nowhere. Remember?"

"What?"

He lay back to trace his memory on the ceiling.

"The day we were married —"

"Yes!"

"Our friends driving and dropping us

off here and we walked down to the drugstore by the pier and bought a tube of toothpaste and two toothbrushes, big bucks, for our honeymoon . . . ? One red toothbrush, one green, to decorate our empty bathroom. And on the way back along the beach, holding hands, suddenly, behind us, two little girls and a boy followed us and sang:

*"Happy marriage day to you,*
*Happy marriage day to you.*
*Happy marriage day,*
    *happy marriage day,*
*Happy marriage day to you . . ."*

She sang it now, quietly. He chimed in, remembering how they had blushed with pleasure at the children's voices, but walked on, feeling ridiculous but happy and wonderful.

"How did they guess? Did we *look* married?"

"It wasn't our clothes! Our faces, don't you think? Smiles that made our jaws ache. We were exploding. They got the concussion."

"Those dear children. I can still hear their voices."

"And so here we are, seventeen

months later." He put his arm around her and gazed at their future on the dark ceiling.

"And here *I* am," a voice murmured.

"Who?" Douglas said.

"Me," the voice whispered. "Sascha."

Douglas looked down at his wife's mouth, which had barely trembled.

"So, at last, you've decided to speak?" said Douglas.

"Yes," came the whisper.

"We wondered," said Douglas, "when we would hear from you." He squeezed his wife gently.

"It's time," the voice murmured. "So here I am."

"Welcome, Sascha," both said.

"Why didn't you talk sooner?" asked Douglas Spaulding.

"I wasn't sure that you *liked* me," the voice whispered.

"Why would you think *that?*"

"First I was, then I wasn't. Once I was only a name. Remember, last year, I was ready to come and stay. Scared you."

"We were broke," said Douglas quietly. "And nervous."

"What's so scary about life?" said Sascha. Maggie's lips twitched. "It's that *other* thing. *Not* being, ever. Not being wanted."

"On the contrary." Douglas Spaulding moved down on his pillow so he could watch his wife's profile, her eyes shut, but her mouth breathing softly. "We love you. But last year it was bad timing. Understand?"

"No," whispered Sascha. "I only understand you didn't want me. And now you *do.* I should leave."

"But you just *got* here!"

"Here I go, anyway."

"Don't, Sascha! Stay!"

"Good-bye." The small voice faded. "Oh, good-bye."

And then silence.

Maggie opened her eyes with quiet panic.

"Sascha's gone," she said.

"He *can't* be!"

The room was still.

"*Can't* be," he said. "It's only a game."

"More than a game. Oh, God, I feel cold. Hold me."

He moved to hug her.

"It's okay."

"No. I had the funniest feeling just now, as if he were real."

"He *is.* He's *not* gone."

"Unless we do something. Help me."

"Help?" He held her even tighter, then shut his eyes, and at last called:

"Sascha?"

Silence.

"I know you're there. You can't hide."

His hand moved to where Sascha might be.

"Listen. Say something. Don't scare us, Sascha. We don't want to be scared or scare you. We need each other. We three against the world. Sascha?"

Silence.

"Well?" whispered Douglas.

Maggie breathed in and out.

They waited.

"Yes?"

There was a soft flutter, the merest exhalation on the night air.

"Yes."

"You're back!" both cried.

Another silence.

"Welcome?" asked Sascha.

"Welcome!" both said.

And that night passed and the next day and the night and day after that, until there were many days, but especially midnights when he dared to declare himself, pipe opinions, grow stronger and firmer and longer in half-heard declarations, as they lay in anticipatory awareness, now she moving her lips, now he taking over, both open as warm, live ventriloquists' mouthpieces. The small voice shifted from one tongue to the other, with soft bouts of laughter at how ridiculous but loving it all seemed, never knowing what Sascha might say next, but letting him speak on until dawn and a smiling sleep.

"What's this about Halloween?" he asked, somewhere in the sixth month.

"Halloween?" both wondered.

"Isn't that a death holiday?" Sascha murmured.

"Well, yes . . ."

"I'm not sure I want to be born on a night like that."

"Well, what night *would* you like to be born on?"

Silence as Sascha floated a while.

"Guy Fawkes," he finally whispered.

"Guy Fawkes??!!"

"That's mainly fireworks, gunpowder plots, Houses of Parliament, yes? *Please to remember the fifth of November?*"

"Do you think you could wait until then?"

"I could try. I don't think I want to start out with skulls and bones. Gunpowder's more like it. I could write about that."

"Will you be a writer, then?"

"Get me a typewriter and a ream of paper."

"And keep us awake with the *typing?*"

"Pen, pencil, and pad, then?"

"Done!"

So it was agreed and the nights passed into weeks and the weeks leaned from summer into the first days of autumn and his voice grew stronger, as did the sound of his heart and the small commotions of his limbs. Sometimes as Maggie slept, his voice would stir her awake and she would reach up to touch her mouth, where the surprise of his dreaming came forth.

"There, there, Sascha. Rest now. Sleep."

"Sleep," he whispered drowsily, "sleep." And faded away.

"Pork chops, please, for supper."

"No pickles with ice cream?" both said, almost at once.

"Pork chops," he said, and more days passed and more dawns arose and he said: "Hamburgers!"

"For *breakfast?*"

"With onions," he said.

October stood still for one day and then . . .

Halloween departed.

"Thanks," said Sascha, "for helping me past *that.* What's up ahead in five nights?"

"Guy Fawkes!"

"Ah, yes!" he cried.

And at one minute after midnight five days later, Maggie got up, wandered to the bathroom, and wandered back, stunned.

"Dear," she said, sitting on the edge of the bed.

Douglas Spaulding turned over, half awake. "Yes?"

"What day is it?" whispered Sascha.

"Guy Fawkes, at last. So?"

"I don't feel well," said Sascha. "Or, no, I feel fine. Full of pep. Ready to go. It's time to say good-bye. Or is it hello? What *do* I mean?"

"Spit it out."

"Are there neighbors who said, no matter when, they'd take us to the hospital?"

"Yes."

"Call the neighbors," said Sascha.

They called the neighbors.

At the hospital, Douglas kissed his wife's brow and listened.

"It's been nice," said Sascha.

"Only the best."

"We won't talk again. Good-bye," said Sascha.

"Good-bye," both said.

At dawn there was a small clear cry somewhere.

Not long after, Douglas entered his wife's hospital room. She looked at him and said, "Sascha's gone."

"I know," he said quietly.

"But he left word and someone else is here. Look."

He approached the bed as she pulled back a coverlet.

"Well, I'll be damned."

He looked down at a small pink face and eyes that for a brief moment flickered bright blue and then shut.

"Who's that?" he asked.

"Your daughter. Meet Alexandra."

"Hello, Alexandra," he said.

"And do you know what the nickname for Alexandra is?" she said.

"What?"

"Sascha," she said.

He touched the small cheek very gently.

"Hello, Sascha," he said.

# ANOTHER FINE MESS

The sounds began in the middle of summer in the middle of the night.

Bella Winters sat up in bed about three A.M. and listened and then lay back down. Ten minutes later she heard the sounds again, out in the night, down the hill.

Bella Winters lived in a first-floor apartment on top of Vendome Heights, near Effie Street in Los Angeles, and had lived there now for only a few days, so it was all new to her, this old house on an old street with an old staircase, made of concrete, climbing steeply straight up from the lowlands below, one hundred and twenty steps, count them. And right now . . .

"Someone's on the steps," said Bella to herself.

"What?" said her husband, Sam, in his sleep.

"There are some men out on the steps," said Bella. "Talking, yelling, not fighting, but almost. I heard them last night, too, and the night before, but . . ."

61

"What?" Sam muttered.

"Shh, go to sleep. I'll look."

She got out of bed in the dark and went to the window, and yes, two men were indeed talking out there, grunting, groaning, now loud, now soft. And there was another noise, a kind of bumping, sliding, thumping, like a huge object being carted up the hill.

"No one could be moving in at this hour of the night, could they?" asked Bella of the darkness, the window, and herself.

"No," murmured Sam.

"It sounds like . . ."

"Like what?" asked Sam, fully awake now.

"Like two men moving —"

"Moving what, for God's sake?"

"Moving a piano. Up those steps."

"At three in the *morning!?*"

"A piano and two men. Just listen."

The husband sat up, blinking, alert.

Far off, in the middle of the hill, there was a kind of harping strum, the noise a piano makes when suddenly thumped and its harp strings hum.

"There, did you *hear?*"

"Jesus, you're right. But why would anyone steal —"

"They're not stealing, they're delivering."

"A *piano?*"

"I didn't make the rules, Sam. Go out and ask. No, don't; I will."

And she wrapped herself in her robe and was out the door and on the sidewalk.

"Bella," Sam whispered fiercely behind the porch screen. "Crazy."

"So what can happen at night to a woman fifty-five, fat, and ugly?" she wondered.

Sam did not answer.

She moved quietly to the rim of the hill. Somewhere down there she could hear the two men wrestling with a huge object. The piano on occasion gave a strumming hum and fell silent. Occasionally one of the men yelled or gave orders.

"The voices," said Bella. "I know them from somewhere," she whispered and moved in utter dark on stairs that were only a long pale ribbon going down, as a voice echoed:

"Here's *another* fine mess you've got us in."

Bella froze. Where have I heard that voice, she wondered, a million *times!*

"Hello," she called.

She moved, counting the steps, and stopped.

And there was no one there.

Suddenly she was very cold. There was nowhere for the strangers to have gone to. The hill was steep and a long way down and a long way up, and they had been burdened with an upright piano, *hadn't* they?

How come I know *upright?* she thought. I only *heard.* But — yes, *upright!* Not only that, but inside a box!

She turned slowly and as she went back up the steps, one by one, slowly, slowly, the voices began to sound again, below, as if, disturbed, they had waited for her to go away.

"What *are* you doing?" demanded one voice.

"I was just —" said the other.

"*Give* me that!" cried the first voice.

That *other* voice, thought Bella, I know that, *too.* And I know what's going to be said next!

"Now," said the echo far down the hill in the night, "just don't stand there, *help* me!"

"Yes!" Bella closed her eyes and swallowed hard and half fell to sit on the steps, getting her breath back as black-and-white pictures flashed in her head. Suddenly it was 1929 and she was very small, in a theater with dark and light pictures looming above the first row where she sat, transfixed, and then laughing, and then transfixed and laughing again.

She opened her eyes. The two voices were still down there, a faint wrestle and echo in the night, despairing and thumping each other with their hard derby hats.

Zelda, thought Bella Winters. I'll call Zelda. She knows everything. She'll tell me what this is. Zelda, yes!

Inside, she dialed Z and E and L and D and A before she saw what she had done and started over. The phone rang a long while until Zelda's voice, angry with sleep, spoke halfway across L.A.

"Zelda, this is Bella!"

"Sam just *died?*"

"No, no, I'm sorry —"

"*You're* sorry?"

"Zelda, I know you're going to think I'm crazy, but . . ."

"Go ahead, be crazy."

"Zelda, in the old days when they made films around L.A., they used lots of places, right? Like Venice, Ocean Park . . ."

"Chaplin did, Langdon did, Harold Lloyd, sure."

"Laurel and Hardy?"

"What?"

"Laurel and Hardy, did *they* use lots of locations?"

"Palms, they used Palms lots, Culver City Main Street, Effie Street."

"*Effie* Street!"

"Don't yell, Bella."

"Did you say *Effie* Street?"

"Sure, and God, it's three in the morning!"

"Right at the *top* of Effie Street!?"

"Hey, yeah, the stairs. Everyone knows them. That's where the music box chased Hardy downhill and ran over him."

"Sure, Zelda, *sure!* Oh, God, Zelda, if you could *see,* hear, what *I* hear!"

Zelda was suddenly wide awake on the line. "What's going *on?* You *serious?"*

"Oh, God, yes. On the steps just now, and last night and the night before maybe, I heard, I hear — two men hauling a — a piano up the hill."

"Someone's pulling your leg!"

"No, no, they're there. I go out and there's nothing. But the steps are haunted, Zelda! One voice says: 'Here's another fine mess you've got us in.' You got to *hear* that man's voice!"

"You're drunk and doing this because you know I'm a nut for them."

"No, no. Come, Zelda. Listen. Tell!"

Maybe half an hour later, Bella heard the old tin lizzie rattle up the alley behind the apartments. It was a car Zelda, in her joy at visiting silent-movie theaters, had bought to lug herself around in while she wrote about the past, always the past, and steaming into Cecil B. DeMille's old place or circling Harold Lloyd's nation-state, or cranking and banging around the Universal backlot, paying her respects to the Phantom's opera stage, or sitting on Ma and Pa Kettle's porch chewing a sandwich lunch. That was Zelda, who once wrote in a silent country in a silent time for *Silver Screen.*

Zelda lumbered across the front porch, a huge body with legs as big as the Bernini columns in front of St. Peter's in Rome, and a face like a harvest moon.

On that round face now was suspicion, cynicism, skepticism, in equal pie-parts. But when she saw Bella's pale stare she cried:

"Bella!"

"You *see* I'm *not* lying!" said Bella.

"I *see!*"

"Keep your voice down, Zelda. Oh, it's scary and strange, terrible and nice. So come on."

And the two women edged along the walk to the rim of the old hill near the old steps in old Hollywood, and suddenly as they moved they felt time take a half turn around them and it was another year, because nothing had changed, all the buildings were the way they were in 1928 and the hills beyond like they were in 1926 and the steps, just the way they were when the cement was poured in 1921.

"Listen, Zelda. *There!*"

And Zelda listened and at first there was only a creaking of wheels down in the dark, like crickets, and then a moan of wood and a hum of piano strings, and then one voice lamenting about this job, and the other voice claiming he had nothing to do with it, and then the thumps as two derby hats fell, and an exasperated voice announced:

"Here's *another* fine mess you've got us in."

Zelda, stunned, almost toppled off the hill. She held tight to Bella's arm as tears brimmed in her eyes.

"It's a trick. Someone's got a tape recorder or —"

"No, I checked. Nothing but the steps, Zelda, the steps!"

Tears rolled down Zelda's plump cheeks.

"Oh, God, that *is* his voice! I'm the expert, I'm the mad fanatic, Bella. That's Ollie. And that other voice, Stan! And you're *not* nuts after all!"

The voices below rose and fell and one cried: "Why don't you do something to *help* me?"

Zelda moaned. "Oh, God, it's so *beautiful.*"

"What does it mean?" asked Bella. "Why are they here? Are they really ghosts, and why would ghosts climb this hill every night, pushing that music box, night after night, tell me, Zelda, why?"

Zelda peered down the hill and shut her eyes for a moment to think. "Why do *any* ghosts go anywhere? Retribution? Revenge? No, not *those* two. Love maybe's the reason, lost loves or something. *Yes?*"

Bella let her heart pound once or twice and then said, "Maybe nobody *told* them."

"Told them *what?*"

"Or maybe they were told a lot but still didn't believe, because maybe in their old years things got bad, I mean they were sick, and sometimes when you're sick you forget."

"Forget *what!?*"

"How much we loved them."

"They *knew!*"

"*Did* they? Sure, we told each other, but maybe not enough of us ever wrote or waved when they passed and just yelled *'Love!'* you think?"

"Hell, Bella, they're on TV every *night!*"

"Yeah, but that don't count. Has anyone, since they left us, come here to these steps and *said?* Maybe those voices down there, ghosts or whatever, have been here every night for years, pushing that music box, and nobody thought, or tried, to just whisper or yell all the love we had all the years. Why not?"

"Why not?" Zelda stared down into the long darkness where perhaps shadows moved and maybe a piano lurched clumsily among the shadows. "You're right."

"If I'm right," said Bella, "and you say so, there's only one thing to do —"

"You mean you and *me?*"

"Who else? Quiet. Come on."

They moved down a step. In the same instant lights came on around them, in a window here, another there. A screen door opened somewhere and angry words shot out into the night:

"Hey, what's going *on?*"

"Pipe down!"

"You know what *time* it is?"

"My God," Bella whispered, "everyone *else* hears now!"

"No, no." Zelda looked around wildly. "They'll spoil everything!"

"I'm calling the cops!" A window slammed.

"God," said Bella, "if the cops come —"

"What?"

"It'll be all wrong. If anyone's going to tell them to take it easy, pipe down, it's gotta be us. We *care, don't* we?"

"God, yes, but —"

"No buts. Grab on. Here we go."

The two voices murmured below and the piano tuned itself with hiccups of sound as they edged down another step and another, their mouths dry, hearts hammering, and the night so dark they could see only the faint streetlight at the stair bottom, the single street illumination so far away it was sad being there all by itself, waiting for shadows to move.

More windows slammed up, more screen doors opened. At any moment there would be an avalanche of protest, incredible outcries, perhaps shots fired, and all this gone forever.

Thinking this, the women trembled and held tight, as if to pummel each other to speak against the rage.

"Say something, Zelda, quick."

"*What?*"

"Anything! They'll get hurt if we don't —"

"*They?*"

"You know what I mean. Save them."

"Okay. Jesus!" Zelda froze, clamped her eyes shut to find the words, then opened her eyes and said, "Hello."

"Louder."

"Hello," Zelda called softly, then loudly.

Shapes rustled in the dark below. One of the voices rose while the other fell and the piano strummed its hidden harp strings.

"Don't be afraid," Zelda called.

"That's good. Go on."

"Don't be afraid," Zelda called, braver now. "Don't listen to those others yelling. We won't hurt you. It's just us. I'm Zelda, you wouldn't remember, and this here is Bella, and we've known you forever, or since we were kids, and we love you. It's late, but we thought you should know. We've loved you ever since you were in the desert or on that boat with ghosts or trying to sell Christmas trees door-to-door or in that traffic where you tore the headlights off cars, and we still love you, right, Bella?"

The night below was darkness, waiting.

Zelda punched Bella's arm.

"Yes!" Bella cried, "what she *said*. We love you."

"We can't think of anything else to say."

"But it's enough, yes?" Bella leaned forward anxiously. "It's *enough?*"

A night wind stirred the leaves and grass around the stairs and the shadows below that had stopped moving with the music box suspended between them as they looked up and up at the two women, who suddenly began to cry. First tears fell from Bella's cheeks, and when Zelda sensed them, she let fall her own.

"So now," said Zelda, amazed that she could form words but managed to speak anyway, "we want you to know, you don't have to come back anymore. You don't have to climb the hill every night, waiting. For what we said just now is it, isn't it? I mean you wanted to hear it here on this hill, with those steps, and that piano, yes, that's the whole thing, it had to be that, didn't it? So now here we are and there you are and it's said. So rest, dear friends."

"Oh, there, Ollie," added Bella in a sad, sad whisper. "Oh, Stan, Stanley."

The piano, hidden in the dark, softly hummed its wires and creaked its ancient wood.

And then the most incredible thing happened. There was a series of shouts and then a huge banging crash as the music box, in the dark, rocketed down the hill, skittering on the steps, playing chords where it hit, swerving, rushing, and ahead of it, running, the two shapes pursued by the musical beast, yelling, tripping, shouting, warning the Fates, crying out to the gods, down and down, forty, sixty, eighty, one hundred steps.

And half down the steps, hearing, feeling, shouting, crying themselves, and now laughing and holding to each other, the two women alone in the night wildly clutching, grasping, trying to see, almost sure that they *did* see, the three things ricocheting off and away, the two shadows rushing, one fat, one thin, and the piano blundering after, discordant and mindless, until they reached the street, where, instantly, the one overhead streetlamp died as if struck, and the shadows floundered on, pursued by the musical beast.

And the two women, abandoned, looked down, exhausted with laughing until they wept and weeping until they laughed, until suddenly Zelda got a terrible look on her face as if shot.

"My God!" she shouted in panic, reaching out. "Wait. We didn't mean, we don't want — don't go *forever!* Sure, go, so the neighbors here sleep. But once a year, you *hear?* Once a year, one night a year from tonight, and every year after that, come back. It shouldn't bother anyone so much. But we got to tell you all over again, huh? Come back and bring the box with you, and we'll be here waiting, won't we, Bella?"

"Waiting, yes."

There was a long silence from the steps leading down into an old black-and-white, silent Los Angeles.

"You think they heard?"

They listened.

And from somewhere far off and down, there was the faintest explosion like the engine of an old jalopy knocking itself to life, and then the merest whisper of a lunatic music from a dark theater when they were very young. It faded.

After a long while they climbed back up the steps, dabbing at their eyes with wet Kleenex. Then they turned for a final time to stare down into the night.

"You know something?" said Zelda. "I think they *heard*."

# THE ELECTROCUTION

She let him tie the black silk over her eyes and he knotted it and jerked it so tight that she gasped and said, "Loosen it, damn you, Johnny, loosen it, or I won't go on!"

"Sure," he said easily, and she smelled his sharp breath; while beyond, the crowd rustled against the rope barrier and the carnival tent flapped in the night wind, and far off, there was a drift of calliope music and the rattle of a trap drum.

Dimly, through the black silk, she could see the men, the boys, the few women, a good crowd, paying out dimes to see her strapped in this electric chair, the electrodes on her wrists and neck, waiting.

"There." Johnny's voice whispered through the blindfold. "That better?"

She said nothing, but her hands gripped the ends of the wooden chair. She felt her pulse beating in her arms and neck. Outside, the pitchman yelled through his small cardboard megaphone and slapped his cane across the banner where Electra's portrait shivered in the wind: yellow hair, hard blue eyes, sharp chin, seated in her death-chair like someone come for tea.

With the black silk blinding her, it was easier to let her mind run back to wherever it wanted to go . . .

The carnival was either setting up in a new town or letting go; its brown tents inhaling by day, exhaling its stale air by night as the canvases slid rustling down along the dark poles. And then?

Last Monday night this young man with the long arms and the eager pink face bought three tickets to the side-show and stood watching Electra three times as the electricity burned through her like blue fire while this young man strained at the rope barrier, and memorized her every move as she sat high up there on the platform, all fire and pale flesh.

He came four nights in a row.

"You got an audience, Ellie," said Johnny on the third night.

"So I see," she said.

"Don't pay no attention," said Johnny.

"I won't," she said. "Why should I? Don't worry."

After all, she'd done the act for years. Johnny slammed on the power, and it filled her from ankle to elbows to ears as he handed her the bright sword and she thrust it out blindly over the audience, smiling under her half mask, to let them tap shoulders and brows as the blue sparks crackled and spat. On the fourth night she shoved the sword far out toward the young man with the sweating pink face, first among the crowd. The young man raised his hand swiftly, eagerly, as if to seize the blade. Blue sparks leaped the gap, but his hand didn't flinch or stop as he grabbed on and took the fire in his fingers and then his fist and then his wrist and his arm into his body.

His eyes, in the light, flared with blue alcohol flame, fed by the sword, whose fire in passing lit her arm and face and body. He stretched his hand still farther out, his waist jammed against the rope, silent and tense. Then Johnny cried, "*Every*body touch it! Every one!" And Electra lifted the blade out on the air for others to feel and stroke, while Johnny cursed. Through the blindfold she saw the terrible illumination which would not leave the young man's face.

The fifth night, instead of touching the young man's fingers, she tapped the blazing tip of the sword against the palm of his hand, brushing and burning until he shut his eyes.

That night she walked out on the lake pier after the show and did not look back as she moved, but listened and began to smile. The lake shook against the rotting piles. The carnival lights made wandering, uneasy roads on the black water. The Ferris wheel whirled high and around, with its faint screams, and far away the calliope steamed and sobbed "Beautiful Ohio." She slowed her walking. She put out her right foot, slowly, then her left, then she stopped and turned her head. And as she turned she saw the shadow, and his arms moved around her. A long time later she leaned back in his arms and stared up into his healthy, excited pink face, and said, "My God, you're more dangerous than my chair!"

"Is your name really Electra?" he said.

The next night as the power leaped through her, she stiffened, shuddered, and clamped her lips in her teeth, moaning. Her legs stirred; her hands groped and scratched the chair arms.

"What's wrong!" Beyond the blindfold, Johnny cried out, "What?"

And cut the power.

"I'm all right," she gasped. The crowd murmured. "It's nothing. Go on! Now!"

And he hit the switch.

The fire crawled through her and again she clenched her teeth and threw her head back against the chair. A face rushed out of the dark, and a body with it, to press against her. The power exploded. The electric chair stopped, then melted.

Johnny, a million miles off in the dark, handed her the sword. Her limp, twitching hand dropped it. He handed it back and instinctively she shoved it far out into the night.

Someone, out there in the roaring darkness, touched the blade. She could imagine his eyes burning there, his lips parted as the power jolted him. He was pressed against the rope, hard, hard against the rope, and could not breathe or cry out or pull back!

The power died. The smell of lightning stayed.

"That's it!" someone cried.

Johnny left her to squirm out of the leather straps, jumped off the low platform, and walked out toward the midway. Convulsively, she tore off the bonds, trembling. She ran from the tent, not looking back to see if the young man was still there against the rope.

She fell upon the cot of the trailer behind the tent, perspiring and shaking, and was still crying when Johnny stepped in to look down at her.

"What's the matter?" he said.

"Nothing, nothing, Johnny."

"What was that you pulled out there just now?"

"Nothing, nothing."

"Nothing, nothing," he said. "Like hell it is." His face twisted. "Like hell! You haven't done anything like that for years!"

"I was nervous!"

"Years it's been," he said. "When we were first married you did that. You think I forgot how when I switched the power on this same happened like tonight? You been sitting in that chair for three years like someone listening to a radio. And tonight, and *tonight!*" he cried, choking, standing over her, his fists tightened. "Damn it, *tonight.*"

"Please, please, Johnny. I was nervous."

"What were you thinking there in the chair?" he demanded, leaning down wildly. "What did you think about?"

"Nothing, Johnny, nothing." He grabbed her hair. "Please!"

He threw her head down, turned, walked out, and stopped outside. "I know what you were thinking," he said. "I know." And she heard his footsteps fade away.

And the night passed and the day and another night with another crowd.

But nowhere in the crowd did she see *his* face. Now, in the blackness, with the blindfold tight to her face, she sat in the electric chair and waited while Johnny described the wonders of the Skeleton Man over on the next platform, and still she waited and stared at everyone who entered the tent. Johnny walked around the Skeleton Man, all stiffness, describing the living skull and the terrible bones, and at last the crowd rustled, turned, led by Johnny, his voice like a battered brass horn as he jumped up onto the platform with her so violently that she jerked aside and licked her red lips.

And now the knot of the blindfold was

tied tighter and yet tighter as he bent to whisper:

"*Miss* him?"

She said nothing, but held her head up. The crowd stirred below, like animals in a straw stable.

"He's not here," he whispered and locked the electrodes on her arms. She was silent. He whispered again, "He'll never come back." He fitted the black skullcap over her hair. She trembled. "Afraid?" he wondered quietly. "What of?" He snapped the straps around her ankles. "Don't be afraid. Good clean electricity." A gasp escaped her lips. He stood up. "I hit him," he said softly, touching her blindfold. "Hit him so hard I broke his front teeth. Then I knocked him against a wall and hit him again and again —" He stopped and shouted. "Ladies and gentlemen, witness the most astounding act in carnival history! Here you see a penitentiary electric chair exactly like those used in our biggest prisons. Perfect for the destruction of *criminals!*" With this last word she fell forward, fingers scratching the wood as he cried, "Before your very eyes, this dear lady will be electrocuted!"

The crowd murmured, and she thought of the tesla transformer under the platform and how Johnny might have fixed it so she got amperage, not voltage. Accident, bad accident. Shame. Amperage, not voltage.

She wrenched her right hand free of its leather strap and heard the power switch slam shut as the blue fire seized and shook her, screaming!

The audience applauded and whistled and stomped. Oh, she thought wildly, this is good, my death? Great! More applause! More screams!

Out of the black spaces a body fell. "Hit him so hard I broke his teeth!" The body jerked. "Then I hit him and hit him again!" The body fell, was picked up, fell again. She screamed high and long as a million unseen mouths stung and bit her. Blue flames seized her heart. The young man's body writhed and exploded in bone shrapnel, flame, and ash.

Calmly, Johnny handed her the sword.

"Now," he said.

Being safe was like a blow to the stomach.

She sobbed, fumbling at the sword,

quivering and jerking, unable to move. The power hummed and the crowd stuck out their hands, some like spiders, some like birds leaping away wherever the sword sizzled and spat.

The power still lived in her bones as all over the carnival grounds the lights dimmed.

*Click.* The switch lay in its Off bed.

She sank in upon herself, the sweat running around her nose and her sagging mouth. Gasping, she fought free to pull the blindfold away.

The crowd had gone off to another platform, another miracle, where the Fat Lady called and they obeyed.

Johnny's hand lay on the switch. He dropped his hand, stood there watching her, his dark eyes cold, not flickering.

The tent lights looked dirty, old, yellow, and unclean. She stared blindly at the retreating crowd, Johnny, the tent, the lights. She looked shrunken in the chair. Half of her had poured out through the wires, flushed into the copper cable that fled over the town, leaping from high pole to pole. She lifted her head as if it weighed ninety pounds. The clean light had come, entered into and slid through her, and blasted out again; but it was not the same light anymore. She had changed it; she saw how she had made it. And she shivered because the light was discolored.

Johnny's mouth opened. She didn't hear him at first. He had to repeat what had to be said.

"You're dead," he said firmly. And again: "You're dead."

And sitting there in the electric chair, trapped by the leather straps, with a wind from the tent flaps playing over her face, evaporating the wetness, staring at him and seeing the dark in his eyes, she gave the only answer it was possible to give.

"Yes," she said, eyes shut. "Oh, yes. I *am.*"

# HOPSCOTCH

Vinia woke to the sound of a rabbit running down and across an endless moonlit field; but it was only the soft, quick beating of her heart. She lay on the bed for a moment, getting her breath. Now the sound of the running faded and was gone at a great distance. At last she sat up and looked down from her second-story bedroom window and there below, on the long sidewalk, in the faint moonlight before dawn, was the hopscotch.

Late yesterday, some child had chalked it out, immense and endlessly augmented, square upon square, line after line, numeral following numeral. You could not see the end of it. Down the street it built its crazy pattern, 3, 4, 5, on up to 10, then 30, 50, 90, on away to turn far corners. Never in all the children's world a hopscotch like this! You could jump forever toward the horizon.

Now in the very early, very quiet morning, her eyes traveled and jumped, paused and hopped, along that pre-sumptuous ladder of chalk-scratches and she heard herself whisper:

"Sixteen."

But she did not run on from there.

The next square waited, she knew, with the scribbled blue-chalk 17, but her mind flung out its arms and bal-anced, teetering, poised with her numb foot planted across the 1 and the 6, and could go no further.

Trembling, she lay back down.

The room was like the bottom of a cool well all night and she lay in it like a white stone in a well, enjoying it, float-ing in the dark yet clear element of half dreams and half wakening. She felt the breath move in small jets from her nostrils and she felt the immense sweep of her eyelids shutting and opening again and again. And at last she felt the fever brought into her room by the presence of the sun beyond the hills.

Morning, she thought. It might be a special day. After all, it's my birthday. Anything might happen. And I hope it does.

The air moved the white curtains like a summer breath.

"Vinia . . . ?"

A voice was calling. But it couldn't be a voice. Yet — Vinia raised herself — there it was again.

"Vinia . . . ?"

She slipped from bed and ran to the window of her high second-story bedroom.

There on the fresh lawn below, calling up to her in the early hour, stood James Conway, no older than she, seventeen, very seriously smiling, waving his hand now as her head appeared.

"Jim, what're you doing here?" she said, and thought, Does he know *what* day this is?

"I've been up an hour already," he replied. "I'm going for a walk, starting early, all day. Want to come along?"

"Oh, but I couldn't . . . my folks won't be back till late tonight, I'm alone, I'm supposed to stay . . ."

She saw the green hills beyond the town and the roads leading out into summer, leading out into August and rivers and places beyond this town and this house and this room and this particular moment.

"I can't go . . ." she said faintly.

"I can't hear you!" he protested mildly, smiling up at her under a shielding hand.

"Why did you ask me to walk with you, and not someone else?"

He considered this for a moment. "I don't know," he admitted. He thought it over again, and gave her his most pleasant and agreeable look. "Because, that's all, just because."

"I'll be down," she said.

"Hey!" he said.

But the window was empty.

They stood in the center of the perfect, jeweled lawn, over which one set of prints, hers, had run, leaving marks, and another, his, had walked in great slow strides to meet them. The town was silent as a stopped clock. All the shades were still down.

"My gosh," said Vinia, "it's early. It's crazy-early. I've never been up this early and out this early in years. Listen to everyone sleeping."

They listened to the trees and the whiteness of the houses in this early whispering hour, the hour when mice went back to sleep and flowers began untightening their bright fists.

"Which way do we go?"

"Pick a direction."

Vinia closed her eyes, whirled, and

pointed blindly. "Which way am I point-ing?"

"North."

She opened her eyes. "Let's go north out of town, then. I don't suppose we should."

"Why?"

And they walked out of town as the sun rose above the hills and the grass burned greener on the lawns.

There was a smell of hot chalk high-way, of dust and sky and waters flowing in a creek the color of grapes. The sun was a new lemon. The forest lay ahead with shadows stirring like a million birds under each tree, each bird a leaf-darkness, trembling. At noon, Vinia and James Conway had crossed vast meadows that sounded brisk and starched underfoot. The day had grown warm, as an iced glass of tea grows warm, the frost burning off, left in the sun.

They picked a handful of grapes from a wild barbed-wire vine. Holding them up to the sun, you could see the clear grape thoughts suspended in the dark amber fluid, the little hot seeds of con-templation stored from many afternoons of solitude and plant philosophy. The grapes tasted of fresh, clear water and something that they had saved from the morning dews and the evening rains. They were the warmed-over flesh of April ready now, in August, to pass on their simple gain to any passing stranger. And the lesson was this; sit in the sun, head down, within a prickly vine, in flickery light or open light, and the world will come to you. The sky will come in its time, bringing rain, and the earth will rise through you, from beneath, and make you rich and make you full.

"Have a grape," said James Conway. "Have *two.*"

They munched their wet, full mouths.

They sat on the edge of a brook and took off their shoes and let the water cut their feet off to the ankles with an exquisite cold razor.

My feet are gone! thought Vinia. But when she looked, there they were, underwater, living comfortably apart from her, completely acclimated to an amphibious existence.

They ate egg sandwiches Jim had brought with him in a paper sack.

"Vinia," said Jim, looking at his sandwich before he bit it. "Would you mind if I kissed you?"

"I don't know," she said, after a moment. "I hadn't thought."

"Will you think it over?" he asked.

"Did we come on this picnic just so you could kiss me?" she asked suddenly.

"Oh, don't get me wrong! It's been a swell day! I don't want to spoil it. But if you should decide, later, that it's all right for me to kiss you, would you tell me?"

"I'll tell you," she said, starting on her second sandwich, "if I ever decide."


The rain came as a cool surprise.

It smelled of soda water and limes and oranges and the cleanest, freshest river in the world, made of snow-water, falling from the high, parched sky.

First there had been a motion, as of veils, in the sky. The clouds had enveloped each other softly. A faint breeze had lifted Vinia's hair, sighing and evaporating the moisture from her upper lip, and then, as she and Jim began to run, the raindrops fell down all about without touching them and then at last began to touch them, coolly, as they leaped green-moss logs and darted among vast trees into the deepest, muskiest cavern of the forest. The forest sprang up in wet murmurs overhead, every leaf ringing and painted fresh with water.

"This way!" cried Jim.

And they reached a hollow tree so vast that they could squeeze in and be warmly cozy from the rain. They stood together, arms about each other, the first coldness from the rain making them shiver, raindrops on their noses and cheeks, laughing. "Hey!" He gave her brow a lick. "Drinking water!"

"Jim!"

They listened to the rain, the soft envelopment of the world in the velvet clearness of falling water, the whispers in deep grass, evoking odors of old, wet wood and leaves that had lain a hundred years, moldering and sweet.

Then they heard another sound. Above and inside the hollow warm darkness of the tree was a constant humming, like someone in a kitchen, far away, baking and crusting pies contentedly, dipping in sweet sugars and snowing in baking powders, someone in a warm, dim, summer-rainy kitchen making a vast supply of food, happy at it, humming between lips over it.

"Bees, Jim, up there! Bees!"

"Shh!"

Up the channel of moist, warm hollow they saw little yellow flickers. Now the last bees, wettened, were hurrying home from whatever pasture or meadow or field they had covered, dipping by Vinia and Jim, vanishing up the warm flue of summer into hollow dark.

"They won't bother us. Just stand still."

Jim tightened his arms; Vinia tightened hers. She could smell his breath with the wild tart grapes still on it. And the harder the rain drummed on the tree, the tighter they held, laughing, at last quietly letting their laughter drain away into the sound of the bees home from the far fields. And for a moment, Vinia thought that she and Jim might be caught by a sudden drop of great masses of honey from above, sealing them into this tree forever, enchanted, in amber, to be seen by anyone in the next thousand years who strolled by, while the weather of all ages rained and thundered and turned green outside the tree.

It was so warm, so safe, so protected here, the world did not exist, there was raining silence, in the sunless, forested day.

"Vinia," whispered Jim, after a while. "May I now?"

His face was very large, near her, larger than any face she had ever seen.

"Yes," she said.

He kissed her.

The rain poured hard on the tree for a full minute while everything was cold outside and everything was tree-warmth and hidden away inside.

It was a very sweet kiss. It was very friendly and comfortably warm and it tasted like apricots and fresh apples and as water tastes when you rise at night and walk into a dark, warm summer kitchen and drink from a cool tin cup. She had never imagined that a kiss could be so sweet and immensely tender and careful of her. He held her not as he had held her a moment before, hard, to protect her from the green rain weather, but he held her now as if she were a porcelain clock, very carefully and with consideration. His eyes were closed and the lashes were glistening dark; she saw this in the instant she opened her eyes and closed them again.

The rain stopped.

It was a moment before the new silence shocked them into an awareness of the climate beyond their world. Now there was nothing but the suspension of water in all the intricate branches of the forest. Clouds moved away to show the blue sky in great quilted patches.

They looked out at the change with some dismay. They waited for the rain to come back, to keep them, by necessity, in this hollow tree for another minute or an hour. But the sun appeared, shining through upon everything, making the scene quite commonplace again.

They stepped from the hollow tree slowly and stood with their hands out, balancing, finding their way, it seemed, in these woods where the water was drying fast on every limb and leaf.

"I think we'd better start walking," said Vinia. "That way."

They walked off into the summer afternoon.

They crossed the town limits at sunset and walked hand in hand in the last glowing of the summer day. They had talked very little the rest of the afternoon, and now as they turned down one street after another, they looked at the passing sidewalk under their feet.

"Vinia," he said at last. "Do you think this is the beginning of something?"

"Oh, gosh, Jim, I don't know."

"Do you think maybe we're in love?"

"Oh, I don't know that either!"

They passed down into the ravine and over the bridge and up the other side to her street.

"Do you think we'll ever be married?"

"It's too early to tell, isn't it?" she said.

"I guess you're right." He bit his lip. "Will we go walking again soon?"

'I don't know. I don't know. Let's wait and see, Jim."

The house was dark, her parents not home yet. They stood on her porch and she shook his hand gravely.

"Thanks, Jim, for a really fine day," she said.

"You're welcome," he said.

They stood there.

Then he turned and walked down the steps and across the dark lawn. At the far edge of lawn he stopped in the shadows and said, "Good night."

He was almost out of sight, running, when she, in turn, said good night.

In the middle of the night, a sound wakened her.

She half sat up in bed, trying to hear it again. The folks were home, everything was locked and secure, but it hadn't been them. No, this was a special sound. And lying there, looking out at the summer night that had, not long ago, been a summer day, she heard the sound again, and it was a sound of hollowing warmth and moist bark and empty, tunneled tree, the rain outside but comfortable dryness and secretness inside, and it was the sound of bees come home from distant fields, moving upward in the flue of summer into wonderful darkness.

And this sound, she realized, putting her hand up in the summer-night room to touch it, was coming from her drowsy, half-smiling mouth.

Which made her sit bolt upright, and very quietly move downstairs, out through the door, onto the porch, and across the wet-grass lawn to the sidewalk, where the crazed hopscotch chalked itself way off into the future.

Her bare feet hit the first numbers, leaving moist prints up to 10 and 12, thumping, until she stopped at 16, staring down at 17, hesitating, swaying. Then she gritted her teeth, made fists, reared back, and . . .

Jumped right in the middle of the square 17.

She stood there for a long moment, eyes shut, seeing how it felt.

Then she ran upstairs and lay out on the bed and touched her mouth to see if a summer afternoon was breathing out of it, and listening for that drowsy hum, the golden sound, and it was there.

And it was this sound, eventually, which sang her to sleep.

# THE FINNEGAN

To say that I have been haunted for the rest of my life by the affair Finnegan is to grossly understate the events leading up to that final melancholy. Only now, at threescore and ten, can I write these words for an astonished constabulary who may well run with picks and shovels to unearth my truths or bury my lies.

The facts are these:

Three children went astray and were missed. Their bodies were found in the midst of Chatham Forest and each bore no marks of criminal assassination, but all had suffered their lifeblood to be drained. Only their skin remained like that of some discolored vineyard grapes withered by sunlight and no rain.

From the withered detritus of these innocents rose fresh rumors of vampires or similar beasts with similar appetites. Such myths always pursue the facts to stun them in their tracks. It could only have been a tombyard beast, it was said, that fed on and destroyed three lives and ruined three dozen more.

The children were buried in the most holy ground. Soon after, Sir Robert Merriweather, pretender to the throne of Sherlock Holmes but modestly refusing the claim, moved through the ten dozen doors of his antique house to come forth to search for this terrible thief of life. With myself, I might add, to carry his brandy and bumbershoot and warn him of underbrush pitfalls in that dark and mysterious forest.

Sir Robert Merriweather, you say?

Just that. Plus the ten times ten plus twelve amazing doors in his shut-up house.

Were the doors used? Not one in nine. How had they appeared in Sir Robert's old manse? He had shipped them in, as a collector of doors, from Rio, Paris, Rome, Tokyo, and mid-America. Once collected, he had stashed them, hinged, to be seen from both sides, on the walls of his upper and lower chambers. There he conducted tours of these odd portals for such antique fools as were ravished by the sight of the curiously overdone, the undersimplified, the rococo, or some First Empire cast aside by Napoleon's nephews or seized from Hermann Goering, who had in turn ransacked the Louvre. Others, pelted by Oklahoma dust storms, were jostled home in flat-beds cushioned by bright posters from carnivals buried in the windblown deso-lations of 1936 America. Name your least favorite door, it was *his.* Name the best quality, he owned it also, hidden and safe, true beauties behind obliv-ion's portals.

I had come to see his doors, not the deaths. At his behest, which was a command, I had bought my curiosity a steamship ticket and arrived to find Sir Robert involved not with ten dozen doors, but some great *dark* door. A mysterious portal, still un-found. And beneath? A tomb.

Sir Robert hurried the grand tour, opening and shutting panels rescued from Peking, long buried near Etna, or filched from Nantucket. But his heart, gone sick, was not in this, what should have been delightful, tour.

He described the spring rains that drenched the country to make things green, only to have people to walk out in that fine weather and one week find the body of a boy emptied of life through two incisions in his neck, and in the next weeks, the bodies of the two girls. People shouted for the police and sat drinking in pubs, their faces long and pale, while mothers locked their children home where fathers lectured on the dooms that lay in Chatham Forest.

"Will you come with me," said Sir Robert at last, "on a very strange, sad picnic?"

"I will," I said.

So we snapped ourselves in weatherproofs, lugged a hamper of sandwiches and red wine, and plunged into the forest on a drear Sunday.

There was time, as we moved down a hill into the dripping gloom of the trees, to recall what the papers had said about the vanished children's bloodless flesh, the police thrashing the forest ten dozen times, clueless, while the surrounding estates slammed their doors drum-tight at sunset.

"Rain. Damn. Rain!" Sir Robert's pale face stared up, his gray mustache quivering over his thin mouth. He was sick and brittle and old. "Our picnic will be *ruined!*"

"Picnic?" I said. "Will our killer join us for eats?"

"I pray to God he will," Sir Robert said. "Yes, pray to God he will."

We walked through a land that was now mists, now dim sunlight, now forest, now open glade, until we came into a silent part of the woods, a silence made of the way the trees grew wetly together and the way the green moss lay in swards and hillocks. Spring had not yet filled the empty trees. The sun was like an arctic disk, withdrawn, cold, and almost dead.

"This is the place," said Sir Robert at last.

"Where the children were found?" I inquired.

"Their bodies empty as empty can be."

I looked at the glade and thought of the children and the people who had stood over them with startled faces and the police who had come to whisper and touch and go away, lost.

"The murderer was never apprehended?"

"Not this clever fellow. How observant are you?" asked Sir Robert.

"What do you want observed?"

"There's the catch. The police slipped up. They were stupidly anthropomorphic about the whole bloody mess, seeking a killer with two arms, two legs, a suit of clothes, and a knife. So hypnotized with their human concept of the killer that they overlooked one obvious unbelievable fact about this place. *So!*"

He gave his cane a quick light tap on the earth.

Something happened. I stared at the ground. "Do that again," I whispered.

"You *saw* it?"

"I thought I saw a small trapdoor open and shut. May I have your cane?"

He gave me the cane. I tapped the ground.

It happened again.

"A spider!" I cried. "Gone! God, how quick!"

"Finnegan," Sir Robert muttered.

"What?"

"You know the old saying: in again, out again, Finnegan. Here."

With his penknife, Sir Robert dug in the soil to lift an entire clod of earth, breaking off bits to show me the tunnel. The spider, in panic, leaped out its small wafer door and fell to the ground.

Sir Robert handed me the tunnel. "Like gray velvet. Feel. A model builder, that small chap. A tiny shelter, camouflaged, and him alert. He could hear a fly walk. Then pounce out, seize, pop back, *slam* the lid!"

"I didn't know you loved Nature."

"Loathe it. But this wee chap, there's much we share. Doors. Hinges. Wouldn't consider other arachnids. But my love of portals drew me to study this incredible carpenter." Sir Robert worked the trap on its cobweb hinges. "What craftsmanship! And it *all* ties to the tragedies!"

"The murdered children?"

Sir Robert nodded. "Notice any special thing about this forest?"

"It's too quiet."

"Quiet!" Sir Robert smiled weakly. "Vast *quantities* of silence. No familiar birds, beetles, crickets, toads. Not a rustle or stir. The police didn't notice. Why should they? But it was this absence of sound and motion in the glade that prompted my wild theory about the murders."

He toyed with the amazing structure in his hands.

"What would you say if you could imagine a spider *large* enough, in a hideout *big* enough, so that a running child might hear a vacuumed sound, be seized, and vanish with a soft thud below. How say you?" Sir Robert stared at the trees. "Poppycock and bilge? Yet, why *not?* Evolution, selection, growth, mutations, and — *pfft!*"

Again he tapped with his cane. A trapdoor flew open, shut.

"Finnegan," he said.

The sky darkened.

"Rain!" Casting a cold gray eye at the clouds, he stretched his frail hand to touch the showers. "Damn! Arachnids *hate* rain. And so will our huge dark Finnegan."

"Finnegan!" I cried irritably.

"I *believe* in him, yes."

"A spider larger than a *child?!*"

"*Twice* as large."

The cold wind blew a mizzle of rain over us. "Lord, I hate to leave. Quick, before we go. *Here.*"

Sir Robert raked away the old leaves with his cane, revealing two globular gray-brown objects.

"What *are* they?" I bent. "Old cannon-balls?"

"No." He cracked the grayish globes. "Soil, through and through."

I touched the crumbled bits.

"Our Finnegan excavates," said Sir Robert. "To make his tunnel. With his large rakelike chelicerae he dislodges soil, works it into a ball, carries it in his jaws, and drops it beyond his hole."

Sir Robert displayed half a dozen pellets on his trembling palm. "Normal balls evicted from a tiny trapdoor tunnel. Toy-size." He knocked his cane on the huge globes at our feet. "Explain *those!*"

I laughed. "The *children* must've made them with mud!"

"Nonsense!" cried Sir Robert irritably, glaring about at trees and earth. "By God, somewhere, our dark beast lurks beneath his velvet lid. We might be *standing* on it. Christ, don't stare! His door has beveled rims. Some architect, this Finnegan. A genius at camouflage."

Sir Robert raved on and on, describing the dark earth, the arachnid, its fiddling legs, its hungry mouth, as the wind roared and the trees shook.

Suddenly, Sir Robert flung up his cane.

"No!" he cried.

I had no time to turn. My flesh froze, my heart stopped.

Something snatched my spine.

I thought I heard a huge bottle uncorked, a lid sprung. Then this monstrous thing crawled down my back.

"Here!" cried Sir Robert. "Now!"

He struck with his cane. I fell, dead weight. He thrust the thing from my spine. He lifted it.

The wind had cracked the dead tree branch and knocked it onto my back.

Weakly, I tried to rise, shivering. "Silly," I said a dozen times. "Silly. Damn awful silly!"

"Silly, no. Brandy, yes!" said Sir Robert. "Brandy?"

The sky was very black now. The rain swarmed over us.

Door after door after door, and at last into Sir Robert's country house study. A warm, rich room, where a fire smoldered on a drafty hearth. We devoured our sandwiches, waiting for the rain to cease. Sir Robert estimated that it would stop by eight o'clock, when, by moonlight, we might return, ever so reluctantly, to Chatham Forest. I remembered the fallen branch, its spidering touch, and drank both wine and brandy.

"The silence in the forest," said Sir Robert, finishing his meal. "What murderer could achieve such a silence?"

"An insanely clever man with a series of baited, poisoned traps, with liberal quantities of insecticide, might kill off every bird, every rabbit, every insect," I said.

"Why should he do that?"

"To convince us that there is a large spider nearby. To perfect his act."

"We are the only ones who have noticed this silence; the police did not. Why should a murderer go to all that trouble for nothing?"

"Why *is* a murderer? you might well ask."

"I am not convinced." Sir Robert topped his food with wine. "This creature, with a voracious mouth, has cleansed the forest. With nothing left, he seized the children. The silence, the murders, the prevalence of trapdoor spiders, the large earth balls, it all *fits*."

Sir Robert's fingers crawled about the desktop, quite like a washed, manicured spider in itself. He made a cup of his frail hands, held them up.

"At the bottom of a spider's burrow is a dustbin into which drop insect remnants on which the spider has dined. Imagine the dustbin of our Grand Finnegan!"

I imagined. I visioned a Great Legged thing fastened to its dark lid under the forest and a child running, singing in the half-light. A brisk insucked whisk of air, the song cut short, then nothing but an empty glade and the echo of a softly dropped lid, and beneath the dark earth the spider, fiddling, cabling, spinning the stunned child in its silently orchestrating legs.

What would the dustbin of such an incredible spider resemble? What the remnants of many banquets? I shuddered.

"Rain's letting up." Sir Robert nodded his approval. "Back to the forest. I've mapped the damned place for weeks. All the bodies were found in one half-open glade. That's where the assassin, if it was a man, arrives! Or where the unnatural silk-spinning, earth-tunneling architect of special doors abides his tomb."

"*Must* I hear all this?" I protested.

"Listen more." Sir Robert downed the last of his burgundy. "The poor children's prolapsed corpses were found at thirteen-day intervals. Which means that every two weeks our loathsome eight-legged hide-and-seeker must feed. Tonight is the fourteenth night after the last child was found, nothing but skin. Tonight our hidden friend *must* hunger afresh. So! Within the hour, I shall introduce you to Finnegan the great and horrible!"

"All of which," I said, "makes me want to drink."

"Here I go." Sir Robert stepped through one of his Louis the Fourteenth portals. "To find the last and final and most awful door in all my life. You will follow."

Damn, *yes!* I followed.

The sun had set, the rain was gone, and the clouds cleared off to show a cold and troubled moon. We moved in our own silence and the silence of the exhausted paths and glades while Sir Robert handed me a small silver pistol.

"Not that that would help. Killing an outsize arachnid is sticky. Hard to know where to fire the first shot. If you miss, there'll be no time for a second. Damned things, large or small, move in the *instant!*"

"Thanks." I took the weapon. "I need a drink."

"Done." Sir Robert handed me a silver

brandy flask. "Drink as needed."

I drank. "What about you?"

"I have my own special flask." Sir Robert lifted it. "For the right time."

"Why wait?"

"I must surprise the beast and mustn't be drunk at the encounter. Four seconds before the thing grabs me, I will imbibe of this dear Napoleon stuff, spiced with a rude surprise."

"Surprise?"

"Ah, wait. You'll see. So will this dark thief of life. Now, dear sir, here we part company. I this way, you yonder. Do you mind?"

"Mind when I'm scared gutless? What's that?"

"Here. If I should vanish." He handed me a sealed letter. "Read it aloud to the constabulary. It will help them locate me and Finnegan, lost and found."

"Please, no details. I feel like a damned fool following you while Finnegan, *if* he exists, is underfoot snug and warm, saying, 'Ah, those idiots above running about, freezing. I think I'll *let* them freeze.' "

"One hopes not. Get away now. If we walk together, he won't jump up. Alone, he'll peer out the merest crack, glom the scene with a huge bright eye, flip down again, *ssst,* and one of us gone to darkness."

"Not me, please. Not me."

We walked on about sixty feet apart and beginning to lose one another in the half moonlight.

"Are you there?" called Sir Robert from half the world away in leafy dark.

"I wish I weren't," I yelled back.

"Onward!" cried Sir Robert. "Don't lose sight of me. Move closer. We're near on the site. I can intuit, I almost *feel* —"

As a final cloud shifted, moonlight glowed brilliantly to show Sir Robert waving his arms about like antennae, eyes half shut, gasping with expectation.

"Closer, closer," I heard him exhale. "Near on. Be still. Perhaps . . ."

He froze in place. There was something in his aspect that made me want to leap, race, and yank him off the turf he had chosen.

"Sir Robert, oh, God!" I cried. "Run!"

He froze. One hand and arm orchestrated the air, feeling, probing, while his other hand delved, brought forth his silver-coated flask of brandy. He held it high in the moonlight, a toast to doom.

Then, afflicted with need, he took one, two, three, my God, *four* incredible swigs!

Arms out, balancing the wind, tilting his head back, laughing like a boy, he swigged the last of his mysterious drink.

"All right, Finnegan, below and beneath!" he cried. "Come *get* me!"

He stomped his foot.

Cried out victorious.

And *vanished.*

It was all over in a second.

A flicker, a blur, a dark bush had grown up from the earth with a whisper, a suction, and the thud of a body dropped and a door shut.

The glade was empty.

"Sir Robert. Quick!"

But there was no one to quicken.

Not thinking that *I* might be snatched and vanished, I lurched to the spot where Sir Robert had drunk his wild toast.

I stood staring down at earth and leaves with not a sound save my heart beating while the leaves blew away to reveal only pebbles, dry grass, and earth.

I must have lifted my head and bayed

to the moon like a dog, then fell to my knees, fearless, to dig for lids, for tunneled tombs where a voiceless tangle of legs wove themselves, binding and mummifying a thing that had been my friend. This is his final door, I thought insanely, crying the name of my friend.

I found only his pipe, cane, and empty brandy flask, flung down when he had escaped night, life, everything.

Swaying up, I fired the pistol six times here into the unanswering earth, a dumb thing gone stupid as I finished and staggered over his instant graveyard, his locked-in tomb, listening for muffled screams, shrieks, cries, but heard none. I ran in circles, with no ammunition save my weeping shouts. I would have stayed all night, but a downpour of leaves, a great spidering flourish of broken branches, fell to panic and suffer my heart. I fled, still calling his name to a silence lidded by clouds that hid the moon.

At his estate, I beat on the door, wailing, yanking, until I recalled: it opened inward, it was unlocked.

Alone in the library, with only liquor to help me live, I read the letter that Sir Robert had left behind:

*My dear Douglas:*

*I am old and have seen much but am not mad. Finnegan exists. My chemist had provided me with a sure poison that I will mix in my brandy for our walk. I will drink all. Finnegan, not knowing me as a poisoned morsel, will give me a swift invite. Now you see me, now you don't. I will then be the weapon of his death, minutes after my own. I do not think there is another outsize nightmare like him on earth. Once gone, that's the end.*

*Being old, I am immensely curious. I fear not death, for my physicians tell me that if no accidents kill me, cancer will.*

*I thought of giving a poisoned rabbit to our nightmare assassin. But then I'd never know where he was or if he really existed. Finnegan would die unseen in his monstrous closet, and I never the wiser. This way, for one victorious moment, I will know. Fear for me. Envy me. Pray for me. Sorry to abandon you without farewells. Dear friend, carry on.*

I folded the letter and wept.

No more was ever heard of him.

Some say Sir Robert killed himself, an actor in his own melodrama, and that one day we shall unearth his brooding, lost, and Gothic body and that it was he who killed the children and that his preoccupation with doors and hinges, and more doors, led him, crazed, to study this one species of spider, and wildly plan and build the most amazing door in history, an insane burrow into which he popped to die, before my eyes, thus hoping to perpetuate the incredible Finnegan.

But I have found no burrow. I do not believe a man could construct such a pit, even given Sir Robert's overwhelming passion for doors.

I can only ask, would a man murder, draw his victims' blood, build an earthen vault? For what motive? Create the *finest* secret exit in all time? Madness. And what of those large grayish balls of earth supposedly tossed forth from the spider's lair?

Somewhere, Finnegan and Sir Robert lie clasped in a velvet-lined unmarked crypt, deep under. Whether one is the paranoiac alter ego of the other, I cannot say. But the murders have ceased, the rabbits once more rush in Chatham Forest, and its bushes teem with butterflies and birds. It is another spring, and the children run again through a loud glade, no longer silent.

Finnegan and Sir Robert, *requiescat in peace.*

# THAT WOMAN ON
# THE LAWN

Very late at night he heard the weeping on the lawn in front of his house. It was the sound of a woman crying. By its sound he knew it was not a girl or a mature woman, but the crying of someone eighteen or nineteen years old. It went on, then faded and stopped, and again started up, now moving this way or that on the late-summer wind.

He lay in bed listening to it until it made his eyes fill with tears. He turned over, shut his eyes, let the tears fall, but could not stop the sound. Why should a young woman be weeping long after midnight out there?

He sat up and the weeping stopped.

At the window, he looked down. The lawn was empty but covered with dew. There was a trail of footsteps across the lawn to the middle where someone had stood turning, and another trail going off toward the garden around the house.

The moon stood full in the sky and

122

filled the lawn with its light, but there was no more sadness and only the footprints there.

He stepped back from the window, suddenly chilled, and went down to heat and drink a cup of chocolate.

He did not think of the weeping again until dusk the next day, and even then thought that it must be some woman from a house nearby, unhappy with life, perhaps locked out and in need of a place to let her sadness go.

Yet . . . ?

As the twilight deepened, coming home he found himself hurrying from the bus, at a steady pace which astonished him. Why, why all this?

Idiot, he thought. A woman unseen weeps under your window, and here at sunset the next day, you almost run.

Yes, he thought, but her *voice!*

Was it beautiful, then?

No. Only familiar.

Where had he heard such a voice before, wordless in crying?

Who could he ask, living in an empty house from which his parents had vanished long ago?

He turned in at his front lawn and stood still, his eyes shadowed.

What had he expected? That whoever she was would be waiting here? Was he that lonely that a single voice long after midnight roused all his senses?

No. Simply put: he must know who the crying woman was.

And he was certain she would return tonight as he slept.

He went to bed at eleven, and awoke at three, panicked that he had missed a miracle. Lightning had destroyed a nearby town or an earthquake had shaken half the world to dust, and he had slept through it!

Fool! he thought, and slung back the covers and moved to the window, to see that indeed he had overslept.

For there on the lawn were the delicate footprints.

And he hadn't even *heard* the weeping!

He would have gone out to kneel in the grass, but at that moment a police car motored slowly by, looking at nothing and the night.

How could he run to prowl, to probe, to touch the grass if that car came by again? What doing? Picking clover blossoms? Weeding dandelions? What, what?

His bones cracked with indecision. He would go down, he would not.

Already the memory of that terrible weeping faded the more he tried to make it clear. If he missed her one more night, the memory itself might be gone.

Behind him, in his room, the alarm clock rang.

Damn! he thought. What time *did* I set it for?

He shut off the alarm and sat on his bed, rocking gently, waiting, eyes shut, listening.

The wind shifted. The tree just outside the window whispered and stirred.

He opened his eyes and leaned forward. From far off, coming near, and now down below, the quiet sound of a woman weeping.

She had come back to his lawn and was not forever lost. Be very quiet, he thought.

And the sounds she made came up on the wind through the blowing curtains into his room.

Careful now. Careful but quick.

He moved to the window and looked down.

In the middle of the lawn she stood and wept, her hair long and dark on her shoulders, her face bright with tears.

And there was something in the way her hands trembled at her sides, the way her hair moved quietly in the wind, that shook him so that he almost fell.

He knew her and yet did *not.* He had seen her before, but had never seen.

Turn your head, he thought.

Almost as if hearing this, the young woman sank to her knees to half kneel on the grass, letting the wind comb her hair, head down and weeping so steadily and bitterly that he wanted to cry out: Oh, no! It kills my heart!

And as if she had heard, quite suddenly her head lifted, her weeping grew less as she looked up at the moon, so that he saw her face.

And it was indeed a face seen somewhere once, but *where?*

A tear fell. She blinked.

It was like the blinking of a camera and a picture taken.

"God save me!" he whispered. "No!"

He whirled and stumbled toward the closet to seize down an avalanche of boxes and albums. In the dark he scrabbled, then pulled on the closet light, tossed aside six albums until finally, dragging another forth and riffling pages, he gave a cry, stopped, and held a photo close, then turned and moved blindly to the window.

There he stared down at the lawn and then at the photograph, very old, very yellowed with age.

Yes, yes, the same! The image struck his eyes and then his heart. His whole body shook, made an immense pulsation, as he leaned at the album, leaned on the window frame, and almost shouted:

You! How dare you come back! How dare you be young! How dare you be *what?* A girl untouched, wandering late on my lawn!? You were *never* that young! Never! Damn, oh, damn your warm blood, damn your wild soul!

But this he did not shout or say.

For something in his eyes, like a beacon, must have flashed.

The crying of the young woman on the lawn stopped.

She looked up.

At which instant the album fell from his fingers, through the burst-wide screen, and down like a dark bird fluttering to strike the earth.

127

The young man gave a muted cry, whirled, and ran.

"No, no!" he cried aloud. "I didn't *mean* — come back!"

He was down the stairs and out on the porch in a matter of seconds. The door slammed behind him like a gunshot. The explosion nailed him to the rail, half down to the lawn, where there was nothing to be seen but footprints. Either way, up the street lay empty sidewalks and shadows under trees. A radio played off in an upstairs window in a house behind trees. A car passed, murmuring, at a far intersection.

"Wait," he whispered. "Come back. I shouldn't have *said* —"

He stopped. He had said nothing, but only *thought* it. But his outrage, his jealousy?

She had felt that. She had somehow heard. And now . . . ?

She'll never come back, he thought. Oh God!

He sat on the porch steps for a while, quietly biting his knuckle.

At three in the morning, in bed, he thought he heard a sigh and soft footsteps in grass, and waited. The photo album lay closed on the floor. Even though it lay shut, he could see and know her face. And it was utterly impossible, utterly insane.

His last thought before sleep was: ghost.

The strangest ghost that ever walked.

The ghost of someone dead.

The ghost of someone who died very old.

But somehow come back not as her old self.

But a ghost that was somehow young.

Weren't ghosts always, when they returned, the same age as when they died?

No.

Not this one anyway.

"Why . . . ?" he whispered.

And dream took over the whisper.

One night passed and then another and another, and there was nothing on the lawn but the light of a moon that changed its face from outright stare to half grimace.

He waited.

The first night a more than ordinarily casual cat crossed the yard at two A.M.

The second night a dog trotted by, wearing his tongue half out of his

129

mouth like a loosely tied red cravat, smiling at trees.

The third night a spider spent from twelve-twenty-five until four A.M. building a baroque clockface on the air between lawn and trees, which a bird broke in passing at dawn.

He slept most of Sunday and awoke with a fever that was not an illness at dusk.

Late in the twilight of the fifth day, the color of the sky somehow promised her return, as did the way the wind leaned against the trees and the look of the moon when it finally rose to set the scene.

"All right," he said, half aloud. *"Now."*

But at midnight, nothing.

"Come on," he whispered.

One o'clock, nothing.

You must, he thought.

No, you *will.*

He slept for ten minutes and woke suddenly at two-ten, knowing that when he went to the window —

She would be there.

She was.

At first, he didn't see her, and groaned, and then, in the shadow of the great oak far out on the edge of the lawn, he saw something move, and one foot came out, and she took a step and stood very still.

He held his breath, quieted his heart, told himself to turn, walk, and take each step down with precision, numbering them, fifteen, fourteen, thirteen, moving in darkness with no rush, six, five, four, and at last one. He opened the front screen door with only a whisper, and was on the porch without frightening what might be out beyond waiting for him.

Quietly, he moved down the porch steps to the edge of the lawn, like one who stands on the rim of a pond. Out in the center of that pond, the young woman stood, trapped like someone on thin ice that might at any moment break and drop her through.

She did not see him. And then . . .

She did a thing that was a signal. Tonight her hair was fixed in a knot at the back of her head. She lifted her white arms in a gesture and with one touch of her fingers, a touch of snow, loosened her hair.

It fell in a dark banner, to blow and repattern itself across her shoulders, which trembled with their shadows.

The wind stirred her hair in the night and moved it about her face and on her uplifted hands.

The shadows laid down by the moon under every tree leaned as if called by the motion.

The entire world shifted in its sleep.

The wind blew as the young woman waited.

But no footsteps sounded along the white sidewalks. No front doors opened far down the street. No windows were raised. No motion caused front porches to creak and shift.

He took another step out onto the small meadow of night.

"Who are you — ?" she gasped, and stepped back.

"No, no," he said softly. "It's all right."

Another trembling had taken over her body. Where before it had been some hope, some anticipation, now it was fear. One hand stopped her hair from blowing; the other half shielded her face.

"I'll stand right here," he said. "Believe me."

She waited a long while, staring at him until her shoulders relaxed and the lines around her mouth vanished. Her whole body sensed the truth of his words.

"I don't understand," she said.

"I don't either."

"What are you doing here?"

"I don't know."

"What am *I* doing here?"

"You came to meet someone," he said.

"Did I?"

The town clock struck three in the morning far away. She listened to it, her face shadowed by the sound.

"But it's so late. People don't walk around late on front lawns!"

"They do if they *must*," he said.

"But why?"

"Maybe we can find out, if we talk."

"About what, *what?!*"

"About why you're here. If we talk long enough, we may know. I know why I'm here, of course. I heard you crying."

"Oh, I'm so ashamed."

"Don't be. Why are people ashamed of tears? I cry often. Then I start laughing. But the crying must come first. Go ahead."

"What a strange man you are."

Her hand fell away from her hair. Her

other hand moved away so her face was illuminated by a small and growing curiosity.

"I thought I was the only one who knew about crying," she said.

"Everyone thinks that. It's one of those little secrets we keep from each other. Show me a serious man and I'll show you a man who has never wept. Show me a madman and I'll show you a man who dried his tears a long time ago. Go ahead."

"I think I'm done," she said.

"Any time, start over."

She burst out a tiny laugh. "Oh, you *are* strange. Who are you?"

"We'll come to that."

She peered across the lawn at his hands, his face, his mouth, and then at his eyes.

"Oh, I *know* you. But from *where?!*"

"That would spoil it. You wouldn't believe, anyway."

"I would!"

Now it was his turn to laugh quietly. "You're very young."

"No, nineteen! *Ancient!*"

"Girls, by the time they go from twelve to nineteen, are full of years, yes. I don't know; but it must be so. Now, please, why are you out here in the middle of the night?"

"I —" She shut her eyes to think in on it. "I'm waiting."

"Yes?"

"And I'm sad."

"It's the waiting that makes you sad, yes?"

"I think, no, yes, no."

"And you don't quite know what you're waiting for?"

"Oh, I wish I could be sure. All of me's waiting. I don't know, *all* of me. I don't understand. I'm impossible!"

"No, you're everyone that ever grew up too fast and wanted too much. I think girls, women, like you have slipped out at night since time began. If it wasn't here in Green Town, it was in Cairo or Alexandria or Rome or Paris in summer, anywhere there was a private place and late hours and no one to see, so they just rose up and out, as if someone had called their name —"

"I was called, yes! That's *it!* Someone *did* call my name! It's *true.* How did you know? Was it *you!*"

"No. But someone we both know. You'll know his name when you go back to bed tonight, wherever that is."

"Why, in that house, behind you," she said. "That's my house. I was born in it."

"Well" — he laughed — "so was *I*."

"You? How can that be? Are you sure?"

"Yes. Anyway, you heard someone calling. You had to come out —"

"I did. Many nights now. But, always, no one's here. They *must* be there, or why would I hear them?"

"One day there'll be someone to fit the voice."

"Oh, don't joke with me!"

"I'm not. Believe. There will be. That's what all those other women heard in other years and places, middle of summer, dead of winter, go out and risk cold, stand warm in snow banks, and listen and look for strange footprints on the midnight snow, and only an old dog trotting by, all smiles. Damn, damn."

"Oh, yes, damn, damn." And her smile showed for a moment, even as the moon came out of the clouds and went away. "Isn't it silly?"

"No. Men do the same. They take long walks when they're sixteen, seventeen. They don't stand on lawns, waiting, no. But, my God, how they *walk!* Miles and miles from midnight until dawn and come home exhausted and explode and die in bed."

"What a shame that those who stand and wait and those who walk all night can't —"

"Meet?"

"Yes; don't you think it's a shame?"

"They *do,* finally."

"Oh, no, I shall never meet anyone. I'm old and ugly and terrible and I don't know how many nights I've heard that voice making me come here and there's nothing and I just want to die."

"Oh, lovely young girl," he said gently. "Don't die. The cavalry is on its way. You will be saved."

There was such certainty in his voice that it made her glance up again, for she had been looking at her hands and her own soul in her hands.

"You *know,* don't you?" she asked.

"Yes."

"You truly *know?* You tell the *truth?*"

"Swear to God, swear by all that's living."

"Tell me more!"

"There's little more to tell."

"Tell me!"

"Everything will be all right with you.

Some night soon, or some day, someone will call and they'll really be there when you come to find. The game will be over."

"Hide-and-seek, you mean? But it's gone on too long!"

"It's almost over, Marie."

"You know my name!"

He stopped, confused. He had not meant to speak it.

"How did you know, who are you?" she demanded.

"When you get back to sleep tonight, you'll know. If we say too much, you'll disappear, or I'll disappear. I'm not quite sure which of us is real or which is a ghost."

"Not me! Oh, surely not me. I can feel myself. I'm here. Why, look!" And she showed him the remainder of her tears brushed from her eyelids and held on her palms.

"Oh, that's real, all right. Well, then, dear young woman, *I* must be the visitor. I come to tell you it will all go right. Do you believe in special ghosts?"

"Are you *special?*"

"One of us is. Or maybe both. The ghost of young love or the ghost of the unborn."

"Is that what *I* am, *you* are?"

"Paradoxes aren't easy to explain."

"Then, depending on how you look at it, you're impossible, and so am I."

"If it makes it easier, just think I'm not really here. Do you believe in ghosts?"

"I think I do."

"It comes to me to imagine, then, that there are special ghosts in the world. Not ghosts of dead people. But ghosts of want and need, or I guess you might say desire."

"I don't understand."

"Well, have you ever lain in bed late afternoons, late nights and dreamed something so much, awake, you felt your soul jump out of your body as if something had yanked a long, pure white sheet straight out the window? You want something so much, your soul leaps out and follows, my God, fast?"

"Why . . . yes. Yes!"

"Boys do that, men do that. When I was twelve I read Burroughs' Mars novels. John Carter used to stand under the stars, hold up his arms to Mars, and ask to be taken. And Mars grabbed his soul, yanked him like an aching

139

tooth across space, and landed him in dead Martian seas. That's boys, that's men."

"And girls, women?"

"*They* dream, yes. And their ghosts come out of their bodies. Living ghosts. Living wants. Living needs."

"And go to stand on lawns in the middle of winter nights?"

"That's about it."

"Am I a ghost, then?"

"Yes, the ghost of *wanting* so much it kills but doesn't kill you, shakes and almost breaks you."

"And you?"

"I must be the answer-ghost."

"The answer-ghost. What a funny name!"

"Yes. But you've *asked* and I know the *answer.*"

"Tell me!"

"All right, the answer is this, young girl, young woman. The time of waiting is almost over. Your time of despair will soon be through. Very soon, now, a voice will call and when you come out, both of you, your ghost of want and your body with it, there will be a man to go with the voice that calls."

"Oh, please don't tell me that if it isn't

true!" Her voice trembled. Tears flashed again in her eyes. She half raised her arms again in defense.

"I wouldn't dream to hurt you. I only came to tell."

The town clock struck again in the deep morning.

"It's late," she said.

"Very late. Get along, now."

"Is that all you're going to say?"

"You don't need to know any more."

The last echoes of the great clock faded.

"How strange," she murmured. "The ghost of a question, the ghost of an answer."

"What better ghosts can there be?"

"None that I ever heard of. We're twins."

"Far nearer than you think."

She took a step, looked down, and gasped with delight. "Look, oh, look. I *can* move!"

"Yes."

"What was it you said, boys walk all night, miles and miles?"

"Yes."

"I could go back in, but I can't sleep now. I must walk, too."

"Do that," he said gently.

"But where shall I *go?*"

"Why," he said, and he suddenly knew. He knew where to send her and was suddenly angry with himself for knowing, angry with her for asking. A burst of jealousy welled in him. He wanted to race down the street to a certain house where a certain young man lived in another year and break the window, burn the roof. And yet, oh, yet, if he *did* that!?

"Yes?" she said, for he had kept her waiting.

Now, he thought, you must tell her. There's no escape.

For if you don't tell her, angry fool, you yourself will never be born.

A wild laugh burst from his mouth, a laugh that accepted the entire night and time and all his crazed thinking.

"So you want to know where to go?" he said at last.

"Oh, yes!"

He nodded his head. "Up to that corner, four blocks to the right, one block to the left."

She repeated it quickly. "And the final number?!"

"Eleven Green Park."

"Oh, thank you, thank you!" She ran

a few steps, then stopped, bewildered. Her hands were helpless at her throat. Her mouth trembled. "Silly. I hate to leave."

"Why?"

"Why, because . . . I'm afraid I'll never see *you* again!"

"You will. Three years from now."

"Are you sure?"

"I won't look quite the same. But it'll be me. And you'll know me forever."

"Oh, I'm glad for that. Your face *is* familiar. I somehow know you well."

She began to walk slowly, looking over at him as he stood near the porch of the house.

"Thanks," she said. "You've saved my life."

"And my own along with it."

The shadows of a tree fell across her face, touched her cheeks, moved in her eyes.

"Oh, Lord! Girls lie in bed nights listing the names for their future children. Silly. Joe. John. Christopher. Samuel. Stephen. And right now, Will." She touched the gentle rise of her stomach, then lifted her hand out halfway to point to him in the night. "Is your name Will?"

"Yes."

Tears absolutely burst from her eyes. He wept with her.

"Oh, that's fine, fine," she said at last. "I can go now. I won't be out here on the lawn anymore. Thank God, thank *you.* Good night."

She went away into the shadows across the lawn and along the sidewalk down the street. At the far corner he saw her turn and wave and walk away.

"Good night," he said quietly.

I am not born yet, he thought, or she has been dead many years, which is it? which?

The moon sailed into clouds.

The motion touched him to step, walk, go up the porch stairs, wait, look out at the lawn, go inside, shut the door.

A wind shook the trees.

The moon came out again and looked upon a lawn where two sets of footprints, one going one way, one going another in the dew, slowly, slowly, as the night continued, vanished.

By the time the moon had gone down the sky there was only an empty lawn and no sign, and much dew.

The great town clock struck six in the morning. Fire showed in the east. A cock crowed.

# THE VERY GENTLE MURDERS

Joshua Enderby awoke in the middle of the night because he felt someone's fingers at his throat.

In the rich darkness above him he sensed but could not see his wife's frail, skelatinous weight seated on his chest while she dabbled and clenched tremblingly again and again at his neck.

He opened his eyes wide. He realized what she was trying to do. It was so ridiculous he almost cried out with laughter!

His rickety, jaundiced, eighty-five-year-old wife was trying to strangle him!

She panted forth a rum-and-bitters smell as she perched there, toppling like a drunken moth, tinkering away as if he were a toy. She sighed irritably and her skinny fingers began to sweat as she gasped, "Why *don't* you, oh, why *don't* you?"

Why don't I *what?* he wondered idly, lying there. He swallowed and this faint action of his Adam's apple dislodged her feeble clutch. Why don't I *die,* is *that* it? he cried silently. He lay another few moments, wondering if she'd gain strength enough to do him in. She didn't.

Should he snap on the light to confront her? Wouldn't she look a silly ass, a skinny chicken aloft sidesaddle on her hated husband's amazed body, and him laughing?

Joshua Enderby groaned and yawned. "Missy?"

Her hands froze on his collarbone.

"Will you —" He turned, pretending half sleep. "Will you — please" — he yawned — "move to *your* side — of the bed? Eh? Good girl."

Missy moved off in the dark. He heard ice tinkle. She was having another shot of rum.

At noon the next day, enjoying the weather and waiting for luncheon guests to arrive, old Joshua and Missy traded drinks in the garden pavilion. He handed her Dubonnet; she gave him sherry.

There was a moment of silence as both eyed the stuff and hesitated to sip. He handled his glass in such a way that his large white diamond ring sparked and glittered on his palsied hand. Its light made him flinch and at last he gathered his phlegm.

"Missy," he said. "You haven't long to live, you know."

Missy was hidden behind jonquils in a crystal bowl and now peered out at her mummified husband. Both perceived that the other's hands shook. She wore a cobalt dress, heavily iced with luncheon jewels, little glittery planets under each ear, a scarlet design for a mouth. The ancient whore of Babylon, he thought dryly.

"How odd, my dear, how very odd," Missy said with a polite scrape of her voice. "Why, only last night —"

"You were *thinking* of me?"

"We must talk."

"Yes, we must." He leaned like a wax mannequin in his chair. "No rush. But if I do you in, or if you do me in (it matters not which), let's protect each other, yes? Oh, don't look at me in amaze, my dear. I was perfectly aware of your little gallop last night on my ribs, fumbling with my esophagus, feeling the tumblers click, or whatever."

"Dear me." Blood rose in Missy's powdery cheeks. "Were you awake all during? I'm mortified. I think I shall have to go lie down."

"Nonsense." Joshua stopped her. "If I die, you should be shielded so no one'll accuse you. Same with me, if *you* die. Why go to all the trouble of trying to — eliminate — each other if it just means a gallows-drop or a french fry."

"Logical enough," she agreed.

"I suggest a — a series of mash notes to each other. Umm, lavish displays of sentiment before friends, gifts, *et cetera.* I'll run up bills for flowers, diamond bracelets. You purchase fine leather wallets and gold-ferruled canes for *me.*"

"You have a head for things, I must say," she admitted.

"It will help allay suspicion if we appear madly, anciently in love."

"You know," she said tiredly, "it doesn't matter, Joshua, which of us dies first, except that I'm *very* old and would like to do *one* thing right in my life. I've always been such a dilettante. I've never liked you. Loved you, yes, but that's ten million years back. You never were a friend. If it weren't for the children —"

"Motives are bilge," he said. "We are two querulous old pots with nothing to do but kick off, and make a circus of *that.* But how much better the dying game if we write a few rules, act it neatly, with no one the wiser. How long has this assassination plot of yours been active?"

She beamed. "Remember the opera last week? You slipped from the curb? That car almost nailed you?"

"Good Lord." He laughed. "I thought someone shoved *both* of us!" He leaned forward, chuckling. "Okay. When you fell in the bath last month? *I* greased the tub!"

Unthinkingly, she gasped, drank part of her Dubonnet, then froze.

Reading her mind, he stared at his own drink.

"This isn't poisoned, by any chance?" He sniffed his glass.

"Don't be silly," she replied, touching her Dubonnet with a lizard's doubtful tongue. "They'd find the residue in what's left of your stomach. Just be sure you double-check your shower tonight. I have kited the temperature, which might bring on a seizure."

"You *didn't!*" he scoffed.

"I've *thought* about it," she confessed.

The front-door chimes rang, but not

with their usual joy, sounding more funereal. Nonsense! Joshua thought. Bosh! thought Missy, then brightened:

"We have forgotten our luncheon guest! That's the Gowrys! He's a bore, but be nice! Fix your collar."

"It's damned tight. Too much starch. One more plot to strangle me?"

"I wish I *had* thought of that. Double time, now!"

And they marched, arm in arm, with idiot laughter, off to meet the half-forgotten Gowrys.

Cocktails were served. The old relics sat side by side, hands laced like school chums, laughing with weak heartiness at Gowry's dire jokes. They leaned forward to show him their porcelain smiles, saying, "Oh, that's a *good* one!" loudly, and, softly, *sotto voce,* to each other: "Thought of anything *new?*" "Electric razor in your bath?" "Not bad, not bad!"

"And then *Pat* said to Mike!" cried Mr. Gowry.

From the corner of his mouth Joshua whispered to Missy, "You know, I dislike you with something approaching the colossal proportions of first love. You have taught me mayhem. How?"

"When the teacher is ready, the pupil will arrive," whispered Missy.

Laughter rose in tumbling, whirling waves. The room was giddy, airy, light. "So Pat says to Mike, do it *yourself!*" boomed Gowry.

"Oh, *ho!*" everyone exploded.

"Now, dear." Missy waved at her ancient husband. "Tell one of *your* jokes. Oh, but *first*," she remembered cleverly, "trot down-cellar, darling, and fetch the brandy."

Gowry sprang forward with wild courtesy. "*I* know where it is!"

"Oh, Mr. Gowry, *don't!*"

Missy gestured frantically.

Mr. Gowry ran from the room.

"Oh, dear, dear me," cried Missy.

A moment later, Gowry uttered a loud shriek from the basement, followed by a thunderous crash.

Missy hippety-hopped out, only to reappear moments later, her hand clutched to her throat. "Heavens to Betsy," she wailed. "Come look. I *do* believe Mr. Gowry has pitched himself straight down the cellar stairs!"

The next morning Joshua Enderby shuffled into the house lugging a large green velvet board some five feet by three, on which pistols were clasped in display.

"Here I am!" he shouted.

Missy appeared with a rum Collins in one bracelet-jangly hand, her cane thumping in the other. "What's *that?*" she demanded.

"First, how's old Gowry?"

"Broken leg. Wished it had been his vocal cords."

"Shame about that top cellar step gone loose, eh?" The old man hooked the green velvet board to the wall. "Good thing Gowry lurched for the brandy, not I."

"Shame." The wife drank thirstily. "Explain."

"I'm in the antique-gun-collecting business." He waved at the weapons in their neat leather nests.

"I don't see —"

"With a collection of guns to clean — *bang!*" He beamed. "Man shoots wife while oiling matchlock garter pistol. Didn't know it was loaded, says weeping spouse."

"Touché," she said.

An hour later, while oiling a revolver, he almost blew his brains out.

His wife came thumping in and froze. "Hell. You're still alive."

"Loaded, by God!" He lifted the weapon in a trembling hand. "*None were* loaded! Unless —"

"Unless — ?"

He seized three more weapons. "*All* loaded! *You!*"

"Me," she said. "While you ate lunch. I suppose I'll have to give you tea now. Come along."

He stared at the bullet hole in the wall. "Tea, hell," he said. "Where's the *gin?!*"

It was *her* turn for a shopping spree. "There are ants in the house." She rattled her full shopping bag and set out ant-paste pots in all the rooms, sprinkled ant powders on windowsills, in his golf bag, and over his gun collection. From other sacks she drew rat poisons, mouse-killers, and bug-exterminators. "A bad summer for roaches." She distributed these liberally among the foods.

"That's a double-edged sword," he observed. "You'll fall on it!"

"Bilge. The victim mustn't *choose* his demise."

"Yes, but no violence. I wish a serene face for the coroner."

"Vanity. Dear Josh, your face will twist like a corkscrew with one heaping teaspoon of Black Leaf Forty in your midnight cocoa!"

"I," he shot back, "know a recipe that will break you out in a thousand lumps before expiring!"

She quieted. "Why, Josh, I wouldn't *dream* of using Black Leaf Forty."

He bowed. "I wouldn't dream of using the thousand-lump recipe."

"Shake," she said.

Their assassins game continued. He bought huge rattraps to hide in the halls. "You run barefoot so: *small* wounds, *large* infections!"

She in turn stuck the sofas full of antimacassar pins. Wherever he laid a hand it drew blood. "Ow! Damn!" He sucked his fingers. "Are these Amazon Indian blowgun darts?"

"No. Just plain old rusty lockjaw needles."

"Oh," he said.

Though he was aging fast, Joshua Enderby dearly loved to drive. You could see him motoring with feeble wildness up and down the hills of Beverly, mouth gaped, eyes blinking palely.

One afternoon he phoned from Malibu. "Missy? My God, I almost dove from a cliff. My right front wheel flew off on a straightaway!"

"I planned it for a *curve!*"

"Sorry."

"Got the idea from Action News. Loosen car's wheel lugs: tomato *surprise.*"

"Never mind about careless old me," he said. "What's new with you?"

"Rug slipped on the hall stairs. Maid fell on her prat."

"Poor Lila."

"I send her everywhere ahead now. She bucketed down like a laundry bag. Lucky she's all fat."

"We'll kill that one between us if we're not careful."

"Do you *think?* Oh, I *do* like Lila *so.*"

"Lay Lila off for a spell. Hire someone new. If we catch *them* in our crossfire, won't be so sad. Hate to think of Lila smashed under a chandelier or —"

"Chandelier!" Missy shrieked. "You been fiddling with my grandma's Fountainbleu Palace crystal hangings? Listen here, mister. You're not to *touch* that chandelier!"

"Promise," he muttered.

"Good grief! Those lovely crystals! If they fell and missed me, I'd hop on one leg to cane you to death, then wake you up and cane you *again!*"

*Slam* went the phone.

Joshua Enderby stepped in from the balcony at supper that night. He'd been smoking. He looked at the table. "Where's your strawberry crumpet?"

"I wasn't hungry. I gave it to the new maid."

"Idiot!"

She glared. "Don't tell me you poisoned that crumpet, you old S.O.B.?"

There was a crash from the kitchen.

Joshua went to look and returned. "She's not new anymore," he said.

They stashed the new maid in an attic trunk. No one telephoned to ask for her.

"Disappointing," observed Missy on the seventh day. "I felt certain there'd be a tall, cold man with a notebook and another with a camera and flashbulbs flashing. Poor girl was lonelier than we *guessed.*"

Cocktail parties streamed wildly through the house. It was Missy's idea. "So we can pick each other off in a forest of obstacles; moving targets!"

Mr. Gowry, gamely returning to the house, limping after his tumble of some weeks before, joked, laughed, and didn't quite blow his ear off with one of the dueling pistols. Everyone roared but the party broke up early. Gowry vowed never to return.

Then there was a Miss Kummer, who, staying overnight, borrowed Joshua's electric razor and was almost but not quite electrocuted. She left the house rubbing her right underarm. Joshua promptly grew a beard.

Soon after, a Mr. Schlagel vanished. So did a Mr. Smith. The last seen of these unfortunates was at a Saturday night soiree at the Enderbys' mansion.

"Hide-and-seek?" Friends slapped Joshua's back jovially.

"How *do* you do it? Kill 'em with toadstools, plant 'em like mushrooms?"

"Grand joke, yes!" chortled Joshua. "No, no, ha, not toadstools, but one got locked in our stand-up fridge. Overnight Eskimo Pie. The other tripped on a croquet hoop. Defenestrated through a greenhouse window."

"Eskimo Pie, defenestrated!" hooted the party people. "Dear Joshua, you *are* a card!"

"I speak only the *truth*," Joshua protested.

"What won't you think of next?"

"One wonders what *did* happen to old Schlagel and that rascal Smith."

"What *did* happen to Schlagel and Smith?" Missy inquired some days later.

"Let me explain. The Eskimo Pie was my dessert. But the croquet hoop? No! Did *you* spot it in the wrong place, hoping I'd pop by and lunge through the greenhouse panes?"

Missy turned to stone; he had touched a nerve.

"Well, now, it's time for a wee talk," he said. "Cancel the parties. One more victim and sirens will announce the arrival of the law."

"Yes," Missy agreed. "Our target practice seems to wind up in ricochet. About that croquet hoop. You always take midnight greenhouse walks. Why was that damn fool Schlagel stumbling about out there at two A.M.? Dumb ox.

Is he *still* under the compost?"

"Until I stash him with he-who-is-frozen."

"Dear, dear. No more parties."

"Just you, me and — ah — the chandelier?"

"Ah, no. I've hid the stepladder so you can't climb!"

"Damn," said Joshua.

That night by the fireplace, he poured a few glasses of their best port. While he was out of the room, answering the telephone, she dropped a little white powder in her *own* glass.

"Hate this," she murmured. "Terribly unoriginal. But there won't be an inquest. He looked long dead before he died, they'll say as they shut the lid." And she added a touch more lethal stuff to her port just as he wandered in to sit and pluck up his glass. He eyed it and fixed his wife a grin. "Ah, no, no, you don't!"

"Don't what?" she said, all innocence.

The fire crackled warmly, gently on the hearth. The mantel clock ticked.

"You don't mind, *do* you, my dear, if we exchange drinks?"

"Surely you don't think I poisoned

your drink while you were out?"

"Trite. Banal. But possible."

"Well, then, fussbudget, *trade.*"

He looked surprised but traded glasses.

"Here's *not* looking at you!" both said, and laughed.

They drank with mysterious smiles.

And then they sat with immense satisfaction in their easy chairs, the firelight glimmering on their ghost-pale faces, letting the port warm their almost spidery veins. He stuck his legs out and held one hand to the fire. "Ah." He sighed. "Nothing, nothing quite like port!"

She leaned her small gray head back, dozing, gumming her red-sticky mouth, and glancing at him with half-secretive, lazy eyes. "Poor Lila," she murmured.

"Yes," he murmured. "Lila. Poor."

The fire popped and she at last added, "Poor Mr. Schlagel."

"Yes." He drowsed. "Poor Schlagel. Don't forget Smith."

"And you, old man," she said finally, slowly, slyly. "How do *you* feel?"

"Sleepy."

"*Very* sleepy?"

"Un-huh." He studied her with bright

160

eyes. "And, my dear, what about you?"

"Sleepy," she said behind closed eyes. Then they popped wide. "Why all these questions?"

"Indeed," he said, stirring alert. "Why?"

"Oh, well, because . . ." She examined her little black shoe moving in a low rhythm a long way off below her knee. "I think, or perhaps imagine, I have just destroyed your digestive and nervous systems."

For the moment he was drowsily content and examined the warm fire and listened to the clock tick. "What you mean is that you have just poisoned me?" He dreamed the words. "You *what!?*" He jumped as all the air gusted from his body. The port glass shattered on the floor.

She leaned forward like a fortune-teller eagerly predicting futures.

"I cleverly poisoned my own drink and knew that you'd ask to trade off, so you felt safe. And we *did!*" Her laugh tinkled.

He fell back in his chair, clutching at his face to stop the wild swiveling of his eyes. Then suddenly he remembered something and let out an incredible explosion of laughter.

"Why," cried Missy, "why are you laughing?"

"Because," he gasped, tears streaming down his cheeks, his mouth grinning horribly, "*I* poisoned *my* drink! and hoped for an excuse to change with *you!*"

"Oh, dear," she cried, no longer smiling. "How stupid of us. Why didn't I *guess?*"

"Because both of us are much *too* clever by far!" And he lay back, chortling.

"Oh, the mortification, the embarrassment, I feel stark naked and hate myself!"

"No, no," he husked. "Think instead how much you still hate me."

"With all my withered heart and soul. You?"

"No deathbed forgiveness here, old lily-white iron-maiden wife o' mine. Cheerio," he added faintly, far away.

"If you think I'll say 'Cheerio' back, you're crazed," she whispered, her head rolling to one side, her eyes clamped, her mouth gone loose around the words. "But what the hell. Cheer—"

At which her breath ceased and the

fire burned to ashes as the clock ticked and ticked in the quiet room.

Friends found them strewn in their library chairs the next day, both looking more than usually pleased with their situation.

"A suicide pact," said all. "So great their love they could not bear to let the other vanish alone into eternity."

"I hope," said Mr. Gowry, on his crutches, "my wife will someday join me in similar drinks."

# QUICKER THAN
# THE EYE

It was at a magic show I saw the man
who looked enough like me to be my
twin.

My wife and I were seated at a Saturday night performance, it was summer
and warm, the audience melting in
weather and conviviality. All around I
saw married and engaged couples delighted and then alarmed by the comic
opera of their lives which was being
shown in immense symbol onstage.

A woman was sawed in half. How the
husbands in the audience *smiled.*

A woman in a cabinet vanished. A
bearded magician wept for her in despair. Then, at the tip-top of the balcony,
she appeared, waving a white-powdered
hand, infinitely beautiful, unattainable,
far away.

How the wives grinned their cat grins!

"Look at them!" I said to my wife.

A woman floated in midair . . . a
goddess born in all men's minds by
their own true love. Let not her dainty

feet touch earth. Keep her on that invisible pedestal. Watch it! God, don't tell me how it's done, *anyone!* Ah, look at her float, and *dream.*

And what was that man who spun plates, globes, stars, torches, his elbows twirling hoops, his nose balancing a blue feather, sweating everything at once! What, I asked myself, but the commuter husband, lover, worker, the quick luncher, juggling hour, Benzedrine, Nembutal, bank balances, and budgets?

Obviously, none of us had come to escape the world outside, but rather to have it tossed back at us in more easily digested forms, brighter, cleaner, quicker, neater; a spectacle both heartening and melancholy.

Who in life has not seen a woman disappear?

There, on the black, plush stage, women, mysteries of talc and rose petal, vanished. Cream alabaster statues, sculptures of summer lily and fresh rain melted to dreams, and the dreams became empty mirrors even as the magician reached hungrily to seize them.

From cabinets and nests of boxes, from flung sea-nets, shattering like porcelain as the conjurer fired his gun, the women vanished.

Symbolic, I thought. Why do magicians point pistols at lovely assistants, unless through some secret pact with the male subconscious?

"What?" asked my wife.

"Eh?"

"You were muttering," said my wife.

"Sorry." I searched the program. "Oh! Next comes Miss Quick! The *only* female pickpocket in the world!"

"That can't be true," said my wife quietly.

I looked to see if she was joking. In the dark, her dim mouth seemed to be smiling, but the quality of that smile was lost to me.

The orchestra hummed like a serene flight of bees.

The curtains parted.

There, with no great fanfare, no swirl of cape, no bow, only the most condescending tilt of her head, and the faintest elevation of her left eyebrow, stood Miss Quick.

I thought it was a dog act, when she snapped her fingers.

"Volunteers. All *men!*"

"Sit down." My wife pulled at me.

I had risen.

There was a stir. Like so many hounds, a silently baying pack rose and walked (or did they run?) to the snapping of Miss Quick's colorless fingernails.

It was obvious instantly that Miss Quick was the same woman who had been vanishing all evening.

Budget show, I thought; everyone doubles in brass. I don't like her.

"What?" asked my wife.

"Am I talking out loud again?"

But really, Miss Quick provoked me. For she looked as if she had gone backstage, shrugged on a rumpled tweed walking suit, one size too large, gravy-spotted and grass-stained, and then purposely rumpled her hair, painted her lipstick askew, and was on the point of exiting the stage door when someone cried, "You're *on!*"

So here she was now, in her practical shoes, her nose shiny, her hands in motion but her face immobile, getting it over with . . .

Feet firmly and resolutely planted, she waited, her hands deep in her lumpy tweed pockets, her mouth cool, as the dumb volunteers dogged it to the stage.

This mixed pack she set right with a few taps, lining them up in a military row.

The audience waited.

"That's all! Act's over! Back to your seats!"

Snap! went her plain fingers.

The men, dismayed, sheepishly peering at each other, ambled off. She let them stumble half down the stairs into darkness, then yawned:

"Haven't you forgotten something?"

Eagerly, they turned.

"Here."

With a smile like the very driest wine, she lazily unwedged a wallet from one of her pockets. She removed another wallet from within her coat. Followed by a third, a fourth, a fifth! Ten wallets in all!

She held them forth, like biscuits, to good beasts.

The men blinked. No, those were not their wallets! They had been onstage for only an instant. She had mingled with them only in passing. It was all a joke. Surely she was offering them brand-new wallets, compliments of the show!

But now the men began feeling themselves, like sculptures finding unseen flaws in old, hastily flung together armatures. Their mouths gaped, their hands grew more frantic, slapping their chest-pockets, digging their pockets.

All the while Miss Quick ignored them to calmly sort their wallets like the morning mail.

It was at this precise moment I noticed the man on the far right end of the line, half on the stage. I lifted my opera glasses. I looked once. I looked twice.

"Well," I said lightly. "There seems to be a man there who somewhat resembles me."

"Oh?" said my wife.

I handed her the glasses, casually. "Far right."

"It's not *like* you," said my wife. "It's *you!*"

"Well, almost," I said modestly.

The fellow was nice-looking. It was hardly cricket to look thus upon yourself and pronounce favorable verdicts. Simultaneously, I had grown quite cold. I took back the opera glasses and nodded, fascinated. "Crew cut. Horn-rimmed glasses. Pink complexion. Blue eyes —"

"Your absolute twin!" cried my wife.

And this was true. And it was strange, sitting there, watching myself onstage.

"No, no, no," I kept whispering.

But yet, what my mind refused, my eye accepted. Aren't there two billion people in this world? Yes! All different snowflakes, no two the same! But now here, delivered into my gaze, endangering my ego and my complacency, here was a casting from the same absolutes, the identical mold.

Should I believe, disbelieve, feel proud, or run scared? For here I stood witness to the forgetfulness of God.

"I don't think," said God, "I've made one like *this* before."

But, I thought, entranced, delighted, alarmed: God errs.

Flashes from old psychology books lit my mind.

Heredity. Environment.

"Smith! Jones! Helstrom!"

Onstage, in bland drill-sergeant tones, Miss Quick called roll and handed back the stolen goods.

You borrow your body from all your forebears, I thought. Heredity.

But isn't the body also an environment?

"Winters!"

Environment, they say, surrounds you. Well, doesn't the body surround, with its lakes, its architectures of bone, its overabundances, or wastelands of soul? Does not what is seen in passing window-mirrors, a face either serene snowfalls or a pitted abyss, the hands like swans or sparrows, the feet anvils or hummingbirds, the body a lumpy wheat-sack or a summer fern, do these not, seen, paint the mind, set the image, shape the brain and psyche like clay? They *do!*

"Bidwell! Rogers!"

Well, then, trapped in the same environmental flesh, how fared this stranger onstage?

In the old fashion, I wanted to leap to my feet and call, "What o'clock is it?"

And he, like the town crier passing late with my face, might half mournfully reply, "Nine o'clock, and all's well . . ."

But was all well with *him?*

Question: did those horn-rims cover a myopia not only of light but of spirit?

Question: was the slight obesity pressed to his skeleton symbolic of a similar gathering of tissue in his head?

In sum, did his soul go north while mine went south, the same flesh cloaking us but our minds reacting, one winter, one summer?

"My God," I said, half aloud. "Suppose we're absolutely *identical!*"

"Shh!" said a woman behind me.

I swallowed hard.

Suppose, I thought, he *is* a chain-smoker, light sleeper, overeater, manic-depressive, glib talker, deep/shallow thinker, flesh fancier . . .

No one with that body, that face, could be otherwise. Even our names must be similar.

Our names!

". . . l . . . bl . . . er . . ."

Miss Quick spoke his!

Someone coughed. I missed it.

Perhaps she'd repeat it. But no, he, my twin, moved forward. Damn! He stumbled! The audience laughed.

I focused my binoculars swiftly.

My twin stood quietly, center stage now, his wallet returned to his fumbling hands.

"Stand straight," I whispered. "Don't slouch."

"Shh!" said my wife.

I squared my own shoulders, secretly.

I never knew I looked that fine, I thought, cramming the glasses to my eyes. Surely my nostrils aren't that thinly made, the true aristocrat. Is my skin that fresh and handsome, my chin *that* firm?

I blushed, in silence.

After all, if my wife said that was me, accept it! The lamplight of pure intelligence shone softly from every pore of his face.

"The glasses." My wife nudged me.

Reluctantly I gave them up.

She trained the glasses rigidly, not on the man, but now on Miss Quick, who was busy cajoling, flirting, and repicking the pockets of the nearest men. On occasion my wife broke into a series of little satisfied snorts and giggles.

Miss Quick was, indeed, the goddess Shiva.

If I saw two hands, I saw nine. Her hands, an aviary, flew, rustled, tapped, soared, petted, whirled, tickled as Miss Quick, her face blank, swarmed coldly over her victims; touched without touching.

"What's in this pocket? And *this?* And *here?*"

She shook their vests, pinched their lapels, jingled their trousers: money rang. She punched them lightly with a vindictive forefinger, ringing totals on cash registers. She unplucked coat buttons with mannish yet fragile motions, gave wallets back, sneaked them away. She thrust them, took them, stole them again, while peeling money to count it behind the men's backs, then snatched their watches while holding their hands.

She trapped a live doctor now!

"Have you a thermometer!?" she asked.

"Yes." He searched. His face panicked. He searched again. The audience cued him with a roar. He glanced over to find:

Miss Quick standing with the thermometer in her mouth, like an unlit smoke. She whipped it out, eyed it.

"Temperature!" she cried. "One hundred ten!"

She closed her eyes and gave an insincere shake of her hips.

The audience roared. And now she assaulted her victims, bullied them, tugged at their shirts, rumpled their hair, asked: "Where's your *tie?*"

They clapped their hands to their empty collars.

She plucked their ties from nowhere, tossed them back.

She was a magnet that invisibly drew good-luck charms, saints' medals, Roman coins, theater stubs, handkerchiefs, stickpins, while the audience ran riot, convulsed as these rabbit men stood peeled of all prides and protections.

Hold your hip pocket, she vacuumed your vest. Clutch your vest, she jackpotted your trousers. Blithely bored, firm but evanescent, she convinced you you missed nothing, until she extracted it, with faint loathing, from her own tweeds moments later.

"What's this?!" She held up a letter. " 'Dear Helen: Last night with you —' "

A furious blush as the victim tussled with Miss Quick, snatched the letter, stowed it away. But a moment later, the letter was restolen and reread aloud: " 'Dear Helen: Last night —' "

So the battle raged. One woman. Ten men.

She kissed one, stole his belt.

Stole another's suspenders.

The women in the audience — *whinnied.*

Their men, shocked, joined in.

What a magnificent bully, Miss Quick! How she spanked her dear, idiot-grinning, carry-on-somehow men turned boys as she spun them like cigar-store Indians, knocked them with her brontosaur hip, leaned on them like barberpoles, calling each one cute or lovely or handsome.

This night, I thought, is lunatic! All about me, wives, hilarious with contempt, hysterical at being so shabbily revealed in their national pastimes, gagged for air. Their husbands sat stunned, as if a war were over that had not been declared, fought and lost before they could move. Each, nearby, had the terrible look of a man who fears his throat is cut, and that a sneeze would fill the aisle with heads . . .

Quickly! I thought. *Do* something!

"You, *you* onstage, my twin, dodge! Escape!"

And she was coming *at* him!

"Be firm!" I told my twin. "Strategy! Duck, weave. Zigzag. Don't look where she says. Look where she *doesn't* say! *Go* it! now!"

If I shouted this, or merely ground it to powder in my teeth, I don't recall, for all the men froze as Miss Quick seized my twin by the hand.

"Careful!" I whispered.

Too late. His watch was gone. He didn't know it. Your watch is gone! I thought. He doesn't know what *time* it is! I thought.

Miss Quick stroked his lapel. Back off! I warned myself.

Too late. His forty-dollar pen was gone. He didn't know it. She tweaked his nose. He smiled. Idiot! There went his wallet. Not your nose, fool, your *coat!*

"Padded?" She pinched his shoulder. He looked at his right arm. No! I cried silently, for now she had the letters out of his left coat pocket. She planted a red kiss on his brow and backed off with everything else he had on him, coins, identification, a package of chocolates which she ate, greedily. Use the sense God gave a cow! I shouted behind my face. Blind! *See* what she's doing!

She whirled him round, measured him, and said, "This *yours?*" and returned his tie.

My wife was hysterical. She still held the glasses fixed on every nuance and vibration of loss and deprivation on the poor idiot's face. Her mouth was spoiled with triumph.

177

My God! I cried in the uproar. Get off the stage! I yelled within, wishing I could really yell it. At least get out while you have *some* pride!

The laughter had erupted a volcano in the theater, high and rumbling and dark. The dim grotto seemed lit with unhealthy fever, an incandescence. My twin wanted to break off, like one of Pavlov's dogs, too many bells on too many days: no reward, no food. His eyes were glazed with his insane predicament.

Fall! Jump in the pit! *Crawl* away! I thought.

The orchestra sawed at destiny with violins and Valkyrian trumpets in full flood.

With one last snatch, one last contemptuous wag of her body, Miss Quick grasped my twin's clean white shirt, and yanked it *off.*

She threw the shirt in the air. As it fell, so did his pants. As his pants fell, unbelted, so did the theater. An avalanche of shock soared to bang the rafters and roll over us in echoes, a thundering hilarity.

The curtain fell.

We sat, covered with unseen rubble.

Drained of blood, buried in one up-heaval after another, degraded and autopsied and, minus eulogy, tossed into a mass grave, we men took a minute to stare at that dropped curtain, behind which hid the pickpocket and her victims, behind which a man quickly hoisted his trousers up his spindly legs.

A burst of applause, a prolonged tide on a dark shore. Miss Quick did not appear to bow. She did not need to. She was standing behind the curtain. I could *feel* her there, no smile, no expression. Standing, coldly estimating the caliber of the applause, comparing it to the metered remembrances of other nights.

I jumped up in an absolute rage. I had, after all, failed myself. When I should have ducked, I bobbed; when I should have backed off, I ran in. What an ass!

"What a fine show!" said my wife as we milled through the departing audience.

"Fine!" I cried.

"Didn't you like it?"

"All except the pickpocket. Obvious act, overdone, no subtlety," I said, lighting a cigarette.

"She was a whiz!"

"This way." I steered my wife toward the stage door.

"Of course," said my wife blandly, "that man, the one who looks like you, he was a plant. They call them shills, don't they? Paid by the management to pretend to be part of the audience?"

"No man would take money for a spectacle like that," I said. "No, he was just some boob who didn't know how to be careful."

"What are we doing back here?"

Blinking around, we found we were backstage.

Perhaps I wished to stride up to my twin, shouting, "Half-baked ox! Insulter of all men! Play a flute: you dance. Tickle your chin: you jump like a puppet! Jerk!"

The truth was, of course, I must see my twin close-up, confront the traitor and see where his true flesh differed from mine. After all, wouldn't *I* have done better in his place?!

The backstage was lit in blooms and isolated flushes, now bright, now dark, where the other magicians stood chatting. And there, *there* was Miss Quick!

And there, smiling, was my *twin!*

180

"You did fine, Charlie," said Miss Quick.

My twin's name was Charlie. Stupid name.

Charlie patted Miss Quick's cheek. "*You* did fine, ma'am!"

God, it was *true!* A shill, a confederate. Paid what? Five, ten dollars for letting his shirt be torn off, letting his pants drop with his pride? What a turncoat, traitor!

I stood, glaring.

He glanced up.

Perhaps he saw me.

Perhaps some bit of my rage and impacted sorrow reached him.

He held my gaze for only a moment, his mouth wide, as if he had just seen an old school chum. But, not remembering my name, could not call out, so let the moment pass.

He saw my rage. His face paled. His smile died. He glanced quickly away. He did not look up again, but stood pretending to listen to Miss Quick, who was laughing and talking with the other magicians.

I stared at him and stared again. Sweat oiled his face. My hate melted. My temper cooled. I saw his profile

181

clearly, his chin, eyes, nose, hairline; I memorized it all. Then I heard someone say:

"It was a *fine* show!"

My wife, moving forward, shook the hand of the pickpocketing beast.

On the street, I said, "Well, *I'm* satisfied."

"About what?" asked my wife.

"He doesn't look like me at all. Chin's too sharp. Nose is smaller. Lower lip isn't full enough. Too much eyebrow. Onstage, far off, had me going. But close up, no, no. It was the crew cut and horn-rims fooled us. *Anyone* could have horn-rims and a crew cut."

"Yes," my wife agreed, "anyone."

As she climbed into our car, I could not help but admire her long, lovely legs.

Driving off, I thought I glimpsed that familiar face in the passing crowd. The face, however, was watching *me.* I wasn't sure. Resemblances, I now knew, are superficial.

The face vanished in the crowd.

"I'll never forget," said my wife, "when his pants — *fell!*"

I drove very fast, then drove very slow, all the way home.

# DORIAN IN
# EXCELSUS

"Good evening. Welcome. I see you have my invitation in your hands. Decided to be brave, did you? Fine. Here we are. Grab onto this."

The tall, handsome stranger with the heavenly eyes and the impossibly blond hair handed me a wineglass.

"Clean your palate," he said.

I took the glass and read the label on the bottle he held in his left hand. Bordeaux, it read. St. Emilion.

"Go on," said my host. "It's not poison. May I sit? And might you *drink?*"

"I might," I sipped, shut my eyes, and smiled. "You're a connoisseur. This is the best I've had in years. But why this wine and why the invitation? What am I doing here at Gray's Anatomy Bar and Grill?"

My host sat and filled his own glass. "I am doing a favor to myself. This is a great night, perhaps for both of us. Greater than Christmas or Halloween." His lizard tongue darted into his wine

183

to vanish back into his contentment. "We celebrate my being honored, at last becoming —"

He exhaled it all out:

"Becoming," he said, "a friend to Dorian! Dorian's friend. *Me!*"

"Ah." I laughed. "That explains the name of this place, then? Does Dorian own Gray's Anatomy?"

"More! Inspires and rules over it. And deservedly so."

"You make it sound as if being a friend to Dorian is the most important thing in the world."

"No! In *life!* In all of life." He rocked back and forth, drunk not from the wine but from some inner joy. "Guess."

"At what?"

"How *old* I am!"

"You look to be twenty-nine at the most."

"Twenty-nine. What a lovely sound. Not thirty, forty, or fifty, but —"

I said, "I hope you're not going to ask what sign I was born under. I usually leave when people ask that. I was born on the cusp, August, 1920." I pretended to half rise. He pressed a gentle hand to my lapel.

"No, no, dear boy — you don't understand. Look here. And here." He touched under his eyes and then around his neck. "Look for wrinkles."

"But you have none," I said.

"How observant. None. And that is why I have become this very night a fresh, new, stunningly handsome friend to Dorian."

"I still don't see the connection."

"Look at the backs of my hands." He showed his wrists. "No liver spots. I am *not* turning to rust. I repeat the question, how old am I?"

I swirled the wine in my glass and studied his reflection in the swirl.

"Sixty?" I guessed. "Seventy?"

"Good God!" He fell back in his chair, astonished. "How did you *know?*"

"Word association. You've been rattling on about Dorian. I know my Oscar Wilde, I know my Dorian Gray, which means you, sir, have a portrait of yourself stashed in an attic aging while you yourself, drinking old wine, stay young."

"No, no." The handsome stranger leaned forward. "Not *stayed* young. *Became* young. I was old, very old, and it took a year, but the clock went back and after a year of playing at it, I *achieved* what I set out for."

"Twenty-nine was your target?"

"How clever you are!"

"And once you became twenty-nine you were fully elected as —"

"A Friend to Dorian! Bull's-eye! But there is *no* portrait, no attic, no *staying* young. It's *becoming* young again's the ticket."

"I'm still puzzled!"

"Child of my heart, you might possibly be another Friend. Come along. Before the greatest revelation, let me show you the far end of the room and some doors."

He seized my hand. "Bring your wine. You'll need it!" He hustled me along through the tables in a swiftly filling room of mostly middle-aged and some fairly young men, and a few smoke-exhaling ladies. I jogged along, staring back at the EXIT as if my future life were there.

Before us stood a golden door.

"And behind the door?" I asked.

"What always lies behind *any* golden door?" my host responded. *"Touch."*

I reached out to print the door with my thumb.

"What do you feel?" my host inquired.

186

"Youngness, youth, beauty." I touched again. "All the springtimes that ever were or ever will be."

"Jeez, the man's a poet. Push."

We pushed and the golden door swung soundlessly wide.

"Is this where Dorian is?"

"No, no, only his students, his disciples, his *almost* Friends. Feast your eyes."

I did as I was told and saw, at the longest bar in the world, a line of men, a *lineage* of young men, reflecting and re-reflecting each other as in a fabled mirror maze, that illusion seen where mirrors face each other and you find yourself repeated to infinity, large, small, very small, smallest, GONE! The young men were all staring down the long bar at us and then, as if unable to pull their gaze away, at themselves. You could almost hear their cries of appreciation. And with each cry, they grew younger and younger and more splendid and more beautiful . . .

I gazed upon a tapestry of beauty, a golden phalanx freshly out of the Elysian fields and hills. The gates of mythology swung wide and Apollo and his demi-Apollos glided forth, each more beautiful than the last.

I must have gasped. I heard my host inhale as if he drank my wine.

"Yes, *aren't* they," he said.

"Come," whispered my new friend. "Run the gauntlet. Don't linger; you may find tiger-tears on your sleeve and blood rising. *Now.*"

And he glided, he undulated, me along on his soundless tuxedo slippers, his fingers a pale touch on my elbow, his breath a flower scent too near. I heard myself say:

"It's been written that H. G. Wells attracted women with his breath, which smelled of honey. Then I learned that such breath comes with illness."

"How clever. Do *I* smell of hospitals and medicines?"

"I didn't mean —"

"Quickly. You're rare meat in the zoo. Hup, two, three!"

"Hold on," I said, breathless not from walking fast but from perceiving quickly. "This man, and the next, and the one after *that* —"

"Yes?!"

"My God," I said, "they're almost all the *same, look*-alikes!"

"Bull's-eye, *half* true! And the next

and the next after that, as far behind as we have gone, as far ahead as we might go. All twenty-nine years old, all golden tan, all six feet tall, white of teeth, bright of eye. Each different but beautiful, like *me!*"

I glanced at him and saw what I saw around me. Similar but different beauties. So much youngness I was stunned.

"Isn't it time you told me your name?"

"Dorian."

"But you said you were his *Friend.*"

"I *am. They* are. But we all share his name. This chap here. And the next. Oh, once we had commoner names. Smith and Jones. Harry and Phil. Jimmy and Jake. But then we signed up to become Friends."

"Is that why I was invited? To sign *up?*"

"I saw you in a bar across town a year ago, made queries. A year later, you look the proper age —"

"Proper — ?"

"Well, *aren't* you? Just leaving sixty-nine, arriving at seventy?"

"Well."

"My God! Are you *happy* being seventy?"

"It'll do."

"*Do?* Wouldn't you like to be *really* happy, steal some wild oats? *Sow* them?!"

"That time's over."

"It's *not.* I asked and you came, curious."

"Curious about *what?*"

"This." He bared me his neck again and flexed his pale white wrists. "And all *those!*" He waved at the fine faces as we passed. "Dorian's sons. Don't you want to be gloriously wild and young like them?"

"How can I decide?"

"Lord, you've thought of it all night for years. Soon you could be *part* of this!"

We had reached the far end of the line of men with bronzed faces, white teeth, and breath like H. G. Wells' scent of honey . . .

"Aren't you tempted?" he pursued. "Will you refuse —"

"Immortality?"

"No! To live the next twenty years, die at ninety, and look twenty-nine in the damn tomb! In the mirror over there — what do you see?"

"An old goat among ten dozen fauns."

"Yes!"

"Where do I sign up?" I laughed.

"Do you accept?"

"No, I need more facts."

"Damn! Here's the *second* door. Get *in!*"

He swung wide a door, more golden than the first, shoved me, followed, and slammed the door. I stared at darkness.

"What's this?" I whispered.

"Dorian's Gym, of course. If you work out here all year, hour by hour, day by day, you get younger."

"That's some gym," I observed, trying to adjust my eyes to the dim areas beyond where shadows tumbled, and voices rustled and whispered. "I've heard of gyms that help *keep,* not *make,* you young . . . Now tell me . . ."

"I read your mind. For every old man that became young in there at the bar, is there an attic portrait?"

"Well, *is* there?"

"No! There's only Dorian."

"A single person? Who grows old for *all* of you?"

"Touché! Behold his gym!"

I gazed off into a vast high arena where a hundred shadows stirred and moaned like a tide on a terrible shore.

"I think it's time to leave," I said.

"Nonsense. Come. No one will see you.

They're all . . . *busy.* I am Moses," said the sweet breath at my elbow. "And I hereby tell the Red Sea to *part!*"

And we moved along a path between two tides, each shadowed, each more terrifying with its gasps, its cries, its slippages of flesh, its slapping like waves, its repeated whispers for more, more, ah, God, more!

I ran, but my host grabbed on. "Look right, left, now *right* again!"

There must have been a hundred, two hundred animals, beasts, no, men wrestling, leaping, falling, rolling in darkness. It was a sea of flesh, undulant, a writhing of limbs on acres of tumbling mats, a glistening of skin, flashes of teeth where men climbed ropes, spun on leather horses, or flung themselves up crossbars to be seized down in the tidal flux of lamentations and muffled cries. I stared across an ocean of rising and falling shapes. My ears were scorched by their bestial moans.

"What, my God," I exclaimed, "does it all *mean?*"

"There. *See.*"

And above the wild turbulence of flesh in a far wall was a great window, forty feet wide and ten feet tall, and behind that cold glass Something watching, savoring, alert, one vast stare.

And over all there was the suction of a great breath, a vast inhalation which pulled at the gymnasium air with a constant hungry and invisible need. As the shadows tumbled and writhed, this inhalation tugged at them and the raw air in my nostrils. Somewhere a huge vacuum machine sucked in darkness but did *not* exhale. There were long pauses as the shadows flailed and fell, and then another savoring inhalation. It swallowed breath. In, in, always in, devouring the sweaty air, hungering the passions.

And the shadows were pulled, *I* was pulled, toward that vast glass eye, that immense window behind which a shapeless Something stared to dine on gymnasium airs.

"Dorian?" I guessed.

"Come meet him."

"Yes, but . . ." I watched the wild, convulsive shadows. "What *are* they doing?"

"Go find out. Afraid? Cowards never live. So!"

He swung wide a third door and

whether it was golden hot and alive, I could not feel, for suddenly I lurched into a hothouse as the door slammed and was locked by my blond young friend. *"Ready?"*

"Lord, I must go *home!"*

"Not until you meet," said my host, *"him."*

He pointed. At first I could see nothing. The lights were dim and the place, like the gymnasium, was mostly shadow. I smelled jungle greens. The air stirred on my face with sensuous strokes. I smelled papaya and mango and the wilted odor of orchids mixed with the salt smells of an unseen tide. But the tide was there with that immense inhaled breathing that rose and was quiet and began again.

"I see no one," I said.

"Let your eyes adjust. Wait."

I waited. I watched.

There were no chairs in the room, for there was no need of chairs.

He did not sit, he did not recline, he "prolonged" himself on the largest bed in history. The dimensions might easily have been fifteen feet by twenty. It reminded me of the apartment of a writer I once knew who had completely covered his room with mattresses so that women stumbled on the sill and fell flat out on the springs.

So it was with this nest, with Dorian, immense, a gelatinous skin, a vitreous shape, undulant within that nest.

And if Dorian was male or female, I could not guess. This was a great pudding, an emperor jellyfish, a monstrous heap of sexual gelatin from the exterior of which, on occasion, noxious gases escaped with rubbery sounds; great lips sibilating. That and the sough of that labored pump, that constant inhalation, were the only sounds within the chamber as I stood, anxious, alarmed, but at last impressed by this beached creature, cast up from a dark landfall. The thing was a gelatinous cripple, an octopus without limbs, an amphibian stranded, unable to undulate and seep back to an ocean sewer from which it had inched itself in monstrous waves and gusts of lungs and eruptions of corrupt gas until now it lay, featureless, with a mere x-ray ghost of legs, arms, wrists, and hands with skeletal fingers. At last I could discern, at the far end of this flesh peninsula, what seemed a half-flat face with a frail phantom of skull beneath, an open fissure for an eye, a ravenous nostril, and a red wound which ripped wide to surprise me as a mouth.

And at last this thing, this Dorian, spoke.

Or whispered, or lisped.

And with each lisp, each sibilance, an odor of decay was expelled as if from a vast night-swamp balloon, sunk on its side, lost in fetid water as its unsavory breath rinsed my cheeks. It expelled but one lingering syllable:

*Yessss.*

Yes *what?*

And then it added:

Soooo . . .

"How long . . . how long," I murmured, "has it . . . has *he* been *here?*"

"No one knows. When Victoria was Queen? When Booth emptied his makeup kit to load his pistol? When Napoleon yellow-stained the Moscow snows? Forever's not bad . . . What else?"

I swallowed hard. "Is . . . is he?"

"Dorian? Dorian of the attic? He of the Portrait? And somewhere along the line found portraits not enough? Oil, canvas, no depth. The world needed something that could soak in, sponge the midnight rains, breakfast and lunch on loss, depravity's guilt. Something to truly take in, drink, digest; a pustule, imperial intestine. A rheum oesophagus for sin. A laboratory plate to take bacterial snows. Dorian."

The long archipelago of membranous skin flushed some buried tubes and valves, and a semblance of laughter was throttled and drowned in the aqueous gels.

A slit widened to emit gas and again the single word:

*Yessss* . . .

"He's *welcoming* you!" My host smiled.

"I know, I know," I said impatiently. "But why? I don't even *want* to be here. I'm ill. Why can't we go?"

"Because" — my host laughed — "you were *selected.*"

"Selected?"

"We've had our *eye* on you."

"You mean you've watched, followed, spied on me? Christ, who gave you *permission?*"

"Temper, temper. Not everyone is picked."

"Who said I *wanted* to be picked!?"

"If you could *see* yourself as *we* see

you, you'd know why."

I turned to stare at the vast mound of priapic gelatin in which faint creeks gleamed as the creature wept its lids wide in holes to let it stare. Then all its apertures sealed: the saber-cut mouth, the slitted nostrils, the cold eyes gummed shut so that its skin was faceless. The sibilance pumped with gaseous suctions.

*Yessss,* it whispered.

Lisssst, it murmured.

"And list it *is!*" My host pulled forth a small computer pad which he tapped to screen my name, address, and phone.

He glanced from the pad to reel off such items as wilted me.

"Single," he said.

"Married and *divorced.*"

"*Now* single! No women in your life?"

"I'm walking wounded."

He tapped his pad. "Visiting strange bars."

"I hadn't noticed."

"Creative blindness. Getting to bed late. Sleeping all day. Drinking heavily three nights a week."

"Twice!"

"Going to the gym, look, *every day.* Workouts excessive. Prolonged steam baths, overlong massages. Sudden interest in sports. Endless basketball, soccer, tennis matches *every* night, and half the noons. *That's* hyperventilation!"

"*My* business!"

"And *ours!* You're balanced giddily on the rim. Shove all these facts in that one-armed bandit in your head, yank, and watch the lemons and ripe cherries spin. Yank!"

Jesus God. Yes! Bars. Drinks. Late nights. Gyms. Saunas. Masseurs. Basketball. Tennis. Soccer. Yank. Pull. *Spin!*

"Well?" My host searched my face, amused. "Three jackpot cherries in a row?"

I shuddered.

"Circumstance. No court would convict me."

"*This* court *elects* you. We tell palms to read ravenous groins. *Yes?*"

Gas steamed up from one shriveled aperture in the restless mound. *Yessss.*

They say that men in the grip of passion, blind to their own darkness, make love and run mad. Stunned by guilt, they find themselves beasts, having done the very thing they were warned *not* to do by church, town, parents, life. In explosive outrage they turn to the sinful lure. Seeing her as unholy provocateur, they kill. Women, in similar rages and guilts, overdose. Eve lies self-slain in the Garden. Adam hangs himself with the Snake as noose.

But here was no passionate crime, no woman, no provocateur, only the great mound of siphoning breath and my blond host. And only words which riddled me with fusillades of arrows. Like an Oriental hedgehog, bristled with shafts, my body exploded with No, No, No. *Echoed* and then real: *"No!"*

*Yessss,* whispered the vapor from the mounded tissue, the skeleton buried in ancient soups.

*Yessss.*

I gasped to see my games, steams, midnight bars, late-dawn beds: a maniac sum.

I rounded dark corridors to confront a stranger so pockmarked, creased, and oiled by passion, so cobwebbed and smashed by drink, that I tried to avert my gaze. The terror gaped his mouth and reached for my hand. Stupidly, I reached to shake his and — rapped glass! A mirror. I stared deep into my own life. I had seen myself in shop windows, dim undersea men running in creeks. Mornings, shaving, I saw my mirrored health. But *this!* This troglodyte trapped in amber. Myself, snapshotted like ten dozen sexual acrobats! And who jammed this mirror at me? My beautiful host, and that corrupt flatulence beyond.

*"You are selected,"* they whispered.

*"I refuse!"* I shrieked.

And whether I shrieked aloud or merely thought, a great furnace gaped. The oceanic mound erupted thunders of gaseous streams. My beautiful host fell back, stunned that their search beneath my skin, behind my mask, had brought revulsion. Always when Dorian cried, "Friend," raw gymnast teams had mobbed to catapult that armless, legless, featureless Sargasso Sea. Before they had smothered to drown in his miasma, to arise, embrace, and wrestle in the dark gymnasium, then run forth young to assault a world.

And I? What had I dared to do, that quaked that membranous sac into regurgitated whistling and broken winds?

"Idiot!" cried my host, all teeth and fists. "Out! Out!"

"Out," I cried, spun to obey, and tripped.

I do not clearly know what happened as I fell. And if it was a swift reaction to the holocaust erupted like vile spit and vomit from that putrescent mound, I cannot say. I knew no lightning shock of murder, yet knew perhaps some summer heat flash of revenge. For *what?* I thought. What are you to Dorian or he to you that frees the hydra behind your face, or causes the slightest twitch of leg, arm, hand, or fingernail, as the last fetid air from Dorian burned my hair and stuffed my nostrils.

It was over in a second.

Something shoved me. Did my secret self, insulted, give that push? I was flung as if on wires, knocked to sprawl at Dorian.

He gave two terrible cries, one of warning, one of despair.

I was recovered so in landing, I did not sink my hands deep in that poisonous yeast, into that multiflorid Man of War jelly. I swear that I touched, raked, scarified him with only one thing: the smallest fingernail of my right hand.

My fingernail!

And so this Dorian was shot and

foundered. And so the mammoth with screams collapsed. And so the nauseous balloon sank, fold on midnight fold, upon its own boneless self, fissuring volcanic sulfurs, immense rectal airs, outgassed whistles, and whimpers of self-pitying despair.

"Christ! What have you *done!?* Murderer! Damn you!" cried my host, riven to stare at Dorian's exhaustions unto death.

He whirled to strike, but ran to reach the door and cry, "Lock this! *Lock!* Whatever happens, for God's sake, don't *open!* Now!" The door slammed. I ran to lock it and turn.

Quietly, Dorian was falling away.

He sank down and down, out of sight. Like a great membranous tent with its poles removed, he vanished into the floor, down flues and vents on all sides of his great platform nest. Vents obviously created for such a massive disease-sac melting into viral fluid and sewer gas. Even as I watched, the last of the noxious clot was sucked into the vents, and I stood abandoned in a room where but a few minutes before an unspeakable strata of discards and half-born fetuses had lain sucking at sins, spoiled bones, and souls to send forth beasts in semblance of beauty. That perverse royalty, that lunatic monarch, gone, all gone. A last choke and throttle from the sewer vent underlined its death.

My God, I thought, even now, that, all that, that terrible miasma, that stuff is on its way to the sea to wash in with bland tides to lie on clean shores where bathers come at dawn . . .

Even now . . .

I stood, eyes shut, waiting.

For what? There had to be a next thing, yes? It came.

There was a trembling, shivering, and then a quaking of the wall, but especially the golden door behind me.

I spun to see as well as hear.

I saw the door shaken, and then bombarded from the other side. Fists pummeled, struck, hammered. Voices cried out and screamed and then shrieked.

I felt a great mass ram the door to shiver, to slam it on its hinges.

I stared, fearful that the door might explode and let in the flood tide of nightmare-ravening, terrified beasts, the kennel of dying things. For now their shrieks as they mauled and rattled to escape, to beg for mercy, were so terrible that I clamped my fists to my ears.

Dorian was gone, but they remained. Shrieks. Screams. Screams. Shrieks. An avalanche of limbs beyond the door struck and fell, yammering.

What must they look like now? I thought. All those bouquets. All those beauties.

The police will come, I thought, soon. But . . .

No matter what . . .

I would not unlock that door.

# NO NEWS, OR
# WHAT KILLED
# THE DOG?

It was a day of holocausts, cataclysms, tornadoes, earthquakes, blackouts, mass murders, eruptions, and miscellaneous dooms, at the peak of which the sun swallowed the earth and the stars vanished.

But to put it simply, the most respected member of the Bentley family up and died.

Dog was his name, and dog he was.

The Bentleys, arising late Saturday morning, found Dog stretched on the kitchen floor, his head toward Mecca, his paws neatly folded, his tail not a-thump but silent for the first time in twenty years.

Twenty years! My God, everyone thought, could it really have been that long? And now, without permission, Dog was cold and gone.

Susan, the younger daughter, woke everyone yelling:

"Something's wrong with Dog. Quick!"

Without bothering to don his bathrobe, Roger Bentley, in his underwear, hurried out to look at that quiet beast on the kitchen tiles. His wife, Ruth, followed, and then their son Skip, twelve. The rest of the family, married and flown, Rodney and Sal, would arrive later. Each in turn would say the same thing:

"No! Dog was *forever*."

Dog said nothing, but lay there like World War II, freshly finished, and a devastation.

Tears poured down Susan's cheeks, then down Ruth Bentley's, followed in good order by tears from Father and, at last, when it had sunk in, Skip.

Instinctively, they made a ring around Dog, kneeling to the floor to touch him, as if this might suddenly make him sit up, smile as he always did at his food, bark, and beat them to the door. But their touching did nothing but increase their tears.

But at last they rose, hugged each other, and went blindly in search of breakfast, in the midst of which Ruth Bentley said, stunned, "We can't just leave him *there*."

Roger Bentley picked Dog up, gently, and moved him out on the patio, in the shade, by the pool.

"What do we do next?"

"I don't know," said Roger Bentley. "This is the first death in the family in years and —" He stopped, snorted, and shook his head. "I mean —"

"You meant exactly what you said," said Ruth Bentley. "If Dog wasn't family, he was nothing. God, I loved him."

A fresh burst of tears ensued, during which Roger Bentley brought a blanket to put over Dog, but Susan stopped him.

"No, no. I want to see him. I won't be able to see him ever again. He's so beautiful. He's so — *old.*"

They all carried their breakfasts out on the patio to sit around Dog, somehow feeling they couldn't ignore him by eating inside.

Roger Bentley telephoned his other children, whose response, after the first tears, was the same: they'd be right over. Wait.

When the other children arrived, first Rodney, twenty-one, and then the older daughter, Sal, twenty-four, a fresh storm of grief shook everyone and then they sat silently for a moment, watching Dog for a miracle.

"What are your plans?" asked Rodney at last.

"I know this is silly," said Roger Bentley after an embarrassed pause. "After all, he's only a dog —"

*"Only!?"* cried everyone instantly.

Roger had to back off. "Look, he deserves the Taj Mahal. What he'll get is the Orion Pet Cemetery over in Burbank."

"Pet Cemetery!?" cried everyone, but each in a different way.

"My God," said Rodney, "that's silly!"

"What's so *silly* about it?" Skip's face reddened and his lip trembled. "Dog, why, Dog was a pearl of . . . rare *price.*"

"Yeah!" added Susan.

"Well, pardon me." Roger Bentley turned away to look at the pool, the bushes, the sky. "I suppose I could call those trash people who pick up dead bodies —"

"Trash people?" exclaimed Ruth Bentley.

"Dead bodies?" said Susan. "Dog isn't a *dead body!*"

"What *is* he, then?" asked Skip bleakly.

They all stared at Dog lying quietly there by the pool.

"He's," blurted Susan at last, "he's . . . he's my *love!*"

Before the crying could start again, Roger Bentley picked up the patio telephone, dialed the Pet Cemetery, talked, and put the phone down.

"Two hundred dollars," he informed everyone. "Not bad."

"For *Dog?*" said Skip. "Not enough!"

"Are you really serious about this?" asked Ruth Bentley.

"Yeah," said Roger. "I've made fun of those places all my life. But, now, seeing as how we'll never be able to visit Dog again —" He let a moment pass. "They'll come take Dog at noon. Services tomorrow."

"Services!" Snorting, Rodney stalked to the rim of the pool and waved his arms. "You won't get me to *that!*"

Everyone stared. Rodney turned at last and let his shoulders slump. "Hell, I'll be there."

"Dog would never forgive you if you didn't." Susan snuffed and wiped her nose.

But Roger Bentley had heard none of this. Staring at Dog, then his family, and up to the sky, he shut his eyes and exhaled a great whisper:

"Oh, my God!" he said, eyes shut. "Do you realize that this is the first terrible thing that's happened to our family? Have we ever been sick, gone to the hospital? Been in an accident?"

He waited.

"No," said everyone.

"Gosh," said Skip.

"Gosh, indeed! You sure as hell notice accidents, sickness, hospitals."

"Maybe," said Susan, and had to stop and wait because her voice broke. "Maybe Dog died just to *make* us notice how lucky we are."

"Lucky?!" Roger Bentley opened his eyes and turned. "Yes! You know what we *are* —"

"The science fiction generation," offered Rodney, lighting a cigarette casually.

"What?"

"You rave on about that, your school lectures, or during dinner. Can openers? Science fiction. Automobiles. Radio, TV, films. Everything! So science fiction!"

"Well, dammit, they are!" cried Roger Bentley and went to stare at Dog, as if the answers were there amongst the last departing fleas. "Hell, not so long

211

ago there were no cars, can openers, TV. Someone had to dream them. Start of lecture. Someone had to build them. Mid-lecture. So science fiction dreams became finished science fact. Lecture *finis!*"

"I *bet!*" Rodney applauded politely.

Roger Bentley could only sink under the weight of his son's irony to stroke the dear dead beast.

"Sorry. Dog bit me. Can't help myself. Thousands of years, all we did is die. Now, that time's over. In sum: science fiction."

"Bull." Rodney laughed. "Stop reading that junk, Dad."

"Junk?" Roger touched Dog's muzzle. "Sure. But how about Lister, Pasteur, Salk? Hated death. Jumped to stop it. That's all science fiction was ever about. Hating the way things are, wanting to make things different. Junk?!"

"Ancient history, Pop."

"Ancient?" Roger Bentley fixed his son with a terrible eye. "Christ. When I was born in 1920, if you wanted to visit your family on Sundays you —"

"Went to the *graveyard?*" said Rodney.

"Yes. My brother and sister died when

I was seven. Half of my family gone! Tell me, dear children, how many of *your* friends died while you were growing up. In grammar school? High school?"

He included the family in his gaze, and waited.

"None," said Rodney at last.

"None! You hear that? None! Christ. Six of my best friends died by the time I was ten! Wait! I just remembered!"

Roger Bentley hurried to rummage in a hall closet and brought out an old 78-rpm record into the sunlight, blowing off the dust. He squinted at the label:

"No News, Or What Killed The Dog?"

Everyone came to look at the ancient disc.

"Hey, how old *is* that?"

"Heard it a hundred times when I was a kid in the twenties," said Roger.

"No News, Or What Killed The Dog?" Sal glanced at her father's face.

"This gets played at Dog's funeral," he said.

"You're not *serious?*" said Ruth Bentley.

Just then the doorbell rang.

"That can't be the Pet Cemetery people come to take Dog — ?"

"No!" cried Susan. "Not so *soon!*"

Instinctively, the family formed a wall between Dog and the doorbell sound, holding off eternity.

Then they cried, one more time.

The strange and wonderful thing about the funeral was how many people came.

"I didn't know Dog had so many friends," Susan blubbered.

"He freeloaded all around town," said Rodney.

"Speak kindly of the dead."

"Well, he did, dammit. Otherwise why is Bill Johnson here, or Gert Skall, or Jim across the street?"

"Dog," said Roger Bentley, "I sure wish you could see this."

"He *does.*" Susan's eyes welled over. "Wherever he is."

"Good old Sue," whispered Rodney, "who cries at telephone books —"

"Shut up!" cried Susan.

"Hush, both of you."

And Roger Bentley moved, eyes down, toward the front of the small funeral parlor where Dog was laid out, head on paws, in a box that was neither too rich nor too simple but just right.

Roger Bentley placed a steel needle down on the black record which turned on top of a flake-painted portable phonograph. The needle scratched and hissed. All the neighbors leaned forward.

"No funeral oration," said Roger quickly. "Just *this* . . ."

And a voice spoke on a day long ago and told a story about a man who returned from vacation to ask friends what had happened while he was gone.

It seemed that nothing whatsoever had happened.

Oh, just one thing. Everyone wondered what had killed the dog.

The dog? asked the vacationer. My *dog* died?

Yes, and maybe it was the burned horseflesh did it.

Burned *horseflesh!?* cried the vacationer.

Well, said his informant, when the barn burned, the horseflesh caught fire, so the dog ate the burned horseflesh, died.

The barn!? cried the vacationer. How did it catch fire?

Well, sparks from the house blew over, torched the barn, burned the horseflesh, dog ate them, died.

Sparks from the *house!?* shouted the vacationer. How — ?

It was the curtains in the house, caught fire.

Curtains? Burned!?

From the candles around the coffin. *Coffin!?*

Your aunt's funeral coffin, candles there caught the curtains, house burned, sparks from the house flew over, burned down the barn, dog ate the burned horseflesh —

In sum: no news, or what killed the dog!

The record hissed and stopped.

In the silence, there was a little quiet laughter, even though the record had been about dogs and people dying.

"*Now,* do we get the lecture?" said Rodney.

"No, a sermon."

Roger Bentley put his hands on the pulpit to stare for long moments at notes he hadn't made.

"I don't know if we're here for Dog or ourselves. Both, I suppose. We're the nothing-ever-happened-to-us people. Today is a first. Not that I want a rush of doom or disease. God forbid. Death, come slowly, please."

He turned the phonograph record round and round in his hands, trying to read the words under the grooves.

"No news. Except the aunt's funeral candles catch the curtains, sparks fly, and the dog goes west. In *our* lives, just the opposite. No news for years. Good livers, healthy hearts, good times. So — what's it all *about?*"

Roger Bentley glanced at Rodney, who was checking his wristwatch.

"Someday we must die, also." Roger Bentley hurried on. "Hard to believe. We're spoiled. But Susan was right. Dog died to tell us this, gently, and we *must* believe. And at the same time celebrate. What? The fact that we're the start of an amazing, dumbfounding history of survival that will only get better as the centuries pass. You may argue that the next war will take us all. Maybe.

"I can only say I think you will grow to be old, *very* old people. Ninety years from now, most people will have cured hearts, stopped cancers, and jumped life cycles. A lot of sadness will have gone out of the world, thank God. Will this be easy to do? No. Will we do it?

Yes. Not in all countries, right off. But, finally, in most.

"As I said yesterday, fifty years ago, if you wanted to visit your aunts, uncles, grandparents, brothers, sisters, the graveyard was it. Death was *all* the talk. You *had* to talk it. Time's up, Rodney?"

Rodney signaled his father he had one last minute.

Roger Bentley wound it down:

"Sure, kids still die. But not millions. Old folks? Wind up in Sun City instead of marble Orchard."

The father surveyed his family, bright-eyed, in the pews.

"God, look at you! Then look back. A thousand centuries of absolute terror, absolute grief. How parents stayed sane to raise their kids when half of them died, damned if I know. Yet with broken hearts, they did. While millions died of flu or the Plague.

"So here we are in a new time that we can't see because we stand in the eye of the hurricane, where everything's calm.

"I'll shut up now, with a last word for Dog. Because we loved him, we've done this almost silly thing, this service, but now suddenly we're not ashamed or

218

sorry we bought him a plot or had me speak. We may never come visit him, who can say? But he has a place. Dog, old boy, bless you. Now, everyone, blow your nose."

Everyone blew his nose.

"Dad," said Rodney suddenly, "could — we hear the record again?"

Everyone looked at Rodney, surprised.

"Just," said Roger Bentley, "what I was going to suggest."

He put the needle on the record. It hissed.

About a minute in, when the sparks from the house flew over to burn the barn and torch the horseflesh and kill the dog, there was a sound at the back doorway to the small parlor.

Everyone turned.

A strange man stood in the door holding a small wicker basket from which came familiar, small yapping sounds.

And even as the flames from the candles around the coffin caught the curtains and the last sparks blew on the wind . . .

The whole family, drawn out into the sunlight, gathered around the stranger with the wicker basket, waiting for Father to arrive to throw back the coverlet on the small carrier so they could all dip their hands in.

That moment, as Susan said later, was like reading the telephone book one more time.

# THE WITCH DOOR

It was a pounding on a door, a furious, frantic, insistent pounding, born of hysteria and fear and a great desire to be heard, to be freed, to be let loose, to escape. It was a wrenching at hidden paneling, it was a hollow knocking, a rapping, a testing, a clawing! It was a scratching at hollow boards, a ripping at bedded nails; it was a muffled closet shouting and demanding, far away, and a call to be noticed, followed by a silence.

The silence was the most empty and terrible of all.

Robert and Martha Webb sat up in bed.

"Did you hear it?"

"Yes, again."

"Downstairs."

Now whoever it was who had pounded and rapped and made his fingers raw, drawn blood with his fever and quest to be free, had drawn into silence, listening himself to see if his terror and drumming had summoned any help.

The winter night lay through the house with a falling-snow silence, silence snowing into every room, drifting over tables and floors, and banking up the stairwell.

Then the pounding started again. And then:

A sound of soft crying.

"Downstairs."

"Someone in the house."

"Lotte, do you think? The front door's unlocked."

"She'd have knocked. Can't be Lotte."

"She's the only one it *could* be. She *phoned.*"

They both glanced at the phone. If you lifted the receiver, you heard a winter stillness. The phones were dead. They had died days ago with the riots in the nearest towns and cities. Now, in the receiver, you heard only your own heartbeat. "Can you put me up?" Lotte had cried from six hundred miles away. "Just overnight?"

But before they could answer her, the phone had filled itself with long miles of silence.

"Lotte *is* coming. She sounded hysterical. That *might* be her," said Martha Webb.

"No," said Robert. "I heard that crying other nights, too. Dear God."

They lay in the cold room in this farmhouse back in the Massachusetts wilderness, back from the main roads, away from the towns, near a bleak river and a black forest. It was the frozen middle of December. The white smell of snow cut the air.

They arose. With an oil lamp lit, they sat on the edge of the bed as if dangling their legs over a precipice.

"There's no one downstairs, there *can't* be."

"Whoever it is sounds frightened."

"We're *all* frightened, damn it. That's why we came out here, to be away from cities, riots, all that damned foolishness. No more wiretaps, arrests, taxes, neurotics. Now when we find it at last, people call and upset us. And tonight *this*, Christ!" He glanced at his wife. "You afraid?"

"I don't know. I don't believe in ghosts. This *is* 1999; I'm sane. Or like to *think* I am. Where's your gun?"

"We won't need it. Don't ask me why, but we won't."

They picked up their oil lamps. In another month the small power plant would be finished in the white barns behind the house and there'd be power to spare, but now they haunted the farm, coming and going with dim lamps or candles.

They stood at the stairwell, both thirty-three, both immensely practical.

The crying, the sadness, and the plea came from below in the winter rooms.

"She sounds so damned sad," said Robert. "God, I'm sorry for her, but don't even know who it *is.* Come on."

They went downstairs.

As if hearing their footsteps, the crying grew louder. There was a dull thudding against a hidden panel somewhere.

"The *Witch* Door!" said Martha Webb at last.

"Can't be."

*"Is."*

They stood in the long hall looking at that place under the stairs, where the panels trembled faintly. But now the cries faded, as if the crier was exhausted, or something had diverted her, or perhaps their voices had startled her and she was listening for them to speak again. Now the winter-night house was silent and the man and wife waited with the oil lamps quietly fuming in their hands.

Robert Webb stepped to the Witch Door and touched it, probing for the hidden button, the secret spring. "There can't be anyone in there," he said. "My God, we've *been* here six months, and that's just a cubby. Isn't that what the Realtor said when he sold the place? No one could hide in there and us not know it. We —"

"Listen!"

They listened.

Nothing.

"She's gone, it's gone, whatever it was, hell, that door hasn't been opened in our lifetime. Everyone's forgotten where the spring is that unlocks it. I don't think there *is* a door, only a loose panel, and rats' nests, that's all. The walls, scratching. Why not?" He turned to look at his wife, who was staring at the hidden place.

"Silly," she said. "Good Lord, rats don't cry. That was a voice, asking to be saved. Lotte, I thought. But now I know it wasn't she, but someone else in as much trouble."

Martha Webb reached out and trembled her fingertips along the beveled edge of ancient maple. "*Can't* we open it?"

"With a crowbar and hammer, tomorrow."

"Oh, Robert!"

"Don't 'Oh, Robert' me. I'm tired."

"You *can't* leave her in there to —"

"She's quiet now. Christ, I'm exhausted. I'll come down at the crack of dawn and knock the damned thing apart, okay?"

"All right," she said, and tears came to her eyes.

"Women," said Robert Webb. "Oh, my God, you and Lotte, Lotte and you. If she *is* coming here, *if* she makes it, I'll have a houseful of lunatics!"

"Lotte's *fine!*"

"Sure, but she should keep her mouth shut. It doesn't pay now to say you're Socialist, Democrat, Libertarian, Pro-Life Abortionist, Sinn Fein Fascist, Commie, any damn thing. The towns are bombed out. People are looking for scapegoats and Lotte has to shoot from the hip, get herself smeared and now, hell, on the run."

"They'll jail her if they catch her. Or kill her, yes, kill her. We're lucky to be here with our own food. Thank God we planned ahead, we saw it coming, the starvation, the massacres. We helped ourselves. Now we help Lotte if she makes it through."

Without answering, he turned to the stairs. "I'm dead on my feet. I'm tired of saving anyone. Even Lotte. But hell, if she comes through the front door, she's saved."

They went up the stairs taking the lamps, advancing in an ever-moving aura of trembling white glow. The house was as silent as snow falling. "God," he whispered. "Damn, I don't *like* women crying like that."

It sounded like the whole world crying, he thought. The whole world dying and needing help and lonely, but what can you *do?* Live in a farm like this? Far off the main highway where people don't pass, away from all the stupidity and death? What can you *do?*

They left one of the lamps lit and drew the covers over their bodies and lay, listening to the wind hit the house and creak the beams and parquetry.

A moment later there was a cry from downstairs, a splintering crash, the sound of a door flung wide, a bursting out of air, footsteps rapping all the rooms, a sobbing, almost an exultation, then the front door banged open, the winter wind blowing wildly in, footsteps across the front porch and gone.

"There!" cried Martha. *"Yes!"*

With the lamp they were down the stairs swiftly. Wind smothered their faces as they turned now toward the Witch Door, opened wide, still on its hinges, then toward the front door where they cast their light out upon a snowing winter darkness and saw nothing but white and hills, no moon, and in the lamplight the soft drift and moth-flicker of snowflakes falling from the sky to the mattressed yard.

"Gone," she whispered.

"Who?"

"We'll never know, unless she comes back."

"She won't. Look."

They moved the lamplight toward the white earth and the tiny footprints going off, across the softness, toward the dark forest.

"It *was* a woman, then. But . . . *why?*"

"God knows. Why anything, now in this crazy world?"

They stood looking at the footprints a long while until, shivering, they moved back through the hall to the open Witch Door. They poked the lamp into this hollow under the stairs.

"Lord, it's just a cell, hardly a closet, and look . . ."

Inside stood a small rocking chair, a braided rug, a used candle in a copper holder, and an old, worn Bible. The place smelled of must and moss and dead flowers.

"Is this where they used to hide people?"

"Yes. A long time back they hid people called witches. Trials, witch trials. They hung or burned some."

"Yes, yes," they both murmured, staring into the incredibly small cell.

"And the witches hid here while the hunters searched the house and gave up and left?"

"Yes, oh, my God, yes," he whispered.

"Rob . . ."

"Yes?"

She bent forward. Her face was pale and she could not look away from the small, worn rocking chair and the faded Bible.

"Rob. How old? This house, how old?"

"Maybe three hundred years."

"*That* old?"

"Why?"

"Crazy. Stupid . . ."

"Crazy?"

"Houses, old like this. All the *years*. And more years and more after that. God, *feel!* If you put your hand in, yes? Would you feel it change, silly, and what if I sat in that rocking chair and shut the door, *what?* That woman . . . how long was she *in* there? How'd she get there? From way, way back. Wouldn't it be *strange?*"

"Bull!"

"But *if* you wanted to run away badly enough, wished for it, prayed for it, and people ran after you, and someone hid you in a place like this, a witch behind a door, and heard the searchers run through the house, closer and closer, wouldn't you *want* to get away? Anywhere? To another place? Why not another time? And then, in a house like this, a house so old nobody knows, if you *wanted* and *asked* for it enough, couldn't you run to another year! Maybe" — she paused — "here . . . ?"

"No, no," he muttered. "*Really* stupid!"

But still, some quiet motion within the closeted space caused both, at almost the same instant, to hold their hands out on the air, curious, like people

230

testing invisible waters. The air seemed to move one way and then another, now warm, now cold, with a pulsation of light and a sudden turning toward dark. All this they thought but could not say. There was weather here, now a quick touch of summer and then a winter cold, which could not be, of course, but there it was. Passing along their fingertips, but unseen by their eyes, a stream of shadows and sun ran as invisible as time itself, clear as crystal, but clouded by a shifting dark. Both felt if they thrust their hands deep, they might be drawn in to drown in a mighty storm of seasons within an incredibly small space. All this, too, they thought or almost felt but could not say.

They seized their frozen but sunburned hands back, to stare down and hold them against the panic in their breasts.

"Damn," whispered Robert Webb. "Oh, damn!"

He backed off and went to open the front door again and look at the snowing night where the footprints had almost vanished.

"No," he said. "No, no."

Just then the yellow flash of headlights on the road braked in front of the house.

"Lotte!" cried Martha Webb. "It *must* be! Lotte!"

The car lights went out. They ran to meet the running woman half up the front yard.

"Lotte!"

The woman, wild-eyed, hair wind-blown, threw herself at them.

"Martha, Bob! God, I thought I'd *never* find you! Lost! I'm being followed, let's get inside. Oh, I didn't mean to get you up in the middle of the night, it's good to *see* you! Jesus! Hide the car! Here are the keys!"

Robert Webb ran to drive the car behind the house. When he came back around he saw that the heavy snowfall was already covering the tracks.

Then the three of them were inside the house, talking, holding onto each other. Robert Webb kept glancing at the front door.

"I can't thank you," cried Lotte, huddled in a chair. "You're at risk! I won't stay long, a few hours until it's safe. Then . . ."

"Stay as long as you want."

"No. They'll *follow!* In the cities, the

fires, the murders, everyone starving, I stole gas. Do you have *more?* Enough to get me to Phil Merdith's in Greenborough? I —"

"Lotte," said Robert Webb.

"Yes?" Lotte stopped, breathless.

"Did you see anyone on your way up here? A woman? Running on the road?"

"What? I drove so fast! A *woman?* Yes! I almost hit her. Then she was gone! Why?"

"Well . . ."

"She's not *dangerous?*"

"No, no."

"It *is* all right, my *being* here?"

"Yes, fine, fine. Sit back. We'll fix some coffee —"

"Wait! I'll check!" And before they could stop her, Lotte ran to the front door, opened it a crack, and peered out. They stood with her and saw distant headlights flourished over a low hill and gone into a valley. "They're coming," whispered Lotte. "They might search here. God, where can I hide?"

Martha and Robert glanced at each other.

No, no, thought Robert Webb. God, no! Preposterous, unimaginable, fantastic, so damned coincidental the mind raves at it, crows, hoots, guffaws! No, none of *this!* Get off, circumstance! Get away with your goings and comings on not neat, or too neat, schedules. Come back, Lotte, in ten years, five years, maybe a year, a month, a week, and ask to hide. Even tomorrow show up! But don't come with coincidence in each hand like idiot children and ask, only half an hour after one terror, one miracle, to test our disbelief! I'm not, after all, Charles Dickens, to blink and let this pass.

"What's wrong?" said Lotte.

"I —" said Robert.

"No place to hide me?"

"Yes," he said. "We've a place."

"Well?"

"Here." He turned slowly away, stunned.

They walked down the hall to the half-open paneling.

"This?" Lotte said. "Secret? Did you — ?"

"No, it's been here since the house was built long ago."

Lotte touched and moved the door on its hinges. "Does it work? Will they know where to look and *find* it?"

"No. It's beautifully made. Shut, you

can't tell it's there."

Outside in the winter night, cars rushed, their beams flashing up the road, across the house windows.

Lotte peered into the Witch Door as one peers down a deep, lonely well.

A filtering of dust moved about her. The small rocking chair trembled.

Moving in silently, Lotte touched the half-burned candle.

"Why, it's still *warm!*"

Martha and Robert said nothing. They held to the Witch Door, smelling the odor of warm tallow.

Lotte stood rigidly in the little space, bowing her head beneath the beamed ceiling.

A horn blew in the snowing night. Lotte took a deep breath and said, "Shut the door."

They shut the Witch Door. There was no way to tell that a door was there.

They blew out the lamp and stood in the cold, dark house, waiting.

The cars rushed down the road, their noise loud, and their yellow headlights bright in the falling snow. The wind stirred the footprints in the yard, one pair going out, another coming in, and the tracks of Lotte's car fast vanishing, and at last gone.

"Thank God," whispered Martha.

The cars, honking, whipped around the last bend and down the hill and stopped, waiting, looking in at the dark house. Then, at last, they started up away into the snow and the hills.

Soon their lights were gone and their sound gone with them.

"We were lucky," said Robert Webb.

"But *she's* not."

"She?"

"That woman, whoever she was, ran out of here. *They'll* find her. *Some*body'll find her."

"Christ, that's right."

"And she has no I.D., no proof of herself. And she doesn't know what's *happened* to her. And when she tells them who she is and where she *came* from!"

"Yes, yes."

"God help her."

They looked into the snowing night but saw nothing. Everything was still. "You can't escape," she said. "No matter what you do, no one can escape."

They moved away from the window and down the hall to the Witch Door and touched it.

"Lotte," they called.

The Witch Door did not tremble or move.

"Lotte, you can come out now."

There was no answer; not a breath or a whisper.

Robert tapped the door. "Hey in there."

"Lotte!"

He knocked at the paneling, his mouth agitated.

"Lotte!"

"Open it!"

"I'm trying, damn it!"

"Lotte, we'll get you out, wait! Every-thing's all *right!*"

He beat with both fists, cursing. Then he said, "Watch out!" took a step back, raised his leg, kicked once, twice, three times; vicious kicks at the paneling that crunched holes and crumbled wood into kindling. He reached in and yanked the entire paneling free. "Lotte!"

They leaned together into the small place under the stairs.

The candle flickered on the small table. The Bible was gone. The small rocking chair moved quietly back and forth, in little arcs, and then stood still.

"Lotte!"

They stared at the empty room. The candle flickered.

"Lotte," they said.

"You don't believe . . ."

"I don't know. Old houses are *old* . . . old . . ."

"You think Lotte . . . she . . . ?"

"I don't know, I don't know."

"Then she's safe at least, safe! Thank God!"

"Safe? Where's she *gone*? You really *think* that? A woman in new clothes, red lipstick, high heels, short skirt, perfume, plucked brows, diamond rings, silk stockings, safe? Safe!" he said, staring deep into the open frame of the Witch Door.

"Yes, safe. Why not?"

He drew a deep breath.

"A woman of that description, lost in a town called Salem in the year 1680?"

He reached over and shut the Witch Door.

They sat waiting by it for the rest of the long, cold night.

# THE GHOST IN
# THE MACHINE

The talk in the village in the year 1853 was, of course, about the madman above, in his sod-and-brick hut, with an untended garden and a wife who had fled, silent about his madness, never to return.

The people of the village had never drunk enough courage to go see what the special madness was or why the wife had vanished, tear-stained, leaving a vacuum into which atmospheres had rushed to thunder-clap.

And yet . . .

On a sweltering hot day with no cloud to offer shadow comfort and no threat of rain to cool man or beast, the Searcher arrived. Which is to say, Dr. Mortimer Goff, a man of many parts, most of them curious and self-serving, but also traveling the world for some baroque event, or miraculous revelation.

The good doctor came tramping up the hill, stumbling over cobbles that were more stone than paving, having abandoned his coach-and-horses, fearful of crippling them with such a climb.

Dr. Goff, it turned out, had come from London, inhaling fogs, bombarded by storms, and now, stunned by too much light and heat, this good if curious physician stopped, exhausted, to lean against a fence, sight further up the hill, and ask:

"Is this the way to the lunatic?"

A farmer who was more scarecrow than human raised his eyebrows and snorted, "That would be Elijah Wetherby."

"If lunatics have names, yes."

"We call him crazed or mad, but lunatic will do. It sounds like book learning. Are you one of *those?*"

"I own books, yes, and chemical retorts and a skeleton that was once a man, and a permanent pass to the London Historical and Scientific Museum —"

"All well and good," the farmer interrupted, "but of no use for failed crops and a dead wife. Follow your nose. And when you find the fool or whatever you name him, take him with you. We're tired of his shouts and commotions late nights in his iron foundry and anvil menagerie. Rumor says he will soon finish some monster that will run to kill us all."

"Is that true?" asked Dr. Goff.

"No, it lies easy on my tongue. Good day, Doctor, and God deliver you from the lightning bolts that wait for you above."

With this the farmer spaded the earth to bury the conversation.

So the curious doctor, threatened, climbed on, under a dark cloud which did not stop the sun.

And at last arrived at a hut that seemed more tomb than home, surrounded by land more graveyard than garden.

Outside the ramshackle sod-and-brick dwelling a shadow stepped forth, as if waiting, and became an old, very old, man.

"Well, there you are at last!" it cried.

Dr. Goff reared back at this. "You sound, sir, as if you *expected* me!"

"I did," said the old man, "some years ago! What *took* you so long?"

"You are not exactly cheek by jowl with London, sir."

"I am not," the old man agreed and

added, "The name is Wetherby. The *Inventor.*"

"Mr. Wetherby, the Inventor. I am Dr. Goff, the so-called Searcher, for I move in behalf of our good Queen, turning rocks, digging truffles, curious for stuffs that might delight her Majesty or fill her museums, shops, and streets in the greatest city in the world. Have I reached the right place?"

"And just in time, for I am now in my eightieth year and of inconsequential vigor. If you had arrived next year, you might have found me in the church-yard. Do come in!"

At this moment, Dr. Goff heard a gathering of people behind him, all with a most unpleasant muttering, so at Mr. Wetherby's beckoning, he was glad to enter, sit, and watch an almost rare whiskey being poured without invitation. When he had quaffed the glass, Dr. Goff swiveled his gaze about the room.

"Well, where *is* it?"

"Where is what, sir?"

"The lunatic device, the insane machine that goes nowhere but in going might run down a child, a lamb, a priest, a nun, or an old blind dog, *where?*"

242

"So I am that famous, am I?" The old man let a few crumbs of laughter fall from his toothless mouth. "Well, sir. I keep it locked in the goats' shed behind: the outhouse of machines. Finish that to strengthen your sanity when you at last behold the delight and grievance of my long inventive life. So!"

The doctor drank, was replenished and soon out the door, across a small, smooth circle of turf, and to a shed whose door was triple-kept with numerous padlocks and keys. Old Wetherby entered, lit many candles, and beckoned the good doctor in.

He pointed as to a manger. The medical Searcher looked, expecting a mother, crib, and holy babe by the way Wetherby gestured and cried:

"There she *be!*"

"Is it female, then?"

"Come to think, she *is!*"

And there in the candlelight was Wetherby's mechanical pride.

Dr. Goff coughed, to hide his chagrin.

"That, sir, is but a metal frame!"

"But what a frame to hold *velocities!* Ha!"

And the old man, young with fevers, rushed to seize a largish wheel which he transported to fit to the front part of the frame. Then he fetched yet another circular object to fit into the frame's rear.

"Well?" he cried.

"I see two wheels, *half* a cart, and no horse!"

"We will shoot all horses!" exclaimed Wetherby. "My invention, by the tens of thousands, will shy off all horses and banish manures. Do you know, each day in London a thousand tons of horse clods must be cleared, fertilizer wasted, not spread on neighbor fields but dumped as sludge down-Thames. God, how I talk!"

"But, sir, continue. Those look to be spinning wheels, borrowed from nearby farms?"

"They are, but spliced and strengthened with metal to sustain" — Wetherby touched himself — "one hundred twenty pounds. And here's the saddle for that weight." Whereupon he fitted a saddle mid-frame. "And here the stirrups and ribbon to run the back wheel." So saying, he affixed a longish leather ribbon to one stirrup's rotary and tightened it on a spool at the rear.

"Do you begin to perceive, Doctor?"

"I am stranded in ignorance, sir."

"Well, then, be alert, for I now enthrone myself."

And the old man, light as a chimpanzee, slung himself in place on a leather seat mid-frame between the silent spinning wheels.

"I still see no horse, sir."

"*I* am the horse, Doctor. *I* am the horse a-gallop!"

And the old man thrust his feet in the stirrups to churn them up, around, and down; up, around, and down; as the rear wheels, provoked, did likewise, up, down, around, with a lovely hum, fastened in place on the platform planks.

"Aha." The doctor's face brightened. "This is a device to manufacture electrical power? Something from Benjamin Franklin's storm-lightning notebooks?!"

"Gods, no. It *could* make lightnings, yes! But this, sir, not seeming one, *is* a horse, and I its night rider! So!"

And Wetherby pumped and wheezed, wheezed and pumped, and the rear wheels, locked in place, spun faster, faster, with a siren whine.

"All very well," snorted the good doctor, "but the horse, if it *is*, and the rider, if you *are,* seem to be going nowhere! What will you *call* your machine?"

"I have had many nights and years to think." Wetherby pumped and wheezed. "The Velocitor, perhaps." Pump-wheeze. "Or the Precipitor, but no, that sounds as if I might be thrown from my 'horse.' The Galvanizer, yes? Or why not —" Wheeze-pump. "The Landstride or Diminisher, for —" Wheeze-pump. "It does diminish time and distance. Doctor, you know Latin, eh? So, feet to wheel, wheel run by feet — *name* it!"

"The Elijah, your given name, sir, the Elijah."

"But he saw a wheel way in the middle of the air and it was a wheel in a wheel, is that not so?"

"When last I was in church, yes. And you are grounded, that is plain to see. Why not Velocipede, then? Having to do with speed and the applied toe and ankle?"

"Close-on, Dr. Goff, close-on. Why do you stare so fixedly?"

"It comes to mind that great times call forth great inventions. The inventor is child to his year and day. This is not a great time for such as you and yours. Did this century call you forth as its mightiest of all men of genius?"

Old Wetherby let his machine coast for a moment and smiled.

"No, I and my Tilda here, I call her Tilda, will instead be the gravity that calls forth the century. We will influence the year, the decade, and the millennium!"

"It is hard for me to believe," said the medical gentleman, "that you will build a road from your sill to the city on which to glide your not-inconsiderable dream."

"Nay, Doctor, the reverse is true. The city, and the world, when they know me, and this will run a concourse here to deliver me to fame."

"Your head knocks heaven, Mr. Wetherby," said the doctor dryly. "But your roots ache for sustenance, water, minerals, air. You stroke and pump wildly, but go nowhere. Once off that rack, will you not fall on your side, destroyed?"

"Nay, nay." Wetherby, in gusts, pumped again. "For I have discovered some physics, as yet nameless. The faster you propel this bodily device, the less tendency to fall left or right but continue straight, if no obstacles prevent!"

"With only *two* wheels beneath? Prove it. Release your invention, set it free in flight, let us see you sustain your forward motion without breaking your bum!"

"Oh, God, shut up!" cried Wetherby as his kindling legs thrashed the pedals, racketing round as he leaned into a phantom wind, eyes clenched against an invisible storm, and churned the wheels to a frenzy. "Don't you hear? Listen. That whine, that cry, that whisper. The ghost in the machine, which promises things most new, unseen, unrealized, only a dream now but *tomorrow* — Great God, don't you *see?!* If I were on a *real* path this would be swifter than gazelles, a panic of deer! All pedestrians vanquished. All coach-and-horses in dust! Not twenty miles a day, but thirty, forty miles in a single glorious *hour!* Stand off, Time. Beware, meadow-beasts! Here glides, in full plummet, Wetherby with *nothing* to stop him!"

"Aye," said the Searcher dryly, "you pump up a storm on that stand. But, set free, how would you balance on only *two* wheels!?"

"Like this!" cried Wetherby, and with

a thrust of his hands and an uplift of frame, seized the Traveler, the Motion Machine, the Pathfinder, up free of its stand and in an instant plunged through the room and out the door, with Dr. Goff, in full pursuit, yelling:

"Stop! You'll kill yourself!"

"No, exhilarate my heart, oxygenate my blood!" cried Wetherby, and there he was in a chicken-yard he had trampled flat, paths some sixty feet around on which he now flailed his metal machine with scythings of ankle, toe, heel, and leg, sucking air, gusting out great laughs. "See? I do *not* fall! Two legs, two wheels, and: *presto!*"

"My God!" cried Dr. Goff, eyes thrust forth like hard-boiled eggs. "God's truth! How so?!"

"I fly forward faster than I fall downward, an unguessed law of physics. But lo! I almost fly. Fly! Good-bye horses, doomed and dead!"

And with *"dead"* he was overcome with such a delirium of pant and pump, perspiration raining off him in showers, that with a great cry, he wobbled and was flung, a meteor of flesh, over and down on a coop where the chickens, in dumb feather-duster alarms, exploded in shrieks as Wetherby slid in one direction while his vehicle, self-motivated, wheels a-spin, mounted Dr. Goff, who jumped aside, fearful of being spliced.

Wetherby, helped to his feet, protested his trajectory:

"Ignore that! Do you at last understand?"

"Fractures, wounds, broken skulls, yes!"

"No, a future brave with motion, 'tween my legs. You have come a long way, Doctor. Will you adopt and further my machine?"

"Well," said the doctor, already out of the yard, into the house, and to the front door, his face confused, his wits a patch of nettles. "Ah," he said.

"Say you will, Doctor. Or my device dies, and I *with* it!"

"But . . ." said the doctor and opened the outer door, only to draw back, alarmed. "What have I done!" he cried.

Peering over his shoulder, Wetherby expressed further alarm. "Your presence is known, Doctor; the word has spread. A lunatic has come to visit a lunatic."

And it was true. On the road and in the front garden yard were some twelve or twenty farmers and villagers, some with rocks, some with clubs, and with looks of malice or outright hostility caught in their eyes and mouths.

"*There* they are!" someone cried.

"Have you come to take him away?" someone else shouted.

"Yah," echoed the struggling crowd, moving forward.

Thinking quickly, Dr. Goff replied, "Yes. I will take him away!" And turned back to the old man.

"Take me where, Doctor?" whispered Wetherby, clutching his elbow.

"One moment!" cried the doctor to the crowd, which then subsided in murmurs. "Let me think."

Standing back, cudgeling his bald spot, and then massaging his brow for rampant inspiration, Dr. Goff at last exhaled in triumph.

"I have it, by George. A genius of an idea, which will please both villagers, to be rid of you, and you, to be rid of them."

"What, what, Doctor?"

"Why, sir, you are to come down to London under cover of night and I will let you through the side door of my museum with your blasphemous toy of Satan . . ."

"To what purpose?"

"Purpose? Why, sir, I have found the path, the smooth surface, the road you spoke of at some future time!"

"The road, the path, the surface?"

"The museum floors, marble, smooth, lovely, wondrous, ohmigod, for all your needs!"

"Needs?"

"Don't be thick. Each night, as many nights as you wish, to your heart's content, you can ride that wheeled demon round and round, past the Rembrandts and Turners and Fra Angelicos, through the Grecian statues and Roman busts, careful of porcelains, minding the crystals, but pumping away like Lucifer all night till dawn!"

"Oh, dear God," murmured Wetherby, "why didn't *I* think?"

"If you *had* you would've been too shy to *ask!*"

"The only place in the world with roads like future roads, paths like tomorrow's paths, boulevards without cobbles, pure as Aphrodite's cheeks! Smooth as Apollo's rump!"

And here Wetherby unlocked his eyes to let fall tears, pent up for months and long hilltop years.

"Don't cry," said Dr. Goff.

"I must, with joy, or burst. Do you mean it?"

"My good man, here's my *hand!*"

They shook and the shaking let free at least one drop of rain from the good doctor's cheek, also.

"The excitement will kill me," said Wetherby, wiping the backs of his fists across his eyes.

"No better way to die! Tomorrow night?"

"But what will people say as I lead my machine through the streets to your museum?"

"If anyone sees, say you're a gypsy who's stolen treasure from a distant year. Well, well, Elijah Wetherby, I'm off."

"Be careful downhill."

"Careful."

Half out the door, Dr. Goff tripped on a cobble and almost fell as a farmer said:

"Did you see the lunatic?"

"I did."

"Will you take him to a madhouse?"

"Yes. Asylum." Dr. Goff adjusted his cuffs. "Crazed. Worthless. You will see him no more!"

"Good!" said all as he passed.

"Grand," said Goff and picked his way down the stone path, listening.

And uphill was there not a final, joyful, wheel-circling cry from that distant yard?

Dr. Goff snorted.

"Think on it," he said, half aloud, "no more horses, no more *manure!* Think!"

And, thinking, fell on the cobbles, lurching toward London and the future.

# AT THE END
# OF THE
# NINTH YEAR

"Well," said Sheila, chewing on her breakfast toast and examining her complexion, distorted in the side of the coffee urn, "here it is the last day of the last month of the ninth year."

Her husband, Thomas, glanced over the rampart of *The Wall Street Journal*, saw nothing to fasten his regard, and sank back in place. "What?"

"I said," said Sheila, "the ninth year's finished and you have a completely new wife. Or, to put it properly, the old wife's gone. So I don't think we're married anymore."

Thomas floored the *Journal* on his as-yet-untouched scrambled eggs, tilted his head this way and that, and said:

"Not *married?*"

"No, that was another time, another body, another me." She buttered more toast and munched on it philosophically.

"Hold on!" He took a stiff jolt of coffee. "Explain."

"Well, dear Thomas, don't you remember reading as children and later, that every nine years, I *think* it was nine, the body, churning like a gene-chromosome factory, did your entire person over, fingernails, spleen, ankles to elbows, belly, bum, and earlobes, molecule by molecule —"

"Oh, get *to* it," he grumbled. "The point, wife, the *point!*"

"The point, dear Tom," she replied, finishing her toast, "is that with this breakfast I have replenished my soul and psyche, completed the reworking of my entire flesh, blood, and bones. This person seated across from you is *not* the woman you married —"

"I have often *said* that!"

"Be serious."

"Are *you?*" he said.

"Let me finish. If the medical research is true, then at the end of nine years there is not an eyebrow, eyelash, pore, dimple, or skin follicle in this creature here at this celebratory breakfast that in any way is related to that old Sheila Tompkins married at eleven A.M. of a Saturday nine years ago this very hour.

Two different women. One in bondage to a nice male creature whose jaw jumps out like a cash register when he scans the *Journal*. The other, now that it is one minute after the deadline hour, Born Free. So!"

She rose swiftly and prepared to flee.

"Wait!" He gave himself another jolt of coffee. "Where are you going?"

Halfway to the door, she said, "Out. Perhaps away. And who knows: forever!"

"Born free? Hogwash. Come here! Sit down!"

She hesitated as he assumed his lion-tamer's voice. "Dammit. You owe me an explanation. Sit!"

She turned slowly. "For only as long as it takes to draw a picture."

"Draw it, then. Sit!"

She came to stare at her plate. "I seem to have eaten everything in sight."

He jumped up, ran over to the side table, rummaged more omelet, and banged it in front of her.

"There! Speak with your mouth full."

She forked in the eggs. "You do see what I'm driving at, don't you, Tomas-ino?"

"Damnation! I thought you were *happy!*"

"Yes, but not *incredibly* happy."

"That's for maniacs on their honeymoons!"

"Yes, *wasn't* it?" she remembered.

"That was then, this is *now. Well?*"

"I could feel it happening all year. Lying in bed, I felt my skin prickle, my pores open like ten thousand tiny mouths, my perspiration run like faucets, my heart race, my pulse sound in the oddest places, under my chin, my wrists, the backs of my knees, my ankles. I felt like a huge wax statue, melting. After midnight I was afraid to turn on the bathroom light and find a stranger gone mad in the mirror."

"All right, all right!" He stirred four sugars in his coffee and drank the slops from the saucer. "Sum it *up!*"

"Every hour of every night and then all day, I could feel it as if I were out in a storm being struck by hot August rain that washed away the old to find a brand-new me. Every drop of serum, every red and white corpuscle, every hot flash of nerve ending, rewired and restrung, new marrow, new hair for combing, new fingerprints even. Don't *look* at me that way. Perhaps *no* new fingerprints. But all the rest. See? Am I not a fresh-sculpted, fresh-painted work of God's creation?"

He searched her up and down with a razor glare.

"I hear Mad Carlotta maundering," he said. "I see a woman hyperventilated by a midlife frenzy. Why don't you just *say* it? *Do* you want a divorce?"

"Not necessarily."

"Not necessarily?" he shouted.

"I'll just simply . . . go away."

"Where will you go?"

"There must be some place," she said vaguely, stirring her omelet to make paths.

"Is there another man?" he said at last, holding his utensils with fists.

"Not quite yet."

"Thank God for small favors." He let a great breath gust out. "Now go to your room."

"Beg pardon?" She blinked.

"You'll not be allowed out for the rest of this week. Go to your room. No phone calls. No TV. No —"

She was on her feet. "You sound like my father in high school!"

"I'll be damned." He laughed quietly.

"Yes! Upstairs now! No lunch for you, my girl. I'll put a plate by your door at suppertime. When you behave I'll give you your car keys. Meanwhile, march! Pull out your telephone plugs and hand over your CD player!"

"This is outrageous," she cried. "I'm a grown woman."

"*Ingrown*. No progress. *Re-gress.* If that damn theory's true, you didn't add on, just sank back nine years! Out you go! *Up!*"

She ran, pale-faced, to the entry stairs, wiping tears from her eyes.

As she was halfway up, he, putting his foot on the first step, pulled the napkin from his shirt and called quietly, "Wait . . ."

She froze in place but did not look back down at him, waiting.

"Sheila," he said at last, tears running down *his* cheeks now.

"Yes," she whispered.

"I love you," he said.

"I know," she said. "But it doesn't help."

"Yes, it does. Listen."

She waited, halfway up to her room.

He rubbed his hand over his face as if trying to massage some truth out of it. His hand was almost frantic, searching for something hidden around his mouth or near his eyes.

Then it almost burst from him. "Sheila!"

"I'm supposed to go to my room," she said.

*"Don't!"*

"What, then?"

His face began to relax, his eyes to fix on a solution, as his hand rested on the banister leading up to where she stood with her back turned.

"If what you say is true —"

"It *is,*" she murmured. "Every cell, every pore, every eyelash. Nine years —"

"Yes, yes, I know, yes. But listen."

He swallowed hard and that helped him digest the solution which he now spoke very weakly, then quietly, and then with a kind of growing certainty.

"If what you say happened —"

"It did," she murmured, head down.

"Well, then," he said slowly, and then, "It happened to me, *too.*"

"What?" Her head lifted a trifle.

"It doesn't just happen to *one* person, right? It happens to all people, everyone in the world. And if that's true, well, *my* body has been changing along with *yours* during all the last nine years. Every follicle, every fingernail, all the dermis and epidermis or whatever. I never noticed. But it *must* have."

Her head was up now and her back was not slumped. He hurried on.

"And if that's true, good Lord, then I'm new, too. The old Tom, Thomas, Tommy, Tomasino is left behind back there with the shed snakeskin."

Her eyes opened and she listened and he finished.

"So we're both brand-new. You're the new, beautiful woman I've been thinking about finding and loving in the last year. And I'm that man you were heading out to search for. Isn't that right? Isn't that true?"

There was the merest hesitation and then she gave the smallest, almost imperceptible nod.

"Mercy," he called gently.

"That's not my name," she said.

"It is now. New woman, new body, new name. So I picked one for you. Mercy?"

After a moment she said, "What does that make you?"

"Let me think." He chewed his lip and smiled. "How about Frank? Frankly, my dear, I *do* give a damn."

"Frank," she murmured. "Frank and Mercy. Mercy and Frank."

"It doesn't exactly *ring*, but it'll do. Mercy?"

"Yes?"

"Will you marry me?"

"What?"

"I said, will you marry me. Today. An hour from now. Noon?"

She turned at last to look down at him with a face all freshly tanned and washed.

"Oh, yes," she said.

"And we'll run away and be maniacs again, for a little while."

"No," she said, "here is fine. Here is wonderful."

"Come down, then," he said, holding his hand up to her. "We have another nine years before another change. Come down and finish your wedding breakfast. Mercy?"

She came down the steps and took his hand and smiled.

"Where's the champagne?" she said.

# BUG

Looking back now, I can't remember a time when Bug wasn't dancing. Bug is short for jitterbug and, of course, those were the days in the late thirties, our final days in high school and our first days out in the vast world looking for work that didn't exist when jitterbugging was all the rage. And I can remember Bug (his real name was Bert Bagley, which shortens to Bug nicely), during a jazz-band blast at our final aud-call for our high school senior class, suddenly leaping up to dance with an invisible partner in the middle of the front aisle of the auditorium. That brought the house down. You never heard such a roar or such applause. The bandleader, stricken with Bug's oblivious joy, gave an encore and Bug did the same and we all exploded. After that the band played "Thanks for the Memory" and we all sang it, with tears pouring down our cheeks. Nobody in all the years after could forget: Bug dancing in the aisle, eyes shut, hands out to grasp his invisible girlfriend, his legs not connected to his body, just his heart, all over the place. When it was over, nobody, not even the band, wanted to leave. We just stood there in the world Bug had made, hating to go out into that other world that was waiting for us.

It was about a year later when Bug saw me on the street and stopped his roadster and said come on along to my place for a hot dog and a Coke, and I jumped in and we drove over with the top down and the wind really hitting us and Bug talking and talking at the top of his lungs, about life and the times and what he wanted to show me in his front parlor — front parlor, hell, dining room, kitchen, and bedroom.

What was it he wanted me to see?

Trophies. Big ones, little ones, solid gold and silver and brass trophies with his name on them. Dance trophies. I mean they were everywhere, on the floor by his bed, on the kitchen sink, in the bathroom, but in the parlor, especially, they had settled like a locust plague. There were so many of them on the mantel, and in bookcases instead of books, and on the floor, you had to

wade through, kicking some over as you
went. They totaled, he said, tilting his
head back and counting inside his eyelids, to about three hundred and twenty
prizes, which means grabbing onto a
trophy almost every night in the past
year.

"All this," I gasped, "just since we left
high school?"

"Ain't I the cat's pajamas?" Bug cried.

"You're the whole darned department
store! Who was your partner, all those
nights?"

"Not partner, part*ners*," Bug cor-
rected. "Three hundred, give or take a
dozen, different women on three hundred different nights."

"Where do you find three hundred
women, all talented, all good enough,
to win prizes?"

"They weren't talented or all good,"
said Bug, glancing around at his collection. "They were just ordinary, good,
every-night dancers. I won the prizes. I
made them good. And when we got out
there dancing, we cleared the floor.
Everyone else stopped, to watch us
there out in the middle of nowhere, and
we never stopped."

He paused, blushed, and shook his

head. "Sorry about that. Didn't mean to brag."

But he wasn't bragging. I could see. He was just telling the truth.

"You want to know how this all started?" said Bug, handing over a hot dog and a Coke.

"Don't tell me," I said. "I *know*."

"How could you?" said Bug, looking me over.

"The last aud-call at L.A. High, I think they played 'Thanks for the Memory,' but just before that —"

" 'Roll Out the Barrel' —"

"— 'the Barrel,' yes, and there you were in front of God and everyone, jumping."

"I never stopped," said Bug, eyes shut, back in those years. "Never," he said, "stopped."

"You got your life all made," I said.

"Unless," said Bug, "something *happens.*"

What happened was, of course, the war.

Looking back, I remember that in that last year in school, sap that I was, I made up a list of my one hundred and sixty-five *best* friends. Can you imagine that? One hundred and sixty-five, count 'em, best *friends!* It's a good thing I never showed that list to anyone. I would have been hooted out of school.

Anyway, the war came and went and took with it a couple dozen of those listed friends and the rest just disappeared into holes in the ground or went east or wound up in Malibu or Fort Lauderdale. Bug was on that list, but I didn't figure out I didn't really *know* him until half a lifetime later. By that time I was down to half a dozen pals or women I might turn to if I needed, and it was then, walking down Hollywood Boulevard one Saturday afternoon, I heard someone call:

"How about a hot dog and a Coke?"

Bug, I thought without turning. And that's who it was, standing on the Walk of Stars with his feet planted on Mary Pickford and Ricardo Cortez just behind and Jimmy Stewart just ahead. Bug had taken off some hair and put on some weight, but it *was* Bug and I was overjoyed, perhaps too much, and showed it, for he seemed embarrassed at my enthusiasm. I saw then that his suit was not half new enough and his shirt frayed, but his tie was neatly tied and he shook my hand off and we popped into a place where we stood and had that hot dog and that Coke.

"Still going to be the world's greatest writer?" said Bug.

"Working at it," I said.

"You'll get there," said Bug and smiled, meaning it. "You were always good."

"So were you," I said.

That seemed to pain him slightly, for he stopped chewing for a moment and took a swig of Coke. "Yes, sir," he said. "I surely *was.*"

"God," I said, "I can still remember the day I saw all those trophies for the first time. What a family! Whatever — ?"

Before I could finish asking, he gave the answer.

"Put 'em in storage, some. Some wound up with my first wife. Goodwill got the rest."

"I'm sorry," I said, and truly was.

Bug looked at me steadily. "How come *you're* sorry?"

"Hell, I dunno," I said. "It's just, they seemed such a part of you. I haven't thought of you often the last few years or so, to be honest, but when I do, there you are knee-deep in all those cups and mugs in your front room, out in the kitchen, hell, in your *garage!*"

"I'll be damned," said Bug. "What a memory you got."

We finished our Cokes and it was almost time to go. I couldn't help myself, even seeing that Bug had fleshed himself out over the years.

"When —" I started to say, and stopped.

"When what?" said Bug.

"When," I said with difficulty, "when was the last time you danced?"

"Years," said Bug.

"But how long ago?"

"Ten years. Fifteen. Maybe twenty. Yeah, twenty. I don't dance anymore."

"I don't believe that. Bug not dance? Nuts."

"Truth. Gave my fancy night-out shoes to the Goodwill, too. Can't dance in your socks."

"*Can,* and barefoot, too!"

Bug had to laugh at that. "You're really something. Well, it's been nice." He started edging toward the door. "Take care, genius —"

"Not so fast." I walked him out into the light and he was looking both ways as if there were heavy traffic. "You know one thing I never saw and wanted to see? You bragged about it, said you took three hundred ordinary girls out on the dance floor and turned them into Ginger Rogers inside three minutes. But I only saw you once at that aud-call in '38, so I don't believe you."

"What?" said Bug. "You saw the trophies!"

"You could have had those made up," I pursued, looking at his wrinkled suit and frayed shirt cuffs. "Anyone can go in a trophy shop and buy a cup and have his name put on it!"

"You think I did that?" cried Bug.

"I think that, yes!"

Bug glanced out in the street and back at me and back in the street and back to me, trying to decide which way to run or push or shout.

"What's got into you?" said Bug. "Why're you talking like that?"

"God, I don't know," I admitted. "It's just, we might not meet again and I'll never have the chance, or you to prove it. I'd like, after all this time, to see what you talked about. I'd love to see you dance again, Bug."

"Naw," said Bug. "I've forgotten how."

"Don't hand me that. You may have forgotten, but the rest of you knows how. Bet you could go down to the Ambassador Hotel this afternoon, they still have tea dances there, and clear the floor, just like you said. After you're out there nobody else dances, they all stop and look at you and her just like thirty years ago."

"No," said Bug, backing away but coming back. "No, no."

"Pick a stranger, any girl, any woman, out of the crowd, lead her out, hold her in your arms and just skim her around as if you were on ice and dream her to Paradise."

"If you write like that, you'll never sell," said Bug.

"Bet you, Bug."

"I don't bet."

"All right, then. Bet you you can't. Bet you, By God, that you've lost your stuff!"

"Now, hold on," said Bug.

"I mean it. Lost your stuff forever, for good. Bet you. Wanna bet?"

Bug's eyes took on a peculiar shine and his face was flushed. "How much?"

"Fifty bucks!"

"I don't have —"

"Thirty bucks, then. Twenty! You can afford to lose that, *can't* you?"

"Who says I'd lose, dammit?"

"*I* say. Twenty. Is it a deal?"

"You're throwing your money away."

"No, I'm a sure winner, because you can't dance worth shoats and shinola!"

"Where's your money?" cried Bug, incensed now.

"Here!"

"Where's your car!?"

"I don't own a car. Never learned to drive. Where's yours?"

"Sold it! Jesus, no cars. How do we get to the tea dance!?"

We got. We grabbed a cab and I paid and, before Bug could relent, dragged him through the hotel lobby and into the ballroom. It was a nice summer afternoon, so nice that the room was filled with mostly middle-aged men and their wives, a few younger ones with their girlfriends, and some kids out of college who looked out of place, embarrassed by the mostly old-folks music out of another time. We got the last table and when Bug opened his mouth for one last protest, I put a straw in it and helped him nurse a marguerita.

"Why are you *doing* this?" he protested again.

"Because you were just one of one

hundred sixty-five close friends!" I said.

"We were never friends," said Bug.

"Well, today, anyway. There's 'Moonlight Serenade.' Always liked that, never danced myself, clumsy fool. On your feet, Bug!"

He was on his feet, swaying.

"Who do you pick?" I said. "You cut in on a couple? Or there's a few wallflowers over there, a tableful of women. I dare you to pick the least likely and give her lessons, yes?"

That did it. Casting me a glance of the purest scorn, he charged off half into the pretty teatime dresses and immaculate men, searching around until his eyes lit on a table where a woman of indeterminate age sat, hands folded, face thin and sickly pale, half hidden under a wide-brimmed hat, looking as if she were waiting for someone who never came.

*That* one, I thought.

Bug glanced from her to me. I nodded. And in a moment he was bowing at her table and a conversation ensued. It seemed she didn't dance, didn't know *how* to dance, didn't *want* to dance. Ah, yes, he seemed to be saying. Ah, *no*, she seemed to reply. Bug turned, holding her hand, and gave me a long stare and a wink. Then, without looking at her, he raised her by her hand and arm and out, with a seamless glide, onto the floor.

What can I say, how can I tell? Bug, long ago, had never bragged, but only told the truth. Once he got hold of a girl, she was weightless. By the time he had whisked and whirled and glided her once around the floor, she almost took off, it seemed he had to hold her down, she was pure gossamer, the closest thing to a hummingbird held in the hand so you cannot feel its weight but only sense its heartbeat sounding to your touch, and there she went out and around and back, with Bug guiding and moving, enticing and retreating, and not fifty anymore, no, but eighteen, his body remembering what his mind thought it had long forgotten, for his body was free of the earth now, too. He carried himself, as he carried her, with that careless insouciance of a lover who knows what will happen in the next hour and the night soon following.

And it happened, just like he said. Within a minute, a minute and a half at most, the dance floor cleared. As Bug and his stranger lady whirled by with a glance, every couple on the floor stood still. The bandleader almost forgot to keep time with his baton, and the members of the orchestra, in a similar trance, leaned forward over their instruments to see Bug and his new love whirl and turn without touching the floor.

When the "Serenade" ended, there was a moment of stillness and then an explosion of applause. Bug pretended it was all for the lady, and helped her curtsy and took her to her table, where she sat, eyes shut, not believing what had happened. By that time Bug was on the floor again, with one of the wives he borrowed from the nearest table. This time, no one even went out on the floor. Bug and the borrowed wife filled it around and around, and this time even Bug's eyes were shut.

I got up and put twenty dollars on the table where he might find it. After all, he *had* won the bet, hadn't he?

Why had I done it? Well, I couldn't very well have left him out in the middle of the high school auditorium aisle dancing *alone*, could I?

On my way out I looked back. Bug

saw me and waved, his eyes as brimmed full as mine. Someone passing whispered, "Hey, come on, *lookit* this guy!"

God, I thought, he'll be dancing all night.

Me, I could only walk.

And I went out and walked until I was fifty again and the sun was going down and the low June fog was coming in early over old Los Angeles.

That night, just before going to sleep, I wished that in the morning when Bug woke up he would find the floor around his bed covered with trophies.

Or at the very least he would turn and find a quiet and understanding trophy with her head on his pillow, near enough to touch.

# ONCE MORE,
# LEGATO

Fentriss sat up in his chair in the garden in the middle of a fine autumn and listened. The drink in his hand remained unsipped, his friend Black unspoken to, the fine house unnoticed, the very weather itself neglected, for there was a veritable fountain of sound in the air above them.

"My God," he said. "Do you hear?"

"What, the birds?" asked his friend Black, doing just the opposite, sipping his drink, noticing the weather, admiring the rich house, and neglecting the birds entirely until this moment.

"Great God in heaven, listen to them!" cried Fentriss.

Black listened. "Rather nice."

"Clean out your ears!"

Black made a halfhearted gesture, symbolizing the cleaning out of ears. "Well?"

"Damn it, don't be funny. I mean really *listen!* They're singing a tune!"

"Birds usually do."

"No, they don't; birds paste together

bits and pieces maybe, five or six notes, eight at the most. Mockingbirds have repertoires that change, but not entire melodies. *These* birds are different. Now shut up and give over!"

Both men sat, enchanted. Black's expression melted.

"I'll be damned," he said at last. "They *do* go on." He leaned forward and listened intently.

"Yes . . ." murmured Fentriss, eyes shut, nodding to the rhythms that sprang like fresh rain from the tree just above their heads. ". . . ohmigod . . . indeed."

Black rose as if to move under the tree and peer up. Fentriss protested with a fierce whisper:

"Don't spoil it. Sit. Be very still. Where's my pencil? Ah . . ."

Half peering around, he found a pencil and notepad, shut his eyes, and began to scribble blindly.

The birds sang.

"You're not *actually* writing down their song?" said Black.

"What does it look like? Quiet."

And with eyes now open, now shut, Fentriss drew scales and jammed in the notes.

"I didn't know you read music," said Black, astonished.

"I played the violin until my father broke it. Please! There. There. Yes!

"Slower," he whispered. "Wait for me."

As if hearing, the birds adjusted their lilt, moving toward *piano* instead of *bravado.*

A breeze stirred the leaves, like an invisible conductor, and the singing died.

Fentriss, perspiration beading his forehead, stopped scribbling and fell back.

"I'll be damned." Black gulped his drink. "What was *that* all about?"

"Writing a song." Fentriss stared at the scales he had dashed on paper. "Or a tone poem."

"Let me *see* that!"

"Wait." The tree shook itself gently, but produced no further notes. "I want to be sure they're done."

Silence.

Black seized the pages and let his eyes drift over the scales. "Jesus, Joseph, and Mary," he said, aghast. "It *works.*" He glanced up at the thick green of the tree, where no throat warbled, no wing stirred. "What kind of birds *are* those?"

"The birds of forever, the small beasts of an Immaculate Musical Conception. Something," said Fentriss, "has made them with child and its name is song —"

"Hogwash!"

"*Is* it?! Something in the air, in the seeds they ate at dawn, some whim of climate and weather, God! But now they're mine, *it's* mine. A fine tune."

"It *is*," said Black. "But *can't* be!"

"Never question the miraculous when it happens. Good grief, maybe those damned wonderful creatures have been throwing up incredible songs for months, years, but no one *listened*. Today, for the first time, someone *did*. Me! Now, what to *do* with the gift?"

"You don't seriously mean — ?"

"I've been out of work for a year. I quit my computers, retired early, I'm only forty-nine, and have been threatening to knit macramé to give friends to spoil their walls, day after day. Which shall it be, friend, macramé or Mozart?"

"Are *you* Mozart?"

"Just his bastard son."

"Nonsense," cried Black, pointing his face like a blunderbuss at the trees as if he might blast the choir. "That tree,

281

those birds, are a Rorschach test. Your subconscious is picking and choosing notes from pure chaos. There's no discernible tune, no special rhythm. You had me fooled, but I see and hear it now: you've had a repressed desire since childhood to compose. And you've let a clutch of idiot birds grab you by the ears. Put down that pen!"

"Nonsense right back at you." Fentriss laughed. "You're jealous that after twelve layabout years, thunderstruck with boredom, one of us has found an occupation. I shall follow it. Listen and write, write and listen. Sit down, you're obstructing the acoustics!"

"I'll sit," Black exclaimed, "but —" He clapped his hands over his ears.

"Fair enough," said Fentriss. "Escape fantastic reality while I change a few notes and finish out this unexpected birth."

Glancing up at the tree, he whispered:

"Wait for me."

The tree rustled its leaves and fell quiet.

"Crazy," muttered Black.

One, two, three hours later, entering

the library quietly and then loudly, Black cried out:

"What *are* you doing?"

Bent over his desk, his hand moving furiously, Fentriss said:

"Finishing a symphony!"

"The same one you began in the garden?"

"No, the birds began, the birds!"

"The birds, then." Black edged closer to study the mad inscriptions. "How do you know *what* to do with that stuff?"

"They did most. I've added variations!"

"An arrogance the ornithologists will resent and attack. Have you composed before?"

"Not" — Fentriss let his fingers roam, loop, and scratch — "until today!"

"You realize, of course, you're plagiarizing those songbirds?"

"Borrowing, Black, borrowing. If a milkmaid, singing at dawn, can have her hum borrowed by Berlioz, *well!* Or if Dvorak, hearing a Dixie banjo plucker pluck 'Goin' Home,' steals the banjo to eke out his New World, why can't I weave a net to catch a tune? There! Finito. Done! Give us a title, Black!"

"I? Who sings off-key?"

"What about 'The Emperor's Nightin-gale'?"

"Stravinsky."

" 'The Birds'?"

"Hitchcock."

"Damn. How's this: 'It's Only John Cage in a Gilded Bird'?"

"Brilliant. But no one knows who John Cage *was*."

"Well, then, I've *got* it!"

And he wrote:

" 'Forty-seven Magpies Baked in a Pie.' "

"*Blackbirds*, you mean; go back to John Cage."

"Bosh!" Fentriss stabbed the phone. "Hello, Willie? Could you come over? Yes, a small job. Symphonic arrange-ment for a friend, or friends. What's your usual Philharmonic fee? Eh? Good enough. Tonight!"

Fentriss disconnected and turned to gaze at the tree with wonder in it.

"What *next?*" he murmured.

"Forty-seven Magpies," with title shortened, premiered at the Glendale Chamber Symphony a month later with standing ovations, incredible reviews.

Fentriss, outside his skin with joy,

prepared to launch himself atop large, small, symphonic, operatic, whatever fell on his ears. He had listened to the strange choirs each day for weeks, but had noted nothing, waiting to see if the "Magpie" experiment was to be repeated. When the applause rose in storms and the critics hopped when they weren't skipping, he knew he must strike again before the epilepsy ceased.

There followed: "Wings," "Flight," "Night Chorus," "The Fledgling Madrigals," and "Dawn Patrol," each greeted by new thunderstorms of acclamation and critics angry at excellence but forced to praise.

"By now," said Fentriss, "I should be unbearable to live with, but the birds caution modesty."

"Also," said Black, seated under the tree, waiting for a sprig of benison and the merest touch of symphonic manna, "shut up! If all those sly dimwit composers, who will soon be lurking in the bushes, cop your secret, you're a gone poacher."

"Poacher! By God, yes!" Fentriss laughed. "Poacher."

And damn if the first poacher didn't arrive!

Glancing out at three in the morning, Fentriss witnessed a runty shadow stretching up, handheld tape recorder poised, warbling and whistling softly at the tree. When this failed, the half-seen poacher tried dove-coos and then orioles and roosters, half dancing in a circle.

"Damn it to hell!" Fentriss leaped out with a shotgun cry: "Is that Wolfgang Prouty poaching my garden? Out, Wolfgang! Go!"

Dropping his recorder, Prouty vaulted a bush, impaled himself on thorns, and vanished.

Fentriss, cursing, picked up an abandoned notepad.

"Nightsong," it read. On the tape recorder he found a lovely Satie-like birdchoir.

After that, more poachers arrived mid-night to depart at dawn. Their spawn, Fentriss realized, would soon throttle his creativity and still his voice. He loitered full-time in the garden now, not knowing what seed to give his beauties, and heavily watered the lawn to fetch up worms. Wearily he stood guard through sleepless nights, nodding off only to find Wolfgang Prouty's evil minions astride the wall, prompting arias, and one night, by God, perched in the tree itself, humming in hopes of sing-alongs.

A shotgun was the final answer. After its first fiery roar, the garden was empty for a week. That is, until —

Someone came very late indeed and committed mayhem.

As quietly as possible, he cut the branches and sawed the limbs.

"Oh, envious composers, dreadful murderers!" cried Fentriss.

And the birds were gone.

And the career of Amadeus Two with it.

"Black!" cried Fentriss.

"Yes, dear friend?" said Black, looking at the bleak sky where once green was.

"Is your car outside?"

"When last I looked."

"Drive!"

But driving in search didn't do it. It wasn't like calling in lost dogs or tele-phone-poled cats. They must find and cage an entire Mormon tabernacle team of soprano springtime-in-the-Rockies birdseed lovers to prove one in the hand is worth two in the bush.

But still they hastened from block to

block, garden to garden, lurking and listening. Now their spirits soared with an echo of "Hallelujah Chorus" oriole warbling, only to sink in a drab sparrow twilight of despair.

Only when they had crossed and re-crossed interminable mazes of asphalt and greens did one of them finally (Black) light his pipe and emit a theory.

"Did you ever think to wonder," he mused behind a smoke-cloud, "what *season* of the year this *is?*"

"Season of the year?" said Fentriss, exasperated.

"Well, coincidentally, wasn't the night the tree fell and the wee songsters blew town, was not that the first fall night of autumn?"

Fentriss clenched a fist and struck his brow.

"You *mean?*"

"Your friends have flown the coop. Their migration must be above San Miguel Allende just now."

"If they are migratory birds!"

"Do you *doubt* it?"

Another pained silence, another blow to the head.

"Shit!"

"Precisely," said Black.

"Friend," said Fentriss.

"Sir?"

"Drive home."

It was a long year, it was a short year, it was a year of anticipation, it was the burgeoning of despair, it was the revival of inspiration, but at its heart, Fentriss knew, just another Tale of Two Cities, but he did not know what the other city was!

How stupid of me, he thought, not to have guessed or imagined that my songsters were wanderers who each autumn fled south and each springtime swarmed north in A Cappella choirs of sound.

"The waiting," he told Black, "is madness. The phone never stops —"

The phone rang. He picked it up and addressed it like a child. "Yes. Yes. Of course. Soon. When? Very soon." And put the phone down. "You see? That was Philadelphia. They want another Cantata as good as the first. At dawn today it was Boston. Yesterday the Vienna Philharmonic. *Soon,* I say. When? God knows. Lunacy! Where are those angels that once sang me to my rest?"

He threw down maps and weather

charts of Mexico, Peru, Guatemala, and the Argentines.

"How far south? Do I scour Buenos Aires or Rio, Mazatlán or Cuernavaca? And then? Wander about with a tin ear, standing under trees waiting for bird-drops like a spotted owl? Will the Argentine critics trot by scoffing to see me leaning on trees, eyes shut, waiting for the quasi-melody, the lost chord? I'd let no one know the cause of my journey, my search, otherwise pandemoniums of laughter. But in what city, under what kind of tree would I wander to stand? A tree like mine? Do they seek the same roosts? or will anything do in Ecuador or Peru? God, I could waste months guessing and come back with birdseed in my hair and bird bombs on my lapels. What to do, Black? *Speak!*"

"Well, for one thing" — Black stuffed and lit his pipe and exhaled his aromatic concepts — "you might clear off this stump and plant a new tree."

They had been circling the stump and kicking it for inspiration. Fentriss froze with one foot raised. "Say that *again?!*"

"I said —"

"Good grief, you genius! Let me kiss you!"

"Rather not. Hugs, maybe."

Fentriss hugged him, wildly. "Friend!"

"Always was."

"Let's get a shovel and spade."

"You get. I'll watch."

Fentriss ran back a minute later with a spade and pickax. "Sure you won't join me?"

Black sucked his pipe, blew smoke. "Later."

"How much would a full-*grown* tree cost?"

"Too much."

"Yes, but if it were *here* and the birds *did* return?"

Black let out more smoke. "Might be worth it. Opus Number Two: 'In the Beginning' by Charles Fentriss, stuff like that."

" 'In the Beginning,' or maybe *'The Return.'* "

"One of those."

"Or —" Fentriss struck the stump with the pickax. " 'Rebirth.' " He struck again. " *'Ode to Joy.'* " Another strike. " *'Spring Harvest.'* " Another. " *'Let the Heavens Resound.'* How's that, Black?"

"I prefer the other," said Black.

The stump was pulled and the new tree bought.

"Don't show me the bill," Fentriss told his accountant. "Pay it."

And the tallest tree they could find, of the same family as the one dead and gone, was planted.

"What if *it* dies before my choir returns?" said Fentriss.

"What if it *lives*," said Black, "and your choir goes *elsewhere?*"

The tree, planted, seemed in no immediate need to die. Neither did it look particularly vital and ready to welcome small singers from some far southern places.

Meanwhile, the sky, like the tree, was empty.

"Don't they know I'm *waiting?*" said Fentriss.

"Not unless," offered Black, "you majored in cross-continental telepathy."

"I've checked with Audubon. They say that while the swallows *do* come back to Capistrano on a special day, give or take a white lie, other migrating species are often one or two weeks late."

"If I were you," said Black, "I would plunge into an intense love affair to distract you while you wait."

"I am fresh out of love affairs."

"Well, then," said Black, "suffer."

The hours passed slower than the minutes, the days passed slower than the hours, the weeks passed slower than the days. Black called. "No birds?"

"No birds."

"Pity. I can't stand watching you lose weight." And Black disconnected.

On a final night, when Fentriss had almost yanked the phone out of the wall, fearful of another call from the Boston Symphony, he leaned an ax against the trunk of the new tree and addressed it and the empty sky.

"Last chance," he said. "If the dawn patrol doesn't show by seven A.M., it's quits."

And he touched ax-blade against the tree-bole, took two shots of vodka so swiftly that the spirits squirted out both eyes, and went to bed.

He awoke twice during the night to hear nothing but a soft breeze outside his window, stirring the leaves, with not a ghost of song.

And awoke at dawn with tear-filled eyes, having dreamed that the birds had returned, but knew, in waking, it was only a dream.

And yet . . . ?

Hark, someone might have said in an

old novel. List! as in an old play.

Eyes shut, he fine-tuned his ears . . .

The tree outside, as he arose, looked fatter, as if it had taken on invisible ballasts in the night. There were stirrings there, not of simple breeze or probing winds, but of something in the very leaves that knitted and purled them in rhythms. He dared not look but lay back down to ache his senses and try to *know.*

A single chirp hovered in the window.

He waited.

Silence.

Go on, he thought.

Another chirp.

Don't breathe, he thought; don't let them know you're listening.

Hush.

A fourth sound, then a fifth note, then a sixth and seventh.

My God, he thought, is this a substitute orchestra, a replacement choir come to scare off my loves?

Another five notes.

Perhaps, he prayed, they're only tuning *up!*

Another twelve notes, of no special timbre or pace, and as he was about to explode like a lunatic conductor and fire the bunch —

It happened.

Note after note, line after line, fluid melody following spring freshet melody, the whole choir exhaled to blossom the tree with joyous proclamations of return and welcome in chorus.

And as they sang, Fentriss sneaked his hand to find a pad and pen to hide under the covers so that its scratching might not disturb the choir that soared and dipped to soar again, firing the bright air that flowed from the tree to tune his soul with delight and move his hand to remember.

The phone rang. He picked it up swiftly to hear Black ask if the waiting was over. Without speaking, he held the receiver in the window.

"I'll be damned," said Black's voice.

"No, *anointed*," whispered the composer, scribbling Cantata No. 2. Laughing, he called softly to the sky.

"Please. More slowly. *Legato*, not *agitato*."

And the tree and the creatures within the tree obeyed.

*Agitato* ceased.

*Legato* prevailed.

# EXCHANGE

There were too many cards in the file, too many books on the shelves, too many children laughing in the children's room, too many newspapers to fold and stash on the racks . . .

All in all, too much. Miss Adams pushed her gray hair back over her lined brow, adjusted her gold-rimmed pince-nez, and rang the small silver bell on the library desk, at the same time switching off and on all the lights. The exodus of adults and children was exhausting. Miss Ingraham, the assistant librarian, had gone home early because her father was sick, so it left the burden of stamping, filing, and checking books squarely on Miss Adams' shoulders.

Finally the last book was stamped, the last child fed through the great brass doors, the doors locked, and with immense weariness, Miss Adams moved back up through a silence of forty years of books and being keeper of the books, stood for a long moment by the main desk.

She laid her glasses down on the green blotter, and pressed the bridge of her small-boned nose between thumb and forefinger and held it, eyes shut. What a racket! Children who finger-painted or cartooned frontispieces or rattled their roller skates. High school students arriving with laughters, departing with mindless songs!

Taking up her rubber stamp, she probed the files, weeding out errors, her fingers whispering between Dante and Darwin.

A moment later she heard the rapping on the front-door glass and saw a man's shadow outside, wanting in. She shook her head. The figure pleaded silently, making gestures.

Sighing, Miss Adams opened the door, saw a young man in uniform, and said, "It's late. We're closed." She glanced at his insignia and added, "Captain."

"Hold on!" said the captain. "Remember me?"

And repeated it, as she hesitated.

*"Remember?"*

She studied his face, trying to bring light out of shadow. "Yes, I think I do," she said at last. "You once borrowed books here."

"Right."

"Many years ago," she added. "Now I almost have you placed."

As he stood waiting she tried to see him in those other years, but his younger face did not come clear, or a name with it, and his hand reached out now to take hers.

"May I come in?"

"Well." She hesitated. "Yes."

She led the way up the steps into the immense twilight of books. The young officer looked around and let his breath out slowly, then reached to take a book and hold it to his nose, inhaling, then almost laughing.

"Don't mind me, Miss Adams. You ever smell new books? Binding, pages, print. Like fresh bread when you're hungry." He glanced around. "I'm hungry now, but don't even know what for."

There was a moment of silence, so she asked him how long he might stay.

"Just a few hours. I'm on the train from New York to L.A., so I came up from Chicago to see old places, old friends." His eyes were troubled and he fretted his cap, turning it in his long, slender fingers.

She said gently, "Is anything wrong? Anything I can help you with?"

He glanced out the window at the dark town, with just a few lights in the windows of the small houses across the way.

"I was surprised," he said.

"By what?"

"I don't know what I expected. Pretty damn dumb," he said, looking from her to the windows, "to expect that when I went away, everyone froze in place waiting for me to come home. That when I stepped off the train, all my old pals would unfreeze, run down, meet me at the station. Silly."

"No," she said, more easily now. "I think we all imagine that. I visited Paris as a young girl, went back to France when I was forty, and was outraged that no one had waited, buildings had vanished, and all the hotel staff where I had once lived had died, retired, or traveled."

He nodded at this, but could not seem to go on.

"Did anyone know you were coming?" she asked.

"I wrote a few, but no answers. I figured, hell, they're busy, but they'll be *there*. They weren't."

She felt the next words come off her

lips and was faintly surprised. "I'm still here," she said.

"You *are,*" he said with a quick smile. "And I can't tell you how glad I am."

He was gazing at her now with such intensity that she had to look away. "You know," she said, "I must confess you look familiar, but I don't quite fit your face with the boy who came here —"

"Twenty years ago! And as for what *he* looked like, that other one, me, well —"

He brought out a smallish wallet which held a dozen pictures and handed over a photograph of a boy perhaps twelve years old, with an impish smile and wild blond hair, looking as if he might catapult out of the frame.

"Ah, yes." Miss Adams adjusted her pince-nez and closed her eyes to remember. "That one. Spaulding. William Henry Spaulding?"

He nodded and peered at the picture in her hands anxiously.

"Was I a lot of trouble?"

"Yes." She nodded and held the picture closer and glanced up at him. "A fiend." She handed the picture back. "But I loved you."

300

"Did you?" he said and smiled more broadly.

"In spite of you, yes."

He waited a moment and then said, "Do you *still* love me?"

She looked to left and right as if the dark stacks held the answer.

"It's a little early to know, isn't it?"

"Forgive."

"No, no, a good question. Time will tell. Let's not stand like your frozen friends who didn't move. Come along. I've just had some late-night coffee. There may be some left. Give me your cap. Take off that coat. The file index is there. Go look up your old library cards for the hell — heck — of it."

"Are they still *there?*" In amaze.

"Librarians save everything. You never know who's coming in on the next train. Go."

When she came back with the coffee, he stood staring down into the index file like a bird fixing its gaze on a half-empty nest. He handed her one of the old purple-stamped cards.

"Migawd," he said, "I took out a lot of books."

"Ten at a time. I said no, but you took them. And," she added, "*read* them!

Here." She put his cup on top of the file and waited while he drew out canceled card after card and laughed quietly.

"I can't believe. I must not have lived anywhere else but here. May I take this with me, to sit?" He showed the cards. She nodded. "Can you show me around? I mean, maybe I've forgotten something."

She shook her head and took his elbow. "I doubt that. Come on. Over here, of course, is the adult section."

"I begged you to let me cross over when I was thirteen. 'You're not ready,' you said. But —"

"I let you cross over anyway?"

"You did. And much thanks."

Another thought came to him as he looked down at her.

"You used to be taller than me," he said.

She looked up at him, amused.

"I've noticed that happens quite often in my life, but I can still do *this*."

Before he could move, she grabbed his chin in her thumb and forefinger and held tight. His eyes rolled.

He said:

"I remember. When I was really bad you'd hold on and put your face down close and scowl. The scowl did it. After ten seconds of your holding my chin very tight, I behaved for days."

She nodded, released his chin. He rubbed it and as they moved on he ducked his head, not looking at her.

"Forgive, I hope you won't be upset, but when I was a boy I used to look up and see you behind your desk, so near but far away, and, how can I say this, I used to think that you were Mrs. God, and that the library was a whole world, and that no matter what part of the world or what people or thing I wanted to see and read, you'd find and give it to me." He stopped, his face coloring. "You *did*, too. You had the world ready for me every time I asked. There was always a place I hadn't seen, a country I hadn't visited where you took me. I've never forgotten."

She looked around, slowly, at the thousands of books. She felt her heart move quietly. "Did you really call me what you just said?"

"Mrs. God? Oh, yes. Often. Always."

"Come along," she said at last.

They walked around the rooms to-gether and then downstairs to the newspaper files, and coming back up, he suddenly leaned against the banister, holding tight.

"Miss Adams," he said.

"What is it, Captain?"

He exhaled. "I'm scared. I don't want to leave. I'm afraid."

Her hand, all by itself, took his arm and she finally said, there in the shadows, "Sometimes — I'm afraid, too. What frightens *you?*"

"I don't want to go away without saying good-bye. If I never return, I want to see all my friends, shake hands, slap them on the back, I don't know, make jokes." He stopped and waited, then went on. "But I walk around town and nobody knows me. Everyone's gone."

The pendulum on the wall clock slid back and forth, shining, with the merest of sounds.

Hardly knowing where she was going, Miss Adams took his arm and guided him up the last steps, away from the marble vaults below, to a final, brightly decorated room, where he glanced around and shook his head.

"There's no one here, either."

"Do you believe that?"

"Well, where are they? Do any of my old pals ever come visit, borrow books, bring them back late?"

"Not often," she said. "But listen. Do you realize Thomas Wolfe was wrong?"

"Wolfe? The great literary beast? Wrong?"

"The *title* of one of his books."

"*You Can't Go Home Again?*" he guessed.

"That's it. He was wrong. *This* is home. Your friends are still here. This was your summer place."

"Yes. Myths. Legends. Mummies. Aztec kings. Wicked sisters who spat toads. Where I really lived. But I don't see my people."

"Well."

And before he could speak, she switched on a green-shaded lamp that shed a private light on a small table.

"Isn't this nice?" she said. "Most libraries today, too much light. There should be shadows, don't you think? Some mystery, yes? So that late nights the beasts can prowl out of the stacks and crouch by this jungle light to turn the pages with their breath. Am I crazy?"

"Not that I noticed."

"Good. Sit. Now that I know who you are, it all comes back."

"It couldn't possibly."

"No? You'll see."

She vanished into the stacks and came out with ten books that she placed upright, their pages a trifle spread so they could stand and he could read the titles.

"The summer of 1930, when you were, what? ten, you read all of these in one week."

"Oz? Dorothy? The Wizard? Oh, *yes.*"

She placed still others nearby. "*Alice in Wonderland. Through the Looking-Glass.* A month later you reborrowed both. 'But,' I said, 'you've already *read* them!' 'But,' you said, 'not enough so I can speak. I want to be able to *tell* them out *loud.*' "

"My God," he said quietly, "did I say that?"

"You did. Here's more you read a dozen times. Greek myths, Roman, Egyptian. Norse myths, Chinese. You were *ravenous.*"

"King Tut arrived from the tomb when I was three. His picture in the Rotogravure started me. What else have you there?"

"*Tarzan of the Apes.* You borrowed it . . ."

"Three dozen times! *John Carter, Warlord of Mars*, four dozen. My God, dear lady, how come you remember all this?"

"You never left. Summertimes you were here when I unlocked the doors. You went home for lunch but sometimes brought sandwiches and sat out by the stone lion at noon. Your father pulled you home by your ear some nights when you stayed late. How could I forget a boy like that?"

"But still —"

"You never played, never ran out in baseball weather, or football, I imagine. Why?"

He glanced toward the front door. "*They* were waiting for me."

"They?"

"You know. The ones who never borrowed books, never read. They. Them. *Those.*"

She looked and remembered. "Ah, yes. The bullies. Why did they chase you?"

"Because they knew I loved books and didn't much care for them."

"It's a wonder you survived. I used to watch you reading, getting hunchbacked, late afternoons. You looked so lonely."

"No. I had *these*. Company."

"Here's more."

She put down *Ivanhoe*, *Robin Hood*, and *Treasure Island*.

"Oh," he said, "and dear and strange Mr. Poe. How I loved his Red Death."

"You took it so often I told you to keep it on permanent loan unless someone else asked. Someone did, six months later, and when you brought it in I could see it was a terrible blow. A few days later I let you have Poe for another year. I don't recall, did you ever — ?"

"It's out in California. Shall I —"

"No, no. Please. Well, here are *your* books. Let me bring others."

She came out not carrying many books but one at a time, as if each one were, indeed, special.

She began to make a circle inside the other Stonehenge circle and as she placed the books, in lonely splendor, he said their names and then the names of the authors who had written them and then the names of those who had sat across from him so many years ago and read the books quietly or sometimes whispered the finest parts aloud, so beautifully that no one said Quiet or

Silence or even *Shh!*

She placed the first book and there was a wild field of broom and a wind blowing a young woman across that field as it began to snow and someone, far away, called "Kathy" and as the snows fell he saw a girl he had walked to school in the sixth grade seated across the table, her eyes fixed to the windblown field and the snow and the lost woman in another time of winter.

A second book was set in place and a black and beauteous horse raced across a summer field of green and on that horse was another girl, who hid behind the book and dared to pass him notes when he was twelve.

And then there was the far ghost with a snow-maiden face whose hair was a long golden harp played by the summer airs; she who was always sailing to Byzantium where Emperors were drowsed by golden birds that sang in clockwork cages at sunset and dawn. She who always skirted the outer rim of school and went to swim in the deep lake ten thousand afternoons ago and never came out, so was never found, but suddenly now she made landfall here in the green-shaded light and opened Yeats to at last sail home from Byzantium.

And on her right: John Huff, whose name came clearer than the rest, who claimed to have climbed every tree in town and fallen from none, who had raced through watermelon patches treading melons, never touching earth, to knock down rainfalls of chestnuts with one blow, who yodeled at your sun-up window and wrote the same Mark Twain book report in four different grades before the teachers caught on, at which he said, vanishing, "Just call me Huck."

And to *his* right, the pale son of the town hotel owner who looked as if he had gone sleepless forever, who swore every empty house was haunted and took you there to prove it, with a juicy tongue, compressed nose, and throat garglings that sounded the long October demise, the terrible and unutterable fall of the House of Usher.

And next to him was yet another girl.

And next to her . . .

And just beyond . . .

Miss Adams placed a final book and he recalled the fair creature, long ago, when such things were left unsaid, glancing up at him one day when he was an unknowing twelve and she was a wise thirteen to quietly say: "I am Beauty. And you, are *you* the Beast?"

Now, late in time, he wanted to answer that small and wondrous ghost: "No. He hides in the stacks and when the clock strikes three, will prowl forth to drink."

And it was finished, all the books were placed, the outer ring of his selves and the inner ring of remembered faces, deathless, with summer and autumn names.

He sat for a long moment and then another long moment and then, one by one, reached for and took all of the books that had been his, and still were, and opened them and read and shut them and took another until he reached the end of the outer circle and then went to touch and turn and find the raft on the river, the field of broom where the storms lived, and the pasture with the black and beauteous horse and its lovely rider. Behind him, he heard the lady librarian quietly back away to leave him with words . . .

A long while later he sat back, rubbed his eyes, and looked around at the fortress, the encirclement, the Roman encampment of books, and nodded, his eyes wet.

"Yes."

He heard her move behind him.

"Yes, *what?*"

"What you said, Thomas Wolfe, the title of that book of his. Wrong. Everything's *here.* Nothing's changed."

"Nothing will as long as I can help it," she said.

"Don't ever go away."

"I won't if you'll come back more often."

Just then, from below the town, not so very far off, a train whistle blew. She said:

"Is that *yours?*"

"No, but the one soon after," he said and got up and moved around the small monuments that stood very tall and, one by one, shut the covers, his lips moving to sound the old titles and the old, dear names.

"Do we *have* to put them back on the shelves?" he said.

She looked at him and at the double circle and after a long moment said, "Tomorrow will do. Why?"

"Maybe," he said, "during the night,

because of the color of those lamps, green, the jungle, maybe those creatures you mentioned will come out and turn the pages with their breath. And maybe —"

"What else?"

"Maybe my friends, who've hid in the stacks all these years, will come out, too."

"They're already here," she said quietly.

"Yes." He nodded. "They are."

And still he could not move.

She backed off across the room without making any sound, and when she reached her desk she called back, the last call of the night.

"Closing time. Closing time, children."

And turned the lights quickly off and then on and then halfway between; a library twilight.

He moved from the table with the double circle of books and came to her and said, "I can go now."

"Yes," she said. "William Henry Spaulding. You *can*."

They walked together as she turned out the lights, turned out the lights, one by one. She helped him into his coat and then, hardly thinking to do so, he took her hand and kissed her fingers.

It was so abrupt, she almost laughed, but then she said, "Remember what Edith Wharton said when Henry James did what you just did?"

"What?"

" 'The flavor starts at the *elbow*.' "

They broke into laughter together and he turned and went down the marble steps toward the stained-glass entry. At the bottom of the stairs he looked up at her and said:

"Tonight, when you're going to sleep, remember what I called you when I was twelve, and say it out loud."

"I don't remember," she said.

"Yes, you do."

Below the town, a train whistle blew again.

He opened the front door, stepped out, and he was gone.

Her hand on the last light switch, looking in at the double circle of books on the far table, she thought: What *was* it he called me?

"Oh, *yes*," she said a moment later.

And switched off the light.

# FREE DIRT

The cemetery was in the center of the city. On four sides it was bounded by gliding streetcars on glistening blue tracks and cars with exhaust fumes and sound. But, once inside the wall, the world was lost. For half a mile in four directions the cemetery raised midnight trees and headstones that grew from the earth, like pale mushrooms, moist and cold. A gravel path led back into darkness and within the gate stood a Gothic Victorian house with six gables and a cupola. The front-porch light showed an old man there alone, not smoking, not reading, not moving, silent. If you took a deep breath he smelled of the sea, of urine, of papyrus, of kindling, of ivory, and of teak. His false teeth moved his mouth automatically when it wanted to talk. His tiny yellow seed eyes twitched and his poke-hole nostrils thinned as a stranger crunched up the gravel path and set foot on the porch step.

"Good evening!" said the stranger, a

young man, perhaps twenty.

The old man nodded, but his hands lay quietly on his knees.

"I saw that sign out front," the stranger went on. "FREE DIRT, it said."

The old man almost nodded.

The stranger tried a smile. "Crazy, but that sign caught my eye."

There was a glass fan over the front door. A light shone through this glass fan, colored blue, red, yellow, and touched the old man's face. It seemed not to bother him.

"I wondered, free dirt? Never struck me you'd have much left over. When you dig a hole and put the coffin in and refill the hole, you haven't much dirt left, *have* you? I should think . . ."

The old man leaned forward. It was so unexpected that the stranger pulled his foot off the bottom step.

"You *want* some?" said the old man.

"Why, no, no, I was just curious. Signs like that *make* you curious."

"Set down," said the old man.

"Thanks." The young man sat uneasily on the steps. "You know how it is, you walk around and never think how it is to *own* a graveyard."

"And?" said the old man.

316

"I mean, like how much *time* it takes to dig graves."

The old man leaned back in his chair. "On a cool day: two hours. Hot day, four. Very hot day, six. Very cold day, not cold so it freezes, but *real* cold, a man can dig a grave in one hour so he can head in for hot chocolate, brandy *in* the chocolate. Then again, you get a good man on a hot day, he's no better than a bad man in the cold. Might take eight hours to open up, but there's easy-digging soil here. All loam, no rocks."

"I'm curious about winter."

"In blizzards we got a icebox mausoleum to stash the dead, undelivered mail, until spring and a whole *month* of shovels and spades."

"Seeding and planting time, eh?" The stranger laughed.

"*You* might say that."

"Don't you dig in winter *anyhow?* For *special* funerals? *Special* dead?"

"Some yards got a hose-shovel contraption. Pump hot water through the blade; shape a grave quick, like placer mining, even with the ground an ice-pond. We don't cotton to that. Use picks and shovels."

The young man hesitated. "Does it *bother* you?"

"You mean, I get scared ever?"

"Well . . . yes."

The old man at last took out and stuffed his pipe with tobacco, tamped it with a callused thumb, lit it, let out a small stream of smoke.

"No," he said at last.

The young man's shoulders sank.

"Disappointed?" said the old man.

"I thought maybe once . . . ?"

"Oh, when you're young, maybe. One time . . ."

"Then there *was* a time!" The young man shifted up a step.

The old man glanced at him sharply, then resumed smoking. "One time." He stared at the marbled hills and the dark trees. "My grandpa owned this yard. I was born here. A gravedigger's son learns to *ignore* things."

The old man took a number of deep puffs and said:

"I was just eighteen, folks off on vacation, me left to tend things, alone, mow the lawn, dig holes and such. Alone, four graves to dig in October and a cold came hard off the lake, frost on the graves, tombstones like snow,

318

ground froze solid.

"One night I walked out. No moon. Hard grass underfoot, could see my breath, hands in my pockets, walking, listening."

The old man exhaled frail ghosts from his thin nostrils. "Then I heard this sound, deep under. I froze. It was a voice, screaming. Someone woke up buried, heard me walk by, cried out. I just *stood*. They screamed and screamed. Earth banged. On a cold night, ground's like porcelain, rings, you *see?*

"Well —" The old man shut his eyes to remember. "I stood like the wind off the lake stopped my blood. A joke? I searched around and thought, Imagination! No, it was underfoot, sharp, clear. A *woman's* voice. I *knew* all the gravestones." The old man's eyelids trembled. "Could recite them alphabetical, year, month, day. Name *any* year, and I'll tell. How about 1899? Jake Smith departed. And 1923? Betty Dallman lost. And 1933? P. H. Moran! Name a month. August? August last year, buried Henrietta Wells. August 1918? Grandma Hanlon, whole *family!* *Influenza!* Name a day, August fourth?

Smith, Burke, Shelby carried off. Williamson? He's on that hill, pink marble. Douglas? By the creek . . ."

"The *story*," the young man urged.

"Eh?"

"The *story* you were telling."

"Oh, the voice below? Well, I knew all the stones. Standing there, I guessed that voice out of the ground was Henrietta Fremwell, fine girl, twenty-four years, played piano at the Elite Theatre. Tall, graceful, blond. How did I know her voice? I stood where there was only men's graves. Hers was the only woman's. I ran to put my ear on her stone. Yes! Her voice, way down, screaming!

" 'Miss Fremwell!' I shouted.

" 'Miss Fremwell,' I yelled again.

"Deep down I heard her, only weeping now. Maybe she heard me, maybe not. She just cried. I ran downhill so fast I tripped and split my head on a stone, got up, screamed myself! Got to the toolshed, all blood, dragged out the tools, and just stood there in the moonlight with one shovel. The ground was ice solid, solid. I fell back against a tree. It would take three minutes to get back to her grave, and eight hours of cold night to dig to

320

her box. The ground was like glass. A coffin is a coffin; only so much space for air. Henrietta Fremwell had been buried two days before the freeze, been asleep all that time, using up air, and it rained just before the cold spell and the earth over her, soaked with rainwater now, froze. I'd have to dig maybe eight hours. And the way she cried, there wasn't another hour of air left."

The old man's pipe had gone out. He rocked in his chair, back and forth, back and forth, silently.

"But," said the young man, "what did you *do?*"

"Nothing," said the old man.

"Nothing!?"

"Nothing I *could* do. That ground was solid. Six men couldn't have dug that grave. No hot water near. And she might've been screaming *hours* before I heard, so . . ."

"You did — nothing?"

"*Something.* Put the shovel and pick back in the toolshed, locked it and went back to the house and built a fire and drank some hot chocolate, shivering and shivering. Would you have done *different?*"

"I —"

"Would you have dug for eight hours in hard ice rock so's to reach her when she was truly dead of exhaustion, cold, smothered, and have to bury her all *over* again? Then call her folks and *tell them?*"

The young man was silent. On the porch, the mosquitoes hummed about the naked light bulb.

"I see," said the young man.

The old man sucked his pipe. "I think I cried all night because there was nothing I could do." He opened his eyes and stared about, surprised, as if he had been listening to someone else.

"That's quite a story," said the young man.

"No," said the old man, "God's truth. Want to hear more? See that big stone with the ugly angel? That was Adam Crispin's. Relatives fought, got a writ from a judge, dug him up hoping for poison. Found nothing. Put him back, but by that time the dirt from his grave mixed with other dirts. We shoveled in stuff from all around. Next plot, the angel with broken wings? Mary-Lou Phipps. Dug her up to lug her off to Elgin, Illinois. More relatives. Where she'd been, the pit stayed open, oh, three weeks. No funerals. Meanwhile, her dirt got cross-shoveled with others. Six stones over, one stone north, that was Henry Douglas Jones. Became famous sixty years after no one paid attention. Now he's planted under the Civil War monument. *His* grave lay wide two months, nobody wanted to utilize the hole of a Southerner, all of us leaning North with Grant. So *his* dirt got scattered. That give you some notion of what that FREE DIRT sign means?"

The young man eyed the cemetery landscape. "Well," he said, "where *is* that dirt you're handing out?"

The old man pointed with his pipe and the stranger looked and indeed, by a nearby wall was a sizable hillock some ten feet long by about three feet high, loam and grass tufts of many shades of tan, brown, and burnt umber.

"Go look," said the old man.

The young man walked slowly over to stand by the mound.

"Kick it," said the old man. "See if it's real."

The young man kicked and his face paled.

"Did you hear that?" he said.

"What?" said the old man, looking somewhere else.

The stranger listened and shook his head. "Nothing."

"Well, now," said the old man, knocking out the ashes from his pipe. "How much free dirt you need?"

"I hadn't thought."

"Yes, you have," said the old man, "or you wouldn't have driven your lightweight delivery truck up by the cemetery gate. I got cat's ears. Heard your motor just when you stopped. How much?"

"Oh," said the young man uneasily. "My backyard's eighty feet by forty. I could use a good inch of topsoil. So . . . ?"

"I'd say," said the old man, "half of that mound there. Hell, take it all. Nobody wants it."

"You mean —"

"I mean, that mound has been growing and diminishing, diminishing and growing, mixtures up and down, since Grant took Richmond and Sherman reached the sea. There's Civil War dirt there, coffin splinters, satin casket shreds from when Lafayette met the Honor Guard's Edgar Allan Poe. There's funeral flowers, blossoms from ten hundred obsequies. Condolence-card confetti for Hessian troopers, Parisian gunners who never shipped home. That soil is so laced with bonemeal and casket corsages, I should charge *you* to buy the lot. Grab a spade before I *do.*"

"Stay right *there.*" The young man raised one hand.

"I'm not going anywhere," said the old man. "Nor is anyone else nearby."

The half-truck was pulled up by the dirt mound and the young man was reaching in for a spade when the old man said:

"No, I think not."

The old man went on:

"Graveyard spade's best. Familiar metal, familiar soil. Easy digging when like takes to like. So."

The old man's head indicated a spade half stuck in the dark mound. The young man shrugged and moved.

The cemetery spade came free with a soft whispering. Pellets of ancient mound fell with similar whispers.

He began to dig and shift and fill the back of his half-truck as the old man from the corners of his eyes observed:

"It's more than dirt, as I said. War of 1812, San Juan Hill, Manassas, Gettysburg, October flu epidemic 1918, all strewn from graves filled and evicted to be refilled. Various occupants leavened out to dust, various glories melted to mixtures, rust from metal caskets, coffin handles, shoelaces but no shoes, hairs long and short. Ever see wreaths made of hair saved to weave crowns to fix on mortal pictures? All that's left of a smile or that funny look in the eyes of someone who knows she's not alive anymore, ever. Hair, epaulettes, not *whole* ones, but one strand of epaulette, all there along with blood that's gone to silt."

The young man finished, sweating, and started to thrust the spade back in the earth when the old man said:

"Take it. Cemetery dirt, cemetery spade, like takes to like."

"I'll bring it back tomorrow." The young man tossed the spade into the mounded truck.

"No. You got the dirt, so keep the spade. Just don't bring the free dirt *back*."

"Why would I do *that?*"

"Just don't," said the old man, but did

326

not move as the young man climbed in his truck to start the engine.

He sat listening to the dirt mound tremble and whisper in the flatbed.

"What're you waiting for?" asked the old man.

The flimsy half-truck ran toward the last of the twilight, pursued by the ever-encroaching dark. Clouds raced overhead, perturbed by the invisible. Back on the horizon, thunder sounded. A few drops of rain fell on the windshield, causing the young man to ram his foot on the gas and swerve into his home street even as the sun truly died, the wind rose, and the trees around his cottage bent and beckoned.

Climbing out, he stared at the sky and then his house and then the empty garden. A few drops of cold rain on his cheeks decided him; he drove the rattling half-truck into the empty garden, unlatched the metal back-flap, opened it just an inch so as to allow a proper flow, and then began motoring back and forth across the garden, letting the dark stuffs whisper down, letting the strange midnight earth sift and murmur, until at last the truck was empty and he stood in the blowing night, watching the wind stir the black soil.

Then he locked the truck in the garage and went to stand on the back porch, thinking, I won't need water. The storm will soak the ground.

He stood for a long while simply staring at the graveyard mulch, waiting for rain, until he thought, What am I waiting for? *Jesus!* And went in.

At ten o'clock a light rain tapped on the windows and sifted over the dark garden. At eleven it rained so steadily that the gutter drains swallowed and rattled.

At midnight the rain grew heavy. He looked to see if it was eroding the new dark earth but saw only the black muck drinking the downpour like a great black sponge, lit by distant flares of lightning.

Then, at one in the morning, the greatest Niagara of all shuddered the house, rinsed the windows to blindness, and shook the lights.

And then, abruptly, the downpour, the immense Niagara ceased, followed by one great downfell blow of lightning which plowed and pinioned the dark earth close by, near, outside, with explosions of light as if ten thousand flashbulbs had been fired off. Then darkness fell in curtains of thunder, cracking, breaking the bones.

In bed, wishing for the merest dog to hold for lack of human company, hugging the sheets, burying his head, then rising full to the silent air, the dark air, the storm gone, the rain shut, and a silence that spread in whispers as the last drench melted into the trembling soil.

He shuddered and then shivered and then hugged himself to stop the shivering of his cold flesh, and he was thirsty but could not make himself move to find the kitchen and drink water, milk, leftover wine, anything. He lay back, dry-mouthed, with unreasonable tears filling his eyes.

Free dirt, he thought. My God, what a damn-fool night. *Free dirt!*

At two o'clock he heard his wristwatch ticking softly.

At two-thirty he felt his pulse in his wrists and ankles and neck and then in his temples and inside his head.

The entire house leaned into the wind, *listening.*

Outside in the still night, the wind

failed and the yard lay soaked and waiting.

And at last . . . *yes.* He opened his eyes and turned his head toward the shaded window.

He held his breath. What? Yes? Yes? *What?*

Beyond the window, beyond the wall, beyond the house, outside somewhere, a whisper, a murmur, growing louder and louder. Grass growing? Blossoms opening? Soil shifting, crumbling?

A great whisper, a mix of shadows and shades. Something rising. Something moving.

Ice froze beneath his skin. His heart ceased.

Outside in the dark, in the yard.

Autumn had arrived.

October was there.

His garden gave him . . .

A *harvest.*

# LAST RITES

Harrison Cooper was not that old, only thirty-nine, touching at the warm rim of forty rather than the cold rim of thirty, which makes a great difference in temperature and attitude. He was a genius verging on the brilliant, unmarried, unengaged, with no children that he could honestly claim, so having nothing much else to do, woke one morning in the summer of 1999, weeping.

"Why!?"

Out of bed, he faced his mirror to watch the tears, examine his sadness, trace the woe. Like a child, curious after emotion, he charted his own map, found no capital city of despair, but only a vast and empty expanse of sorrow, and went to shave.

Which didn't help, for Harrison Cooper had stumbled on some secret supply of melancholy that, even as he shaved, spilled in rivulets down his soaped cheeks.

"Great God," he cried. "I'm at a funeral, but *who's* dead?!"

He ate his breakfast toast somewhat soggier than usual and plunged off to his laboratory to see if gazing at his Time Traveler would solve the mystery of eyes that shed rain while the rest of him stood fair.

Time Traveler? Ah, yes.

For Harrison Cooper had spent the better part of his third decade wiring circuitries of impossible pasts and as yet untouchable futures. Most men philosophize in their as-beautiful-as-women cars. Harrison Cooper chose to dream and knock together from pure air and electric thunderclaps what he called his Mobius Machine.

He had told his friends, with wine-colored nonchalance, that he was taking a future strip and a past strip, giving them a now half twist, so they looped on a single plane. Like those figure-eight ribbons, cut and pasted by that dear mathematician A. F. Mobius in the nineteenth century.

"Ah, yes, Mobius," friends murmured.

What they really meant was, "Ah, *no*. Good night."

Harrison Cooper was not a mad scientist, but he was irretrievably boring.

Knowing this, he had retreated to finish the Mobius Machine. Now, this strange morning, with cold rain streaming from his eyes, he stood staring at the damned contraption, bewildered that he was not dancing about with Creation's joy.

He was interrupted by the ringing of the laboratory doorbell and opened the door to find one of those rare people, a real Western Union delivery boy on a real bike. He signed for the telegram and was about to shut the door when he saw the lad staring fixedly at the Mobius Machine.

"What," exclaimed the boy, eyes wide, "is *that?*"

Harrison Cooper stood aside and let the boy wander in a great circle around his Machine, his eyes dancing up, over, and around the immense circling figure eight of shining copper, brass, and silver.

"Sure!" cried the boy at last, beaming. "A *Time* Machine!"

"Bull's-eye!"

"When do you leave?" said the boy. "Where will you go to meet which person where? Alexander? Caesar? Napoleon! Hitler?!"

"No, no!"

The boy exploded his list. "Lincoln —"

"More *like* it."

"General Grant! Roosevelt! Benjamin Franklin?"

"Franklin, yes!"

"Aren't you *lucky?*"

"Am I?" Stunned, Harrison Cooper found himself nodding. "Yes, by God, and suddenly —"

Suddenly he knew why he had wept at dawn.

He grabbed the young lad's hand. "Much thanks. You're a catalyst —"

"Cat— ?"

"A Rorschach test — making me draw my *own* list — now gently, swiftly — *out!* No offense."

The door slammed. He ran for his library phone, punched numbers, waited, scanning the thousand books on the shelves.

"Yes, yes," he murmured, his eyes flicking over the gorgeous sun-bright titles. "Some of you. Two, three, maybe four. Hello! Sam? Samuel! Can you get here in five minutes, make it three? Dire emergency. Come!"

He slammed the phone, swiveled to reach out and touch.

"Shakespeare," he murmured. "Willy-

William, will it be — *you?*"

The laboratory door opened and Sam/Samuel stuck his head in and froze.

For there, seated in the midst of his great Mobius figure eight, leather jacket and boots shined, picnic lunch packed, was Harrison Cooper, arms flexed, elbows out, fingers alert to the computer controls.

"Where's your Lindbergh cap and goggles?" asked Samuel.

Harrison Cooper dug them out, put them on, smirking.

"Raise the *Titanic*, then sink it!" Samuel strode to the lovely machine to confront its rather outré occupant. "Well, Cooper, *what?*" he cried.

"I woke this morning in tears."

"Sure. I read the phone book aloud last night. That *did* it!"

"No. You read me *these!*"

Cooper handed the books over.

"Sure! We gabbed till three, drunk as owls on English Lit!"

"To give me tears for *answers!*"

"To what?"

"To their loss. To the fact that they died unknown, unrecognized; to the grim fact that some were only truly recognized, republished, raved over from 1920 on!"

"Cut the cackle and move the buns," said Samuel. "Did you call to sermonize or ask advice?"

Harrison Cooper leaped from his machine and elbowed Samuel into the library.

"You must map my trip for me!"

"Trip? Trip!"

"I go a-journeying, far-traveling, the Grand Literary Tour. A Salvation Army of one!"

"To save lives?"

"No, souls! What good is life if the soul's dead? *Sit!* Tell me all the authors we raved on by night to weep me at dawn. Here's brandy. Drink! Remember?"

"I *do!*"

"List them, then! The New England Melancholic first. Sad, recluse from land, should have drowned at sea, a lost soul of sixty! Now, what *other* sad geniuses did we maunder over —"

"God!" Samuel cried. "You're going to tour *them?* Oh, Harrison, Harry, I love you!"

"Shut up! Remember how you write

jokes? Laugh and think *backwards!* So let us cry and leap up our tear ducts to the source. Weep for Whales to find minnows!"

"Last night I think I quoted —"

"Yes?"

"And then we spoke —"

"Go on —"

"Well."

Samuel gulped his brandy. Fire burned his eyes.

"Write *this* down!"

They wrote and ran.

"What will you do when you get there, Librarian Doctor?"

Harrison Cooper, seated back in the shadow of the great hovering Mobius ribbon, laughed and nodded. "Yes! Harrison Cooper, L.M.D. Literary Meadow Doctor. Curer of fine old lions off their feed, in dire need of tender love, small applause, the wine of words, all in my heart, all on my tongue. Say *'Ah!'* So long. Good-bye!"

"God bless!"

He slammed a lever, whirled a knob, and the machine, in a spiral of metal, a whisk of butterfly ribbon, very simply — vanished.

A moment later, the Mobius Machine gave a twist of its atoms and — returned.

"Voilà!" cried Harrison Cooper, pink-faced and wild-eyed. "It's *done!*"

"So soon?" exclaimed his friend Samuel.

"A minute here, but hours there!"

"Did you succeed?"

"Look! Proof positive."

For tears dripped off his chin.

"What happened? What?!"

"This, and this . . . and . . . *this!*"

A gyroscope spun, a celebratory ribbon spiraled endlessly on itself, and the ghost of a massive window curtain haunted the air, exhaled, and then ceased.

As if fallen from a delivery-chute, the books arrived almost before the footfalls and then the half-seen feet and then the fog-wrapped legs and body and at last the head of a man who, as the ribbon spiraled itself back into emptiness, crouched over the volumes as if warming himself at a hearth.

He touched the books and listened to the air in the dim hallway where dinnertime voices drifted up from below and a door stood wide near his elbow, from which the faint scent of illness came and went, arrived and departed, with the stilted breathing of some patient within the room. Plates and silverware sounded from the world of evening and quiet good health downstairs. The hall and the sickroom were for a time deserted. In a moment, someone might ascend with a tray for the half-sleeping man in the intemperate room.

Harrison Cooper rose with stealth, checking the stairwell, and then, carrying a sweet burden of books, moved into the room, where candles lit both sides of a bed on which the dying man lay supine, arms straight at his sides, head weighting the pillow, eyes grimaced shut, mouth set as if daring the ceiling, mortality itself, to sink and extinguish him.

At the first touch of the books, now on one side, now on the other, of his bed, the old man's eyelids fluttered, his dry lips cracked; the air whistled from his nostrils:

"Who's there?" he whispered. "What time is it?"

"Whenever I find myself growing grim

about the mouth, whenever it is a damp, drizzly November in my soul, then I account it high time to get to sea as soon as I can," replied the traveler at the foot of the bed, quietly.

"What, what?" the old man in the bed whispered swiftly.

"It is a way I have of driving off the spleen and regulating the circulation," quoted the visitor, who now moved to place a book under each of the dying man's hands where his tremoring fingers could scratch, pull away, then touch, Braille-like, again.

One by one, the stranger held up book after book, to show the covers, then a page, and yet another title page where printed dates of this novel surfed up, adrift, but to stay forever on some far future shore.

The sick man's eyes lingered over the covers, the titles, the dates, and then fixed to his visitor's bright face. He exhaled, stunned. "My God, you have the look of a traveler. From *where?*"

"Do the years show?" Harrison Cooper leaned forward. "Well, then — I bring you an Annunciation."

"Such things come to pass only with virgins," whispered the old man. "No virgin lies here buried under his unread books."

"I come to unbury you. I bring tidings from a far place."

The sick man's eyes moved to the books beneath his trembling hands.

"Mine?" he whispered.

The traveler nodded solemnly, but began to smile when the color in the old man's face grew warmer and the expression in his eyes and on his mouth was suddenly eager.

"*Is* there hope, then?"

"There is!"

"I believe you." The old man took a breath and then wondered, "Why?"

"Because," said the stranger at the foot of the bed, "I love you."

"I do not *know* you, sir!"

"But I know you fore and aft, port to starboard, main-topgallants to gunnels, every day in your long life to here!"

"Oh, the sweet sound!" cried the old man. "Every word that you say, every light from your eyes, is foundation-of-the-world true! How can it be?" Tears winked from the old man's lids. "Why?"

"Because I *am* the truth," said the traveler. "I have come a long way to find and say: you are not lost. Your great

341

Beast has only drowned some little while. In another year, lost ahead, great and glorious, plain and simple men will gather at your grave and shout: he breeches, he rises, he breeches, he rises! and the white shape will surface to the light, the great terror lift into the storm and thunderous St. Elmo's fire and you with him, each bound to each, and no way to tell where he stops and you start or where you stop and he goes off around the world lifting a fleet of libraries in his and your wake through nameless seas of sub-sub-librarians and readers mobbing the docks to chart your far journeyings, alert for your lost cries at three of a wild morn."

"Christ's wounds!" said the man in his winding-sheet bedclothes. "To the point, man, the *point!* Do you speak truth!?"

"I give you my hand on it, and pledge my soul and my heart's blood." The visitor moved to do just this, and the two men's fists fused as one. "Take these gifts to the grave. Count these pages like a rosary in your last hours. Tell no one where they came from. Scoffers would knock the ritual beads from your fingers. So tell this rosary in the dark before dawn, and the rosary is this: you will live forever. You are immortal."

"No more of this, no more! Be still."

"I can not. Hear me. Where you have passed a fire path will burn, miraculous in the Bengal Bay, the Indian Seas, Hope's Cape, and around the Horn, past perdition's landfall, as far as living eyes can see."

He gripped the old man's fist ever more tightly.

"I swear. In the years ahead, a million millions will crowd your grave to sleep you well and warm your bones. Do you hear?"

"Great God, you are a proper priest to sound my Last Rites. And will I enjoy my own funeral? I will."

His hands, freed, clung to the books at each side, as the ardent visitor raised yet other books and intoned the dates:

"Nineteen twenty-two . . . 1930 . . . 1935 . . . 1940 . . . 1955 . . . 1970. Can you read and know what it means?"

He held the last volume close to the old man's face. The fiery eyes moved. The old mouth creaked.

"Nineteen ninety?"

"Yours. One hundred years from to-night."

"Dear God!"

"I must go, but I *would* hear. Chapter One. Speak."

The old man's eyes slid and burned. He licked his lips, traced the words, and at last whispered, beginning to weep:

" 'Call me Ishmael.' "

There was snow and more snow and more snow after that. In the dissolving whiteness, the silver ribbon twirled in a massive whisper to let forth in an exhalation of Time the journeying librarian and his bookbag. As if slicing white bread rinsed by snow, the ribbon, as the traveler ghosted himself to flesh, sifted him through the hospital wall into a room as white as December. There, abandoned, lay a man as pale as the snow and the wind. Almost young, he slept with his mustaches oiled to his lip by fever. He seemed not to know nor care that a messenger had invaded the air near his bed. His eyes did not stir, nor did his mouth increase the passage of breath. His hands at his sides did not open to receive. He seemed already lost in a bomb and only his unexpected visitor's voice caused his eyes to roll behind their shut lids.

"Are you forgotten?" a voice asked.

"Unborn," the pale man replied.

"Never remembered?"

"Only. Only in. France."

"Wrote nothing at all?"

"Not worthy."

"Feel the weight of what I place on your bed. No, don't look. *Feel.*"

"Tombstones."

"With names, yes, but not tombstones. Not marble but paper. Dates, yes, but the day after tomorrow and tomorrow and ten thousand after that. And your name on each."

"It will not be."

"*Is.* Let me speak the names. Listen. Masque?"

"Red Death."

"The Fall of —"

"Usher!"

"Pit?"

"Pendulum!"

"Tell-tale?"

"Heart! *My* heart. Heart!"

"Repeat: for the love of God, Montresor."

"Silly."

"Repeat: Montresor, for the love of God."

"For the love of God, Montresor!"

"Do you see this label?"

"I see!"

"Read the date."

"Nineteen ninety-four. No such date."

"Again, and the name of the wine."

"Nineteen ninety-four. Amontillado. And my name!"

"Yes! Now shake your head. Make the fool's-cap bells ring. Here's mortar for the last brick. Quickly. I'm here to bury you alive with books. When death comes, how will you greet him? With a shout and — ?"

*"Requiescat in pace?"*

"Say it again."

*"Requiescat in pace!"*

The Time Wind roared, the room emptied. Nurses ran in, summoned by laughter, and tried to seize the books that weighed down his joy.

"What's he *saying?*" someone cried.

In Paris, an hour, a day, a year, a minute later, there was a run of St. Elmo's fire along a church steeple, a blue glow in a dark alley, a soft tread at a street corner, a turnabout of wind like an invisible carousel, and then footfalls up a stair to a door which opened

346

on a bedroom where a window looked out upon cafes filled with people and far music, and in a bed by the window, a tall man lying, his pale face immobile, until he heard alien breath in his room.

The shadow of a man stood over him and now leaned down so that the light from the window revealed a face and a mouth as it inhaled and then spoke. The single word that the mouth said was:

"Oscar?"

# THE OTHER HIGHWAY

They drove into green Sunday-morning country, away from the hot aluminum city, and watched as the sky was set free and moved over them like a lake they had never known was there, amazingly blue and with white breakers above them as they traveled.

Clarence Travers slowed the car and felt the cool wind move over his face with the smell of cut grass. He reached over to grasp his wife's hand and glanced at his son and daughter in the backseat, not fighting, at least for this moment, as the car moved through one quiet beauty after another in what might be a Sunday so lush and green it would never end.

"Thank God we're doing this," said Cecelia Travers. "It's been a million years since we got away." He felt her hand hug his and then relax completely. "When I think of all those ladies dropping dead from the heat at the cocktail party this afternoon, *well!*"

"Well, indeed," said Clarence Travers. "Onward!"

He pressed the gas pedal and they moved faster. Their progress out of the city had been mildly hysterical, with cars shrieking and shoving them toward islands of wilderness praying for picnics that might not be found. Seeing that he had put the car in the fast lane, he slowed to gradually move himself and his family through the banshee traffic until they were idling along at an almost reasonable fifty miles an hour. The scents of flowers and trees that blew in the window made his move worthwhile. He laughed at nothing at all and said:

"Sometimes, when I get this far out, I think let's just keep driving, never go back to the damned city."

"Let's drive a hundred miles," shouted his son.

"A thousand!" cried his daughter.

"A thousand!" said Clarence Travers. "But one slow mile at a time." And then said, softly, "Hey!"

And as suddenly as if they had dreamed it up, the lost highway came into view. "Wonderful!" said Mr. Clarence Travers.

"*What?*" asked the children.

"Look!" said Clarence Travers, leaning over his wife, pointing. "That's the *old* road. The one they used a long time ago."

"*That?*" said his wife.

"It's awfully small," said his son.

"Well, there weren't many cars then, they didn't need much."

"It looks like a big snake," said his daughter.

"Yeah, the old roads used to twist and turn, all right. Remember?"

Cecelia Travers nodded. The car had slowed and they gazed over at that narrow concrete strip with the green grass buckling it gently here or there and sprays of wildflowers nestling up close to either side and the morning sunlight coming down through the high elms and maples and oaks that led the way toward the forest.

"I know it like the nose on my face," said Clarence Travers. "How would you like to ride on it?"

"Oh, Clarence, now . . ."

"I *mean* it."

"Oh, Daddy, *could* we?"

"All right, we'll do it," he said decisively.

"We can't!" said Cecelia Travers. "It's probably against the law. It can't be safe."

But before his wife could finish, he turned off the freeway and let all the swift cars rush on while he drove, smiling at each bump, down over a small ditch, toward the old road.

"Clarence, please! we'll be arrested!"

"For going ten miles an hour on a highway nobody uses anymore? Let's not kick over any beehives, it's too nice a day. I'll buy you all soda pops if you behave."

They reached the old road.

"See how simple? Now which way, kids?"

"That way, *that* way!"

"Easy as pie!"

And he let the car take them away on the old highway, the great white-gray boa constrictor that lashed now slowly this way in green moss-velvet meadows, looped over gentle hills, and lowered itself majestically into caves of moist-smelling trees, through the odor of cricks and spring mud and crystal water that rustled like sheets of cellophane over small stone falls. They drove slow enough to see the water-spiders' enigmatic etchings on quiet pools behind dams of last October's leaves.

"Daddy, what are those?"

"What, the water-skaters? No one has ever caught one. You wait and wait and put your hand out and bang! The spider's gone. They're the first things in life you can't grab onto. The list gets bigger as you grow old, so start small. Don't believe in them. They're not really there."

"It's fun *thinking* they are."

"You have just stated a deep philosophical truth. Now, drive on, Mr. Travers." And obeying his own command with good humor, he drove on.

And they came to a forest that had been like November all through the winter and now, reluctantly, was putting out green flags to welcome the season. Butterflies in great tosses of confetti leaped from the deeps of the forest to ramble drunkenly on the air, their thousand torn shadows following over grass and water.

"Let's go back now," said Cecelia Travers.

"Aw, Mom," said the son and daughter.

"Why?" said Clarence Travers. "My

God, how many kids back in that damned hot town can say they drove on a road *nobody else* has used in years? Not *one!* Not one with a father brave enough to cross a little grass to take the old way. Right?"

Mrs. Travers lapsed into silence.

"Right there," said Clarence Travers, "over that hill, the highway turns left, then right, then left again, an S curve, and another S. Wait and see."

"Left."

"Right."

"Left."

"An S curve."

The car purred.

"*Another* S!"

"Just like you *said!*"

"Look." Clarence Travers pointed. A hundred yards across the way from them, the freeway suddenly appeared for a few yards before it vanished, screaming behind stacks of playing-card billboards. Clarence Travers stared fixedly at it and the grass between it and this shadowed path, this silent place like the bottom of an old stream where tides used to come but came no more, where the wind ran through nights making the old sound of far traffic.

"You know something," said the wife. "That freeway over there scares me."

"Can we drive home on this old road instead, Dad?" said the son.

"I wish we could."

"I've always been scared," said the wife, watching that other traffic roaring by, gone before it arrived.

"We're *all* afraid," said Clarence Travers. "But you pay your money and take your chance. *Well?*"

His wife sighed. "Damn, get back on that dreadful thing."

"Not quite yet," said Clarence Travers and drove to reach a small, very small village, all quite unexpected, a settlement no more than a dozen white clapboard houses mossed under giant trees, dreaming in a green tide of water and leaf-shadow, with wind shaking the rocking chairs on weathered porches and dogs sleeping in the cool nap of grass-carpeting at noon, and a small general store with a dirty red gas pump out front.

They drew up there and got out and stood, unreal in the sudden lack of motion, not quite accepting these houses lost in the wilderness.

The door to the general store squealed

open and an old man stepped out, blinked at them, and said, "Say, did you folks just come down that old road?"

Clarence Travers avoided his wife's accusing eyes. "Yes, sir."

"No one on that road in twenty years."

"We were out for a lark," said Mr. Travers. "And found a peacock," he added.

"A sparrow," said his wife.

"The freeway passed us by, a mile over there, if you want it," said the old man. "When the new road opened, this town just died on the vine. We got nothing here now but people like me. That is: old."

"Looks like there'd be places here to rent."

"Mister, just walk in, knock out the bats, stomp the spiders, and any place is yours for thirty bucks a month. I own the whole town."

"Oh, we're not *really* interested," said Cecelia Travers.

"Didn't think you *would* be," said the old man. "Too far out from the city, too far off the freeway. And that dirt road there slops over when it rains, all muck and mud. And, heck, it's against the law to use that path. Not that they ever patrol it." The old man snorted, shaking his head. "And not that I'll turn you in. But it gave me a nice start just now to see you coming down that rut. I had to give a quick look at my calendar, by God, and make sure it wasn't 1929!"

Lord, I remember, thought Clarence Travers. This is Fox Hill. A thousand people lived here. I was a kid, we passed through on summer nights. We used to stop here *late late,* and me sleeping in the backseat in the moonlight. My grandmother and grandfather in back with me. It's nice to sleep in a car driving late and the road all white, watching the stars turn as you take the curves, listening to the grown-ups' voices underwater, remote, talking, talking, laughing, murmuring, whispering. My father driving, so stolid. Just to be driving in the summer dark, up along the lake to the Dunes, where the poison ivy grew out on the lonely beach and the wind stayed all the time and never went away. And us driving by that lonely graveyard place of sand and moonlight and poison ivy and the waves tumbling in like dusty ash on the shore, the lake pounding like a locomotive on the sand, coming and going. And me crumpled down and smelling Grand-mother's wind-cooled coat and the voices comforting and blanketing me with their solidity and their always-will-be-here sounds that would go on forever, myself always young and us always riding on a summer night in our old Kissel with the side flaps down. And stopping here at nine or ten for Pista-chio and Tutti-frutti ice cream that tasted, faintly, beautifully, of gasoline. All of us licking and biting the cones and smelling the gasoline and driving on, sleepy and snug, toward home, Green Town, thirty years ago.

He caught himself and said:

"About these houses, would it be much trouble fixing them up?" He squinted at the old man.

"Well, yes and no, most of 'em over fifty years old, lots of dust. You could buy one off me for ten thousand, a real bargain now, you'll admit. If you were an artist, now, a painter, or something like that."

"I write copy in an advertising firm."

"Write stories, too, no doubt? Well, now, you get a writer out here, quiet, no neighbors, you'd do lots of writing."

Cecelia Travers stood silently between

the old man and her husband. Clarence Travers did not look at her, but looked at the cinders around the porch of the general store. "I imagine I *could* work here."

"Sure," said the old man.

"I've often thought," said Mr. Travers, "it's time we got away from the city and took it a little easy."

"Sure," said the old man.

Mrs. Travers said nothing but searched in her purse and took out a mirror.

"Would you like some drinks?" asked Clarence Travers with exaggerated concern. "Three Orange Crushes, make it four," he told the old man. The old man moved inside the store, which smelled of nails and crackers and dust.

When the old man was gone, Mr. Travers turned to his wife, and his eyes were shining. "We've always wanted to do it! *Let's!*"

"Do *what?*" she said.

"Move out here, snap decision, why not? Why? We've promised ourselves every year: get away from the noise, the confusion, so the kids'd have a place to play. And . . ."

"Good grief!" the wife cried.

The old man moved inside the store, coughing.

"Ridiculous." She lowered her voice. "We've got the apartment paid up, you've got a fine job, the kids have school with friends, I belong to some fine clubs. And we've just spent a bundle redecorating. We —"

"Listen," he said, as if she were really listening. "None of that's important. Out here, we can breathe. Back in town, hell, *you* complain . . ."

"Just to have something to *complain* about."

"Your clubs can't be that important."

"It's not clubs, it's *friends!*"

"How many would care if we dropped dead tomorrow?" he said. "If I got hit in that traffic, how many thousand cars would run over me before one stopped to see if I was a man or dog left in the road?"

"Your job . . ." she started to say.

"My God, ten years ago we said, in two more years we'll have enough money to quit and write my novel! But each year we've said *next* year! and next year and *next* year!"

"We've *had* fun, haven't we?"

"Sure! Subways are fun, buses are

fun, martinis and drunken friends are fun. Advertising? Yeah! But I've *used* all the fun there is! I want to *write* about what I've seen now, and there's no better place than this. Look at that house over there! Can't you just see me in the front window banging the hell out of my typewriter?"

"Stop hyperventilating!"

"Hyperventilate? God, I'd jump for joy to quit. I've gone as far as I can go. Come on, Cecelia, let's get back some of the spunk in our marriage, take a chance!"

"The children . . ."

"We'd *love* it here!" said the son.

"I *think*," said the daughter.

"I'm not getting any younger," said Clarence Travers.

"Nor am I," she said, touching his arm. "But we can't play hopscotch now. When the children leave, yes, we'll think about it."

"Children, hopscotch, my God, I'll take my typewriter to the grave!"

"It won't be long. We —"

The shop door squealed open again and whether the old man had been standing in the screen shadow for the last minute, there was no telling. It did not show in his face. He stepped out with four lukewarm bottles of Orange Crush in his rust-spotted hands.

"Here you are," he said.

Clarence and Cecelia Travers turned to stare at him as if he were a stranger come out to bring them drinks. They smiled and took the bottles.

The four of them stood drinking the soda pop in the warm sunlight. The summer wind blew through the grottoes of trees in the old, shady town. It was like being in a great green church, a cathedral, the trees so high that the people and cottages were lost far down below. All night long you would imagine those trees rustling their leaves like an ocean on an unending shore. God, thought Clarence Travers, you could really sleep here, the sleep of the dead and the peaceful-of-heart.

He finished his drink and his wife half finished hers and gave it to the children to argue over, inch by compared inch. The old man stood silent, embarrassed by the thing he may have stirred up among them.

"Well, if you're ever out this way, drop in," he said.

Clarence Travers reached for his wallet.

"No, no!" said the old man. "It's on the house."

"Thank you, thank you very much."

"A pleasure."

They climbed back into their car.

"If you want to get to the freeway," said the old man, peering through the front window into the cooked-upholstery smell of the car, "just take your old dirt road back. Don't rush, or you'll break an axle."

Clarence Travers looked straight ahead at the radiator fixture on the car front and started the motor.

"Good-bye," said the old man.

"Good-bye," the children yelled, and waved.

The car moved away through the town.

"Did you hear what the old man said?" asked the wife.

"What?"

"Did you hear him say which way to the freeway?"

"I heard."

He drove through the cool, shady town, staring at the porches and the windows with the colored glass fringing them. If you looked from the inside of those windows out, people had different-colored faces for each pane you looked through. They were Chinese if you looked through one, Indian through another, pink, green, violet, burgundy, wine, chartreuse, the candy colors, the lemon-lime cool colors, the water colors of the windows looking out on lawns and trees and this car slowly driving past.

"Yes, I heard him," said Clarence Travers.

They left the town behind and took the dirt road to the freeway. They waited their chance, saw an interval between floods of cars hurtling by, swerved out into the stream, and, at fifty miles an hour, were soon hurtling toward the city.

"That's better," said Cecelia Travers brightly. She did not look over at her husband. "*Now* I know where we are."

Billboards flashed by; a mortuary, a pie crust, a cereal, a garage, a hotel. A hotel in the tar pits of the city, where one day is the pitiless glare of the noon sun, thought Mr. Travers, all of the great Erector-set buildings, like prehistoric dinosaurs, will sink down into the bubbling tar-lava and be encased, bone by bone, for future civilizations. And in the stomachs of the electric lizards, inside the iron dinosaurs, the probing scientists of A.D. One Million will find the little ivory bones, the thinly articulated skeletons of advertising executives and clubwomen and children. Mr. Travers felt his eyes flinch, watering. And the scientists will say, so *this* is what the iron cities fed on, is it? and give the bones a kick. So *this* is what kept the iron stomachs full, eh? Poor things, they never had a chance. Probably kept by the iron monsters who needed them in order to survive, who needed them for breakfast, lunch, and dinner. Aphids, in a way, aphids, kept in a great metal cage.

"Look, Daddy, look, *look*, before it's too late!"

The children pointed, yelling. Cecelia Travers did not look. Only the children saw it.

The old highway, two hundred yards away, at their left, sprang back into sight for an instant, wandered aimlessly through field, meadow, and stream, gentle and cool and quiet.

Mr. Travers swung his head sharply

to see, but in that instant it was gone. Billboards, trees, hills rushed it away. A thousand cars, honking, shrieking, shouldered them, and bore Clarence and Cecelia Travers and their captive children stunned and silent down the concourse, onward ever onward into a city that had not seen them leave and did not look to see them return.

"Let's see if this car will do sixty or sixty-five," said Clarence Travers.

It could and did.

# MAKE HASTE
# TO LIVE:
# AN AFTERWORD

When I was eight years old, in 1928, an incredible event occurred on the back wall outside the Academy motion picture theater in Waukegan, Illinois. An advertising broadside, some thirty feet long and twenty feet high, dramatized Blackstone the Magician in half a dozen miraculous poses: sawing a lady in half; tied to an Arabian cannon that exploded, taking him with it; dancing a live handkerchief in midair; causing a birdcage with a live canary to vanish between his fingers; causing an elephant to . . . well, you get the idea. I must have stood there for hours, frozen with awe. I knew then that someday I must become a magician.

That's what happened, didn't it? I'm not a science fiction, fantasy, magic-realism writer of fairy tales and surrealist poems. *Quicker Than the Eye* may well be the best title I have ever conjured for a new collection. I pretend to do one thing, cause you to blink, and in the instant seize twenty bright silks out of a bottomless hat.

How does he do that? may well be asked. I really can't say. I don't write these stories, *they* write *me.* Which causes me to live with a boundless enthusiasm for writing and life that some misinterpret as optimism.

Nonsense. I am merely a practitioner of optimal behavior, which means behave yourself, listen to your Muses, get your work done, and enjoy the sense that you just might live forever.

I don't have to wait for inspiration. It jolts me every morning. Just before dawn, when I would prefer to sleep in, the damned stuff speaks between my ears with my Theater of Morning voices. Yes, yes, I know, that sounds awfully artsy, and no, no, I am *not* preaching some sort of Psychic Summons. The voices exist because I stashed them there every day for a lifetime by reading, writing, and living. They accumulated and began to speak soon after high school.

In other words, I do not greet each day with a glad cry but am forced out of bed by these whispering nags, drag myself to the typewriter, and am soon awake and alive as the no-tion/fancy/concept quits my ears, runs down my elbows and out my fingers. Two hours later, a new story is done that, all night, hid asleep behind my *medulla oblongata.*

That, don't you agree, is not opti-mism. It's behavior. Optimal.

I dare not oppose these morning voices. If I did, they would ransack my conscience all day. Besides, I am as out of control as a car off a cliff. What began as a numbed frenzy before breakfast, ends with elation at noon lunch.

How did I find *these* metaphors? Let me count the ways:

You discover your wife is pregnant with your first child soon to be born, so you name the embryonic presence "Sascha" and converse with this in-creasingly bright fetus that evolves into a story that you love but no one wants. So here it is.

You wonder whatever happened to Dorian Gray's portrait. Your second thoughts grow to an outsize horror by nightfall. You upchuck this hairball into your typewriter.

Some of these stories "happened" to

me. "Quicker Than the Eye" was part of a magic show I attended where, with dismay, I saw someone much like myself being made a fool of onstage.

"No News, or What Killed the Dog?" was a Victrola record I played all day every day when I was five, until the neighbors offered to break me or the record, *choose.*

"That Woman on the Lawn" was first a poem that then turned into a story about my mother as a young and needful woman; a topic we care to discuss only with euphemisms.

"Another Fine Mess" resulted from my writing "The Laurel and Hardy Love Affair." There *had* to be a sequel, because when I arrived in Ireland forty years ago, the *Irish Times* announced LAUREL AND HARDY, ONE TIME ONLY, IN PERSON! FOR THE IRISH ORPHANS. OLYMPIA THEATER, DUBLIN. I rushed to the theater and bought the *last* ticket, front row center!

The curtain rose and there they were, Stan and Ollie, doing all their old, sweet, wondrous routines. I sat with happy tears streaming down my face. Later I went backstage and stood by their dressing room door watching them greet friends. I didn't introduce myself.

I just wanted to warm my hands and heart. After twenty minutes of ambience bathing, I slipped away. Thus "Another Fine Mess."

"Unterderseaboat Doktor" is an example of people not hearing themselves talk. A writer friend at lunch some years back described his psychiatrist, a former submarine captain in Hitler's undersea fleet. "Holy God," I cried, "give me a pencil!" I scribbled a title and finished the tale that night. My writer friend hated me for weeks.

"Last Rites" wrote itself because I am the greatest lover of other writers, old or new, who ever lived. I have never been jealous of any writer, I only wanted to write and dream like them. That makes for an enormous list, some of them first-class ladies as well as writers first class: Willa Cather, Jessamyn West, Katherine Anne Porter, Eudora Welty, and, long before her current fame, Edith Wharton. "Last Rites" shuttles in Time to pay my respects to three of my heroes, Poe, Melville, and a third writer, nameless until the finale. It crazed me to perceive that these giants died thinking they were to be buried unknown and unread. I *had* to invent a Time Machine to celebrate them on their deathbeds.

Some of the stories are self-evident. "At the End of the Ninth Year" is the sort of quasi-scientific factoid we all discuss a dozen times, but neglect to write.

"The Other Highway" lies beside the main route heading north from Los Angeles. It has all but vanished under grass, bushes, trees, and avalanched soil. Here and there you can still bike it for some few hundred yards before it melts into the earth.

"Once More, Legato" spontaneously combusted one afternoon when I heard a treeful of birds orchestrating Berlioz and then Albeniz.

If you know the history of Paris during the 1870s' Commune and Haussmann, who tore it down and built it back to the wonder it is now, and if you have experienced some Los Angeles earthquakes, you could guess the genesis of "Zaharoff/Richter Mark V." During the last High Shake, two years ago, I thought: My God, the damn fools *built* the city on the San Andreas Fault! My next thought: what if they built it that way on *purpose?!*

Two hours later, the story was cooling on the windowsill.

That's not all, but it should do.

My final advice to myself, the boy magician grown old, and you?

When your dawn theater sounds to clear your sinuses: don't delay. Jump. Those voices may be gone before you hit the shower to align your wits.

Speed is everything. The 90-mph dash to your machine is a sure cure for life rampant and death most real.

Make haste to live.

Oh, God, yes.

Live. And write. With great haste.

The employees of Thorndike Press hope you have enjoyed this Large Print book. All our Large Print titles are designed for easy reading, and all our books are made to last. Other Thorndike Large Print books are available at your library, through selected bookstores, or directly from us.

For information about titles, please call:

(800) 223-2336

To share your comments, please write:

Publisher
Thorndike Press
P.O. Box 159
Thorndike, Maine 04986